# NOT OF THIS WORLD

## A GROUP X CASE · BOOK 1

## J. A. BOUMA

EmmausWay
PRESS

# PROLOGUE

Full moons and restless hearts with nothing to do are just what the doc ordered on a night like tonight.

Or the Devil, as the case may be.

What's the saying?

Idle hands are the Devil's workshop. Or is it idle hands are the Devil's tools? Ahh, no, I got it: Idle hands are the Devil's playground.

Oh, bother. All of the above is more than apropos.

For every night—nay, every day!—the streets are alive with possibilities because they're teeming with people, with sheeple, with the unwashed masses who lumber and lurch with outstretched hands searching for a handout of what only I and my brethren can offer. Where the shadows speak of things forbidden yet offer the promise of what we offer.

Life.

Or at least a temporary reprieve from their life. A little dose of something-something to take away the bite of disappointment and regret, to soothe the brokenhearted and broken-spirited, to offer a reprieve for the desperate, the lonely, the downtrodden.

Yessiree, that's my aim, that's my purpose, that's my

unbidden pleasure wandering across the great expanse of this Third Rock from the Sun!

Or so the sheeple believe...

You know what I see when I walk down the street? Any of them, just take your pick. They're all the same.

Tree-lined or trash-lined. Suburban sprawl or urban slum. A dirt country road or cobbled High Street. Makes no difference to me and my gang.

Because, see, they're all the same. They smell the same.

And what do I smell?

Opportunity.

Can sniff it a mile away because I can spot them a mile away.

Shuffling about from cubicle to cubicle. Wandering aimlessly down the clearance aisle at the vanilla department store you could swap for any suburban tchotchke joint selling crap slapped with that "Made in China" label. Darting the rug rats around town from soccer practice to piano lessons. Clearing leaves from the gutters or scraping chewing gum off the bottom of their shoe. Sloping up their toddler's puke or changing their octogenarian mother's soiled undergarments every thankless day.

Sheeple, is what they are. The whole lot of them!

But they're *my* sheeple, you see. The ones whose lives are small and pathetic. The downtrodden and upwardly mobile alike. Doesn't matter whether they're wearing a suit or slumming it in sweats. Whether they call a two-story row house home or the inside of a cardboard box. Makes no difference to me who they are, how they dress, where they live.

Because, see, it's opportunity, all the way down. The whole lot of them are just waiting for me to give them what they want —what they *long for*.

Life.

And the opportunities abound to give 'em what they want. Opportunity to distract and detract. Opportunity to numb away the pain and gain a follower. One that will always come back for

NOT OF THIS WORLD    3

more. One that will stop at nothing to get what I offer. Something that is even better than life.

Escape.

Because when it comes to life on this Third Rock from the Sun, there's nothing more to live for. Nothing more than a needle straight into a vein pulsing with life, just waiting to dull the senses and numb away the pain and frustration of a small life unlived. Or a Chase Sapphire Reserve with a ten-G limit and the empty back seats of a Cadillac Escalade filled to the brim with junk. Even a cocked pistol shoved straight into the kisser, aimed at the brainstem, would do the trick.

I prefer the needle. So does my clientele.

Except…

What's that there?

Oh, yes. A steeple.

A steeple for the sheeple.

Sitting smack dab in the middle of my opportunity. At the intersection of hope and despair. Manned by a pastor or priest. Or suppose *womanned*, as the case may be.

Someone who gives the sheeple something to live for. Something to satiate their God-shaped hole, as one chap put it a few centuries ago.

With a proposition I can't offer…

No matter. Yessiree, opportunity abounds. From sea to shining sea. Or any old street corner will do.

Except…

Who's there? The man bending low to offer a Dasani bottle and sack lunch to the hobo lying in the gutter with a rubber hose still wrapped around his arm?

Father Rafferty, that's who.

Just can't help himself, can he? Doing his darnedest to do unto the least of these, and all that other crap the Name-Who-Shall-Remain-Nameless spouted off two millennia ago.

Now the man's putting an arm around the hobo stinking like a gym bag! Offering him his coat straight from his back, even.

Those words from The Nameless come to mind.

*'I was hungry and you gave me food, I was thirsty and you gave me something to drink, I was a stranger and you welcomed me, I was naked and you gave me clothing.'*

Check, check, and double-check!

And wait, what is this?

The man's pulling something from beneath his cloak, gesturing toward the hobo moaning and groaning something fierce.

At least he was. The fella seems a bit brighter now, with a skip in his step that wasn't there a moment ago.

Before Padre showed his mug in these parts.

Naughty, naughty, Father Rafferty.

He's been a very bad boy. A very bad boy, indeed. Which is ironic, because that gesture was the least of his sins.

Believe me. I know all and see all.

Padre tangoed on the wrong side of the tracks. Should have stuck with hearing confessions and fondling the marbles of altar boys.

No matter.

I can deal—with him or her, with whatever it is standing in the way of my opportunity.

Because I can kill.

And will.

I am Chaos. And I'm just getting started.

# CHAPTER 1

Elijah Fox loved mojitos with a passion that burned bright and strong.

And not just because of the white rum that set his brain buzzing and twitching fingers at ease. It was more than that. More what snowbird grannies and vacationing middle-age managers alike craved in their tropical drink of choice.

Yeah, the crushed mint and lime had something to do with it. As did the sugar (always a downfall) and soda water (loved how the bubbles tickled his tongue and nostrils). The combination of sweetness, tart citrus, and herbaceous mint flavors certainly did the body good. A perfect tropical trifecta, it was.

But it was more than that. It was everything that surrounded the mojito. The furniture, if you will.

The high sun blazing to beat the band in a cloudless sky at the equator, kissing the cheeks and back of the neck with a burn that faded into a golden-brown tan. The white-sand beaches dotted by a rainbow spectrum of umbrellas and beach towels. The crystal-clear ocean water lapping ashore. Even the rug rats scrambling to build sandcastles or collect shells and sea glass.

Ahh, what a life that was.

And it had been Elijah's life too, the past few months. Shirt-less under a beach umbrella on Playa Blanca, olive skin singed by Mother Nature's rays until he perfected the proper sun lotion dosage before he got a wicked-coovey tan (that's a cool-groovy neologism mashup, for the uninitiated). Half-drained mojito in one hand, Kindle with Steven King's latest yarn in the other. Powdery white sand between his toes, with his equally white Jack Russell rescue sandwiched between his legs. Nothing but rays to catch, time to kill, and mojitos to drink before his new gig.

Director of operations for Group X, the investigative arm for the Order of Thaddeus, ancient defender and protector of the Christian faith. With his former partner, Georgina Anderson, from the Federal Bureau of Investigation at his side. The pair had cut their teeth on solving cases of the more paranormal variety that stumped Uncle Sam's men in black.

And there he was: back in Washington, DC, and back in the saddle of an investigative arm solving cases of the more super-natural variety—only this time for Jude Thaddeus, or at least his long-lost religious order.

The Lord sure worked in mysterious, if ironic, ways.

And Elijah was content with that. Had always been, learning at a young age that the wind blows wherever it pleases, including the Spirit's, as John's Gospel quotes Jesus.

Early in his life, he had clung to a daily breadcrumb of Scrip-ture many people take out of context and slap on their life, using it as a sort of rabbit's foot for everything that goes right and wrong in their life. Racing through the DC streets, he quoted Jeremiah 29:11 to himself:

> For surely I know the plans I have for you, says the
> Lord, plans for your welfare and not for harm, to
> give you a future with hope.

For an eight-year-old boy who lived in a five-story cesspool that was more a perpetual porta john than anything resembling a moderately up-kept Motel 6, the verse was the lifeline that kept him going. Of course, no one quotes the rest of the passage, the next three verses:

> *Then when you call upon me and come and pray to me, I will hear you. When you search for me, you will find me; if you seek me with all your heart, I will let you find me, says the Lord, and I will restore your fortunes and gather you from all the nations and all the places where I have driven you, says the Lord, and I will bring you back to the place from which I sent you into exile.*

Sure, the passage reflects the heart of Yahweh for his people, a God who is *'ready to forgive, gracious and merciful, slow to anger and abounding in steadfast love,'* as the Book of Nehemiah and other places in the Hebrew Scriptures testify. But most Westerners who quote the good prophet Jeremiah haven't been exiled to corrupt authoritarian regimes by Yahweh himself!

As he matured in his faith, Elijah preferred the commentary James, the brother of Jesus, offered on the matter in the fourth chapter of his book:

> *Come now, you who say, "Today or tomorrow we will go to such and such a town and spend a year there, doing business and making money." Yet you do not even know what tomorrow will bring. What is your life? For you are a mist that appears for a little while and then vanishes. Instead you ought to say, "If the Lord wishes, we will live and do this or that." As it is, you boast in your arrogance; all such boasting is evil.*

Elijah had learned early on that boasting about tomorrow

was as fruitless as spitting into an Atlantic Ocean wind. Such boastings were liable to come back and smack you in the face, leaving you with nothing but a slimy, goopy mess to clean up. He preferred to leave his options open. Probably far too open, but open, nonetheless.

Now he was planted behind a lumbering Ford Taurus from last century sounding like it smoked a pack a day, racing to start his new life.

Should have bypassed downtown DC to Constitution Avenue edging along the National Mall. Would've been way out of the way, but traffic was better and so was the view. The Mall trifecta got him every time—with Honest Abe perched on his throne peering down the green past the Washington Monument on to the U.S. Capitol Building, its dome shimmering in the daylight.

Forget this…

He revved his BMW motorcycle past the Taurus, zig-zagging between cars until he was making headway toward destiny.

And boy, did he love revving. With all of the potential power in those handlebars, and the 91 horsepower at 4,750 revolutions per minute propelling him forward, giving him all the control he needed to go wherever and whenever—and as fast as ever—he wanted.

Power and control.

The two things in his life he'd never had. Not over his life, certainly not over where it went. Not even his own body, his emotions and brain and body triggered by stimulus and circumstances outside of his control, and leading to less-than-ideal reactions he had little power over.

The self-defeating thought triggered his stimming trick, or tried to anyway. Except his gloved hand gripping the throttle wouldn't allow for it. No way for his thumb to press against his index finger, then his middle, and to his ring finger and pinkie. So, he'd have to settle for the next best thing.

Whistling "Amazing Grace."

Was especially effective inside his helmet, the high pitch music to his ears along with the vibration of his lips a balm to his rising anxiety. Stimming or stimulating for autistic people was like drinking water. Couldn't not do it when the thirst came.

Wasn't sure exactly where it was coming from, this sudden wave thirsting for emotional release. Some of it was the cars and noise and general urban furniture pressing in against him. But his helmet mostly took care of that, the feeling of being removed from it all with the darkened visor and near soundlessness one reason why he'd taken to motorcycling.

He had a hunch, though. And it was called—

"Sweet mother of Melchizedek!" he shouted.

Right before he clutched the handbrake and slammed on the foot brake. And went skidding across the city pavement, searching for a means to a stopping end.

Throwing up a honking complaint from the Taurus, joined by the angry bellow of some city bus.

Didn't matter in the slightest. All that did was the eastern gray squirrel scampering across the road and freezing smack dab in the middle of his lane with sheer frozen fright!

The BMW R18 slid to a halt a few yards from the poor urban critter. Had he kept going, by Elijah's calculation he would've pancaked the little fella in no time flat. With guts and fur and popping eyeballs spread across the road.

Couldn't let that happen. Not on his watch.

The horns flared up again, joined by some choice words that would make his mama blush. But he paid them no mind.

All that mattered was the eastern gray squirrel's safety.

"There you go, little fella. Go eat an acorn for me."

And he did, the urban critter finally snapping out of his squirrel-in-headlights stupor and scampering off the road and up a cherry tree showing the first signs of spring.

Elijah took in a relieved breath, the sweet scent of those cherry flowers dizzying. Another one of God's creatures safe for another day. That is, until some bozo driving a Taurus throws their humanity out the window!

Revving his motorcycle, he let the tires rip, sailing through a yellow-turning-red light on squealing tires and getting back to business.

Where was he?

Oh yes. The new gig, sparking a rise in his anxiety, his gloved fingers searching for relief but his lips doing the stimming heavy lifting instead.

Truth be told, he wasn't entirely sure he'd made the right call. Had always struggled with impulse control, making snap decisions without much thought or concern for risk. Which got him into trouble more often than not. Especially in the orphanage he'd spent most of his childhood stuffed away inside up in those mountains.

But this move was different. Felt different. Like all the other twists and turns in his life, taking him from orphanage to foster family, then on through the gauntlet of families until he arrived at his forever family—then finding his Messiah in Jesus as a Jewish teenager and clear through the ups and downs of college, on to the FBI and on to the other side of getting sacked by Uncle Sam, sending him to Cambridge University and to his last place of employ as a professor at an evangelical Protestant seminary— like all those bends in the maze of his life, this one felt like the Holy Spirit had orchestrated this latest life-shift.

Because if Elijah Fox had learned anything in his thirty-some years on Earth, it's that shift happens. And it's always the Holy Spirit's fault.

And the latest detour in his life journey happened just last year.

The Third Person of the Trinity had worked a number on him during an operation late last year with SEPIO, the more muscular arm of the Order. Silas Grey (Master of the Order of Thaddeus, his new boss) had sought his help untangling a wicked Gordian Knot threatening the Church. His old FBI partner, Gina Anderson (his old-turned-new partner with Group X) had made the connection to help the Order make sense of a conspiracy involving unidentified aerial phenomenon and the existence of extraterrestrial biological entities. More pedantically known as UFOs and aliens.

Both had been a bit of a hobby-horse, his interest in the existence of aliens and what the Bible said about it all getting piqued while working cases in the FBI of a more paranormal nature. Alien abductions, cultic ritual abuse, shape-shifting serial killers, mind-reading con men. You know, your run-of-the-mill criminal crazy with a supernatural edge.

And smack dab in the middle of it all, the Holy Spirit had told Elijah his path was about to change wicked fast.

Not as dramatic the last time that had happened, when he was canned from the FBI or the myriad of crazy twists before that one—when he was bounced around between eleven foster homes before finally finding his forever home, and then became a ward of the Commonwealth of Virginia before that, right after his birth parents abandoned him on account of his autistic outbursts.

Not as dramatic, but still. Was pretty comfy and cozy working his professor gig with Grand River Theological Seminary. Professor of Old Testament studies and biblical theology suited him. Which shouldn't have, given his place on the spectrum. But a funny thing about autism is that not all autistic people are alike.

That was sure lost on Hollywood, which portrays them all as a monolith of unemotional, feckless, socially detached zombies who can't handle anything physical invading their space and fly off the handle when they don't get their way.

Sure, there was some of that in Elijah's own experience; he was self-aware enough about that, mostly thanks to the love and care of his adoptive parents. But as Gina colada (his nickname for his old-now-new partner Gina Anderson) had always insisted: autistic people will confound you.

He'd confounded himself, actually! Elijah discovered that, while he sucked at one-on-one interactions, becoming super self-conscious about what he said and what he didn't know in the midst of a personal conversation, he was a master at public speaking. Could work a room as well as a street-corner prostitute could work—well, a street corner!

Which he knew wasn't kosher, but he thought it anyway.

Surprised him as much as anyone, but it was the social separation between him and his students that allowed him to excel. Helped he had an eidetic memory, too, being able to recall almost anything he read or saw with photographic precision. All of it was what helped him excel as a professor where he couldn't at the FBI—which led to his downfall.

And all of that changed thanks to his new employer, the Order of Thaddeus. And the Holy Spirit; he had something to do with it too.

Hence the three months shack-up on Playa Blanca with his toes in the white sands, sipping mojitos until he passed out, and reading through Stephen King's entire backlist.

Ahh, that was the life. But it wasn't the only life, the only thing he loved. Even the thing he loved the most.

What he loved even more was racing through Washington, DC, on his motorcycle.

Not one of those hippy Harley hogs that smacked of biker cliché. Not a Honda, either, or other Japanese variety. No Yamaha or Kawasaki for him, either.

What Elijah rode was the only motorcycle worth its salt.

A beemer. With two Es and one M. Not a bimmer, with one I and two Ms, which is the American bastardization for cars of the original moniker for BMW motorbikes.

Beemer, that's what he rode. Specifically, a BMW R 18, sporting the dexterity and temerity of a modern cruiser combined with the nostalgic sense of classic beemer design.

Beemer, not bimmer.

It was nearing the middle of the morning, Monday. 8:23 a.m.

exactly. Was getting to the new digs later than he'd wanted. Had always insisted the day was pretty well over by the time 10 a.m. rolled around. Flight back to reality was delayed last night and he'd overslept. But it was what it was.

Arriving at his destination, the sun rising in a clear sky and painting his new digs a brilliant burnt orange, he pulled into a looping driveway off Michigan Avenue and turned into a service entrance on the westside of the Basilica of the National Shrine of the Immaculate Conception. The access driveway ran behind a stone wall and a thick hedgerow, leading to a keycard entrance into an old Order outpost that was now Group X HQ.

Elijah never understood the Protestant fascination with de-ostentatizing their sacred spaces. Strip-mall churches were well and good, carrying the good news of God's crazy love in Jesus to people on the streets. But the big-box monstrosities anchored along highways and spread across suburbs like Kohl's department stores? Why trade the stone and stained glass of the cathedrals their Catholic and Orthodox brothers and sisters built for fog machines and fancy light shows? Ostentatious design and architecture all the way!

Which was ironic, since he grew up in one of those suburban eyesores as the adopted son of an evangelical Protestant pastor—and a Baptist one at that!

Nope. Now smells and bells were his jam. Probably had something to do with his own Jewish people's penchant for cultivating sacred spaces that reeked of burning spices and gums from thuribles throughout Jewish temples—those metal censers suspended from chains, in which incense is burned during worship services. Mostly, it was thanks to his experience of Anglicanism while in England.

Elijah skidded to a stop and slid his motorcycle into an empty spot in a parking lot void of any vehicles. Surprised he was the only one there, but he preferred it that way. Would be an exercise in Yahweh's good graces to carry him through this new assignment, working with a team of others and all.

Dismounting, he took off his helmet and spread a hand across his bed of matted, dark wavy hair, trying his best to make it presentable. Not that he cared. Didn't give a lick about appearances, only how he performed.

Leaving his helmet on his hog, he went to a heavy steel door anchored at the side of the cathedral. Apparently, it had been an old outpost for SEPIO, the muscular arm of the Order of Thaddeus. A Latin acronym for *Sepio, Erudio, Pugno, Inviglio, Observo.*

Protect, instruct, fight for, watch over, heed. Based on Jude 3, Saint Jude Thaddeus' exhortation to *'contend for the once-for-all faith entrusted to God's holy people.'*

As Elijah understood it, around a decade ago, near the start of the Church's existence, the good Apostle had already seen forces inside and outside the faith working against it. So, he launched a religious order about five centuries before that was a Christian thing, historians pegging the first Christian order with Saint Benedict in the 6th century.

For centuries, the Order had worked tirelessly to instantiate Thaddeus's vision for faith-contending—all the while battling nemeses from the shadows of history. Especially one particular bad actor who happened to be headed up by the Order Master's little bro, Nous.

Although formerly a Roman Catholic outfit, the Order of Thaddeus itself was an ecumenical mission, with members from every Christian denomination. Protestant, Catholic, Orthodox, even some Southern Baptists on the force.

And now a Messianic Jew who formerly taught at an evangelical Protestant seminary—

A whirling engine from some grocery-getter behind gave him pause.

Spinning around, a candy apple-red Honda Odyssey rolled into view from around the hedgerow. Elijah's face widened into a grin.

That Messianic Jew was now joined by a charismatic Catholic!

"Gina colada…"

The Honda braked hard in an empty spot next to his beemer, a soprano belting some operatic number heard through the tinted windows.

He darted to his former partner as she climbed out of her pimped-out ride, those wavy ginger locks of hers falling past her shoulders, though the two didn't embrace.

Instead, they both waved a hand, the motion synchronized and almost touching, but not quite. A greeting they had practiced and perfected working together at the Bureau.

Elijah said, "I see our illustrious Order Master replaced your ride. Didn't know they came looking like Santa's sleigh!"

"Custom job," Gina grinned proudly, pressing a hand against the van's body and petting its side. "Named her Fuji, on account of its gorgeous candy apple red sheen."

"Sounds about right. And looks like you put in for an upgrade."

"Figured go big or go home. Besides, the Order footed the bill. Silas Grey came through."

He laughed. "Sort of had to after the last minivan had a run in with FBI bullets!"

"And don't forget that berm and massive oak that tore the van to shreds."

"I'm told such is life in the Order of Thaddeus."

"Lucky us."

He walked back to the door and placed his hand on the security pad. The door unlocked, and Elijah turned to his former partner-in-crime-solving to his new partner-in-*case*-solving.

"Ready, Freda?"

Gina twisted up her face. "Freda? That doesn't rhyme."

"I know. But you're not a dude, so Freddie didn't work."

"*Psht.* Freddie's also a girl's name."

"Oh my cheeps, it is?" he exclaimed.

"Old German version of Alfreda, for elf or magical counselor. Suppose you got the Freda part right."

"How do you like that…"

"Come on, flyboy. Let's get the show on the road."

He nodded and pushed through the door into his new life solving the Church's inexplicable cases.

"Into the void we go…"

# CHAPTER 2

Gina Anderson followed Elijah inside. They were met by a short, sterile-white hallway leading to an elevator.

And she promptly withdrew a packet of gum. Wrigley's Doublemint. "Double your pleasure, double your fun," as the commercials from her '90s childhood had promised. Boy, were they right.

So, she promptly withdrew two sticks wrapped in shimmering foil, unwrapped them to reveal the white sticks of heaven, and shoved them in her mouth. Both. One might be enough for your run-of-the-mill Jane, but two was what the moment required.

A slight flutter overcame her chest at the sight, Gina's acrophobic fear of heights and elevators flaring up. The gum helped. One of the ways she stimmed, or stimulated. The act of chewing two pieces of gum, with the work it took to grind them into a chewy pulp, the fresh spearmint dancing across her taste buds, the smell of minty heaven filling her nostrils—all of it helped focus her attention away from her fears and work through her anxiety at not only descending below thousands of metric tons of bricks and steel and earth. But also being suspended in midair by cables who knew were last inspected for cracks and frays and weaknesses!

The curse of being an autistic person, just like Elijah. She'd managed well enough, her personal spectrum wheel not as complicated as some people she knew similarly challenged with neurodiversity.

But gum helped.

It also reminded her of those silly '90s commercials, the ones featuring twins and that double-your-fun slogan. She could still recall the slogan song, and she began humming it to herself. The one she and her own twin sister Grace had sung together, dancing arm in arm and twirling in their double-wide trailer in a lot outside Toledo, Ohio.

Until her untimely death...

"How's it hanging, Gina colada?" Elijah asked, the elevator door open and waiting for them to enter. "Only way through the portal is down, I'm afraid."

She took a breath and smiled at the nickname he'd given her from back in their FBI days. The one sounding like her go-to tropical pineapple and coconut cocktail. Boy, could she use one of those right then!

Swallowing the minty saliva that had built up, she said, "Fine. Let's hop to it."

He nodded and stepped inside, his own anxious tell starting up.

Thumb to index finger, thumb to middle, thumb to ring finger, thumb to pinkie. Then rinse and repeat.

His phobia was more closed spaces than heights, as it was for her, but it comforted her to know her former partner struggled just like her. Made her feel seen, not so alone. Which had pretty much been the opposite of her half decade at the FBI after he left.

Working that wad of gum over in her mouth, Gina offered up a quick prayer to the good Lord above for his providential care. Who would've thunk Eli and Gina would be partners in crime again. The thought was flat too good to be true!

Punching the lowest floor, the pair traveled three stories beneath the Catholic church and former SEPIO outpost to their awaiting new gig.

"How was your drive over?" Gina asked, small talk not her suit but knowing it was Elijah's jam. Had been years since they'd been partners, and she wasn't sure how it would go after the way they'd left things. Wasn't like climbing back on a pony after getting bucked, that's for sure!

He shrugged. "Almost pancaked a squirrel."

"Egads! But you saved the day, right?"

"Of course. Doc Doolittle lives on."

She smiled at the memory of his nickname back at the Bureau. The fellas never could quite understand him and his love for animals. She understood it came from his dreadful time at the Virginia orphanage, and then being bounced around between foster families. Animals were about the only thing he could love back then, about the only thing that loved him back.

The elevator suddenly lurched with a weightless dip before rising with a sudden heavy groundedness.

Gina sucked in a breath, an electrically charged dread racing through every nerve. She chomped on her gum faster, the ache at her masseter, temporalis, and medial pterygoid jaw muscles about the only thing stabilizing her.

Then a bell chimed, and the elevator doors opened.

"Cheated death once again…" she muttered, following Eli out into a red-brick hallway completely void of any activity.

"Don't you know it," he replied. "I believe we're just down the hallway."

Gina followed, content with him taking the lead even though her mother would have had her head. Mama had been swept up in Third Wave Feminism during childhood, when women were fighting for new rights to party. Not that Gina was poo-pooing the movement of her sisterhood of the traveling pants forebears or anything. She liked voting and working like any run-of-the-mill male variety of the *Homo sapiens* species.

She just wasn't put off by men taking the lead walking down a dank brick hallway that smelled like the sump pump wasn't working. Quite fancied them opening the door for her, actually. Sure beat having to do it herself. And if they wanted to pay for her dinner too—well, more power to 'em!

Not Mama. She burned her bras and panties in a wave of women's marches in downtown Toledo the summer of '99. Since the fam couldn't afford them anyway, Mama was out of luck until the end of the summer when Daddy's paycheck could replace her act of protest.

The thought of her judgment sent Gina chomping harder. Could never get out from underneath that assessing eye of hers. Even three stories beneath a Catholic cathedral. Which would surely set Mama off, given she was raised Lutheran!

Their footfalls echoed through the dimly lit hallway. Air was stale too, with a layer of dust covering the floor. Even caught some cobwebs in the ceiling corners.

Another ping of anxiety wound its way through her chest. Arachnophobia was another of her fears. First thing to go in their new digs would be those cobwebs. A woman's touch should do the trick.

Her mother would not be proud.

Another palm-reading keypad stood guard at double doors, waiting for Eli's hand. When one door unlocked, he opened it to reveal a modest space in disuse.

Flipping a switch, dimmed recess lighting flitted to life around the perimeter, shining down upon narrow tables lining the dark walls commanded by workstations. Back in the day, they would have been manned by agents dutifully executing on SEPIO orders. Now they lay dormant, dust coating the surface and more webs spun between hibernating monitors. A massive dormant screen hung at one end, no longer tracking critical mission updates and relevant news footage. A raised platform with a few chairs stood at the center awaiting someone's control.

Gina folded her arms. "Not much of a workroom, is it?"

Elijah joined her pose. "A good scrubdown should do the trick. And new paint."

Sweeping the room with an assessing gaze of her own, she recalled the history of her new employer in her briefing with Silas Grey, her new boss and Master of the Order of Thaddeus.

A few decades ago, in the face of a number of threats from within and without, the Order realized the Church was quickly coming to a precipice from which it would never be able to walk back, unless they did something to deliberately preserve and protect the once-for-all faith and dogmatic tradition through faithfully passing it along and combating heresy. So, it launched a more kinetic response to their nemesis Nous's shenanigans. Project SEPIO.

Mostly research-based, they also dabble in a bit of propaganda, you could say, seeking to broadcast the memory of the faith using new media, preservation mechanisms, and other exploits. But they also took seriously the P in SEPIO.

Fight for.

Project SEPIO was a sort of Navy SEALs for Jesus, with a kick-ass team of former military and intelligence officers that surrounded the memory of the faith with a hedge, as the Latin *sepio* means. SEPIO was the operational arm of the Order of Thaddeus to fight for the Church's memory. Technically, this more…kinetic aspect of the project fell under the Papal Gendarmerie Corps. The policing unit of the Vatican.

Her and Eli's project was different. Group X, it was called. For *inexplicitus*. Latin for unexplainable—along with inexplicable, incomprehensible, inconceivable. Also had the advantage of mirroring the Greek letter *Chi*, which was the first letter for Christ, an X.

"Takes you back, don't it?" Elijah said, one end of his mouth curled upward.

"Sure does…"

The pair had worked their own set of *inexplicitus* cases for the FBI, the kind of the more paranormal variety. She had been recruited out of the University of Michigan—go Blue! Her thesis on cultic ritual abuse had gotten her noticed by the muckety-mucks up the Bureau food chain, and she was assigned with Eli, a fresh graduate of the Academy. They were handpicked to work the same magic for Group X after their assistance last year.

After everything went down in their last operation with the Order, Silas Grey had realized there was missing a crucial element to the Order's mission to preserve and contend for the once-for-all faith entrusted to God's holy people. An investigative arm to the Order that was separate from the operations part that SEPIO took care of, the more kinetic aspect of the Order.

Which Gina found a gag-worthy euphemism for *violent*. Silas had said it was the Church's forceful response to threats against the faith. A weak excuse, but it was what it was.

Either way, the idea that the Church should have any forceful response to defending the faith was hard to stomach. Her freshman year at U of M, when the Twin Towers fell, was a clear demonstration of the kinds of lengths religious wackadoodles go to defend their faith. Last thing she ever wanted to be was a religious wackadoodle.

But after everything went down last year, with everything she had witnessed that had threatened Christianity's understanding of our place in the world, and the supernatural forces arrayed against the Church—let's just say she became a reluctant participant.

Didn't have a clue why, and she wondered if she'd made the biggest mistake of her life. The FBI had offered her her old job back after nearly taking her and the other SEPIO teammates out at Quantico. Even offered her a commendation and nice cush raise, given her role at exposing the wackadoodle political conspiracy that had embroiled some of their own.

Yet there she was. Helping lead an investigative arm that took seriously the Church's struggle against this present darkness. To wage war against the fallen ones still ravaging this world, investigating the supernatural struggle making itself known and surfacing in ways humanity hadn't seen before.

Of course, she knew why she was there. When Silas made the offer, and she saw another opportunity to work with someone like she had never clicked with before as when they were partners at the Bureau—no *person* in all her life she had clicked with before, her life one of loneliness and one relational disappointment after another from a world that rejected neurodiverse people such as herself.

Obviously, it was a no brainer.

*Yeah, Mama, I followed the boy. So sue me!*

Elijah cleared his throat, the echo snapping her back to the moment.

He had closed his eyes and tipped his head back. "*'For our struggle is not against enemies of blood and flesh,'*" he intoned, quoting from one of the Apostle Paul's letters, "*'but against the rulers, against the authorities, against the cosmic powers of this present darkness, against the spiritual forces of evil in the heavenly places.'*"

"The Book of Ephesians, chapter 6," Gina said, walking to his side.

"Our calling card."

"For spiritual warfare."

"Let's just hope we don't run into any spinning heads—"

"Or pea soup!"

The pair laughed together, *The Exorcist* trope of Regan MacNeil a constant jab from their Bureau counterparts.

Elijah mounted the platform at the center of the room and planted his hands on his hips, then announced: "We've got one job, as far as I'm concerned, Gina colada."

"And what's that?"

"It's like Silas said last year, when he invited us into this gig."

She understood his meaning. "Spiritual warfare."

"Bingo. Which is about fulfilling one task."

"Setting captive people free from the grip of this present supernatural darkness through the gospel of Jesus Christ."

"Both individual and societal."

She recalled something else Silas had said, quoting a well-worn John Stuart Mill maxim: *'Bad men need nothing more to accomplish their ends, than that good men should look on and do nothing.'*

For too long, the Church has sat back in its cozy, quiet comforts of padded pews and fog machines, their high-strung worship songs and rote liturgy. That's all well and good when the world is right and evil isn't knocking on the door. Which really is about a minute of every year, but whatever. Except, as Silas had said, it's in the midst of good people's cozy comfort that wickedness blooms.

Time for the Church to get off its keister and take its firm stand against the darkness, like the Apostle Paul said, and *'withstand on that evil day,'* being *'strong in the Lord and in the great strength of his power.'*

For it was D-Day every day. A Groundhog's Day of D-Days.

And it was up to her and Eli to go against the cosmic powers Paul spoke about, in the more overt, confrontational, stand-your-ground way Silas was envisioning for Group X.

"Only question is," she said, replying to his point about spiritual warfare, "what will that look like?"

He nodded, sitting down in a dusty chair. "For the two of us?"

"For Group X?"

There was a soft knock at the door, making her jump—nearly clear out of her skin!

She spun around, clutching her chest.

"Sorry about that! Didn't mean to startle you."

Silas Grey was at the door, and smartly dressed. A blue-and-white gingham shirt with a button-down collar, sporting dark denim and English tan leather shoes. Even sported a matching English tan leather belt. Fella knew how to dress, and a far cry from when she saw him last mission decked out in a Led

Zeppelin T-shirt and sneakers. A curious manilla envelope was wedged under his arm.

"Don't you look corporate," Elijah said.

Silas startled, glancing down at his attire and blushing a shade. Oh, Eli. Ever the blunt one.

"Well, I think you look nice." She turned to her partner. "Right, Eli?"

He shrugged, looking off toward the ceiling. A tell she knew meant he was avoiding confrontation.

Silas chuckled. "This is what an ecclesial bureaucrat looks like."

Elijah reclined in the chair, throwing his hands behind his head. "What can we do you for?"

"It's what I can do for you two."

"And what's that?" asked Gina.

He pulled the envelope out from under his arm and slapped it down on the U-shaped table.

"Your first case."

Elijah bolted from his chair to a stand, bobbing back and forth on the balls of his feet with unbounded energy.

Guessing a jolt of excitement had just raced through him. Same one making its way through Gina.

The start of a case did that to them both. When the world was a blank slate with wide-open possibilities. When questions were to infinity and beyond, and the answers were less than zilch.

Ahh, heaven…

"Eli…"

Elijah snapped his head toward Silas, who was regarding him with a raised brow.

"You with me?"

He nodded. "Def."

Then he plopped back down in his dusty chair at the table and propped his feet up on the desk. He folded his hands on his lap and grinned.

Gina joined him, taking the other chair when a flash of déjà vu flared up. That happened from time to time. But this wasn't so much a feeling that the moment had happened before as it was a feeling she had had before, one of many.

The feeling of sliding into the driver's seat of a new case that would take her on a wild ride, the two of them together.

Just like old times...

Elijah leaned forward with interest. "What kind of case?"

Silas took a breath, then a beat.

"A dead priest."

Gina tossed him a frown. "Happy first day of work to us..."

# CHAPTER 3

Elijah literally did a double-take with his head. Had he heard him right? A dead man of the cloth, and for their first case? Seemed too on the nose for Group X's first case to investigate the death of one of the Church's own.

And also too close to home…

A clammy coldness swept over him, and he started up his tick. Thumb to index finger, thumb to middle, thumb to ring finger, thumb to pinkie.

One of his stimming routines that helped center him. A way of dealing with stressful situations or a burst of excitement for people like him.

People on the autism spectrum.

Earlier in his life, it had been called Asperger's Syndrome. Nope. Not anymore. At least, not after revelations about Herr Asperger's experiments on children for the Nazi Great Cause. Society switched things up real quick after that little nugget of revelation, making a switcheroo to the Autism Spectrum Disorder lingo.

Even earlier in his life, he had simply been called a retard. And a difficult, out-of-control retard at that. The kind who drove his birth parents to the brink, and then made the guardians at the Commonwealth of Virginia's orphanage and his eleven foster parents want to pull their hair out. And beat him with the backs of their hands, and their belts, even copper pipes and coat hangers when they were within arm's reach.

It wasn't until a psychologist and her pastor husband adopted him that the world finally got him. An Evangelical-Catholic couple from the foothills of Kentucky. Or Kenturkey, as he fondly remembered his teenage childhood, on account of all the wild turkeys running around his property.

An Evangelical Baptist minister and a practicing Catholic adopted an ethnic Jew. Only in America.

At least until one of their untimely deaths…

He wound his stimming tick back to the beginning, his mouth widening into a grin at the opportunity. Then went through it again: Thumb to index finger, thumb to middle, thumb to ring finger, thumb to pinkie.

In this case, it wasn't stress. It was bottled-up thrill ready to open up on a fresh case. The thrill at the chance to right a wrong, to seek justice and right the world. A smidgen of his own world that had been ground to a bloody pulp.

Literally…

Nothing at all in the world like launching headlong into a new investigation when the stakes were high. A wide-open field of possibilities, with twisty (and often twisted) turns that could go in any direction. Like one of those Choose Your Own Adventure books he had loved as a kiddo, where one choice led to the solution and another straight off a cliff.

But a dead priest…Boy, did that make his head spin.

"A priest, as in Roman Catholic?" asked Gina, refocusing him on the moment.

Silas nodded. "That's right."

"Dead?" confirmed Elijah.

"Last I checked. And from what it looks like, murdered."

"Murdered?" Gina exclaimed. "Egads…"

"Oh my cheeps, this is just perfect!" Elijah slapped his hands together and rubbed them, eager to dive into the one case he'd never gotten the chance to resolve at the Bureau. Had come close, real close. But no banana on that front. No thanks to that blowhard Pendergast…

Now was his chance. This was too good to be true…

Silas frowned. "Don't get too excited. The details are still sketchy, and it looks peculiar."

"I think you mean *inexplicitus*," Elijah said wryly, referencing the inspiration behind the X for the Order of Thaddeus's investigative arm.

He nodded. "Exactly. Your old employer has taken the lead on this, so there's that element, which I figured you'd appreciate."

"The Bureau?" Gina said with a start, glancing at Elijah who threw her a raised brow.

"That's right."

"Why?" Elijah asked. "It's not in their jurisdiction."

"It is when there's a whiff of terrorism involved."

*"Terrorism?"* the pair said together.

"Because of the nature of the murder, given it's a priest and all. With all the recent attacks on religious communities over the past few years—synagogues, black congregations, the Amish—the Feds aren't taking any chances with this one. Especially since the victim was a prominent member of the local Catholic community."

Elijah eased back in the dusty chair, an adrenaline ping racing through him now on the cusp of such an exciting new investigation. Not that he was excited about a dead priest or anything. Even felt compelled to cross himself, but that could wait. First things first…

The case file. Which he assumed was the manilla envelope Silas had wedged under his arm before he slapped it down at his spot.

He picked it up. And startled, that adrenaline picking back up with a blooming alarm of confusion.

What the heck…

It was light. Far, far too light for a case file. Not any he'd ever been handed at the FBI when he and Gina were brought in on a case.

Again: What the heck?

Furrowing his brow, he unwound the red twine keeping the manilla envelope closed. One of those Staples specials that had clearly just been bought, the new paper and glue scent an odd juxtaposition with the old, stale basement smell of the ops center. He fought with the dang thing but finally succeeded, sliding open the flap.

And pulling out a single sheet of paper. Same Staples special.

His breath seized in his chest at the sight; his heart rate jolted forward at its meaning.

At the top was printed a case number: X-00001. How original. He and Gina were listed as the investigative agents, along with some details about the case he didn't pay any attention to. Because it wasn't enough.

Not nearly. No way, no how!

Where was the rest of it? All the other pieces that would give him what he needed to solve the case and put the world to rights —put his own world to rights by gaining some small measure of justice for a minister who'd been murdered for their testimony?

He tossed the paper to the table and widened the envelope's mouth, stuffing his head inside and searching for more.

Nope. Bupkis.

Nothing but that sweet Staples-paper air, which was now reeking of betrayal.

Elijah picked the paper back up and held it by a corner with a frown. As if it were one of the dirty diapers he'd helped change back at the orphanage.

"What's this?"

Silas answered, "The case file for your assignment."

"Nope. It's a piece of paper with toner applied to it in an organized fashion."

"Uhh, I suppose that's literally so. It's a one-page brief with the details of the case."

"Where's the rest of it? The crime details, the blood and DNA analysis, the witness list—th-th-the *case*?"

Silas chuckled. "That's why you get paid the big bucks."

"Nope! We don't. We get paid to put the pieces together. To solve an unsolvable crime. That's what we did at the FBI. We need a case file. This is just a piece of paper in a manilla envelope!"

"Sorry…" their boss mumbled. "But that's all we got. If you just read the one-page briefing, you'll get all the—"

Elijah scoffed and stood, throwing the brief across the table and bobbing on the balls of his feet. He knew he was getting worked up, but this wasn't the way it was supposed to be!

When he and Gina worked cases together at the FBI, they'd been handed an entire briefing book—sometimes boxes—chuck full of all the necessary pieces they could use to put the pieces of the puzzle together. Sure, the picture was incomplete, and they had a jumbled mess, with some of the clues amounting to nothing more than a throwaway comment from a 7-Eleven attendant. But they still had all the necessary pieces, in the case file! Rarely did they have to work from scratch.

Like this!

"I need some air…" Elijah announced, his chest feeling constricted with a rising sense of anxiety about his ability to solve the case, his head exploding with insecure voices telling him he couldn't do it.

Couldn't seek the justice he'd been searching for two decades.

That little announcement sent Gina into motion. Knew it would. It was his watch word from back in the day when he felt himself spiraling into a messy meltdown that would do no one any good.

He stormed out of the operations center and into the brick hallway smelling of a basement that took him back to that

Virginia orphanage. Place always smelled like a basement. Damp and full of rot, walls blackened by mildew, the smell only outmatched by urine-stained sheets and poo-streaked walls, and that blasted Thursday night meatloaf special.

The scent took him back to those dark days when there was no escape, when the walls closed in on him and he had no control over his life.

Now was then; this was that!

Elijah threw his hands to his head and paced the vacant hallway, his footfalls echoing. Just like those long, narrow hallways in Virginia made of cinder block and peeling white paint and warped wood paneling, buzzing flies and creeping cockroaches and mice scampering past his feet without a care in the world.

He startled, swearing he saw movement. Swore he saw something ready to scamper across his path right up his pant leg!

But he realized it was just his own shadow.

Elijah smirked and shook his head, pressing his palms against the rough brick and heaving a sigh. Startled by his own shadow. About the long and short of his sad story…

He pushed off and sloughed off his black leather jacket, unbuttoning the top button to his white shirt and loosening his green bow tie. The one his widowed adoptive mother had bought him for his first day on the job as a professor at Grand River Theological Seminary.

What the heck had he done, quitting that safe and secure job for one that gave him nothing more than a blasted one-page case file?

"Eli?" a voice called to him.

He spun around, sucking in a startled breath. It was Gina colada, standing just outside the ops center entrance—her hands up, palms flat and facing him.

He swallowed and went to her, putting up his own palms right at hers. Except not touching her. That was a no-no, for them both. But it was a way for them to connect when the shiznit hit the fan. Whether professionally in the heat of an investigative moment, or personally in the heat of an emotional breakdown brought on by buried insecurities that were rearing their ugly head at the start of a new case.

Like right then.

"We've got this, Eli," Gina reassured. She added: "You've got this."

"But it's a one-page brief! It's not supposed to be like this!"

"I know, but we did it before."

"I know, I remember. I also remember what happened when we went on nothing more than a one-page brief! Sounds like the same dang case, too…"

"That was then, Eli. This is now."

Elijah protested, "But—"

"Butts are for toilets," Gina said with interruption. "I say we can do this. Right this time. After all, it is a new day."

Elijah stood with palms nearly pressed against his partner's, his friend's, but not quite. Thirsting for a mojito and the feel of white sand between his toes.

With his hands chilled and wet from the cold, perspiring glass; his tongue dancing with the delightful tastes of lime and mint; his head light with white rum, his body relaxing under the same; his feet finding relief from the grittiness of the white granular material that had accumulated on the beach from crushed rocks under the weight of thousands of pounds of pressure over millions of days.

Instead, he was beginning to shiver in a dim subterranean hallway, mouth dry and fingers itching for stimulation.

But then a verse flashed in his mind's eye. The one he had raised his nose at earlier on the drive in. The one from the prophet Jeremiah, voicing Yahweh's words of comfort to his people in exile.

Elijah closed his eyes as the verse washed over him: *'For surely I know the plans I have for you, says the Lord, plans for your welfare and not for harm, to give you a future with hope.'*

Wasn't exiled exactly, but he got the point.

The heart of God still beat for him with a crazy love he never before experienced until he was adopted. First into his forever family, then into the family of God in Yeshua, in Jesus the Christ who he had realized was the Messiah.

And Yahweh's welfare-concerned, future-oriented, hope-filled plans for Elijah happened to include giving up his cush professor job and returning to a profession that had left him high and dry—only this time investigating the Church's cases. He knew it was true, deep down.

The Holy Spirit had told him so.

Which meant he could handle whatever Group X threw at him. Even case files filled with nothing more than one-page briefs, and two investigators who had nothing going for them than their prayers and intuition.

So he snapped back his hands from Gina's, the building pressure in his chest and head deflating. Like someone had been blowing up a party balloon to its stretching point only to let it go flying across the room.

Gina sighed and smiled, letting her hands fall to her sides. She knew he was good to go. She always did. And he usually had her to thank.

She said, "How about we get back on the pony, partner."

Elijah held her gaze a beat, then another—his fears melting into resolution.

"Giddy up," he said, rushing past her to that blasted one-page case file.

For justice.

For Dad.

# CHAPTER 4

Gina followed Elijah leading the way back inside the old SEPIO operations center, her partner making for the U-shaped table without making eye contact with Silas.

She held back, leaning against a workstation computer desk coated with enough dust to send her into a catatonic allergic fit. Good thing she'd dosed up on Flonase that morning.

After what had gone down with Eli, though...Now she'd wished she'd dosed up on Red Bull. Because she was having flashbacks from their last case together, and all that went down.

Their first Group X case smacked of their last one. And her memory of it was etched in stone.

It was all so personal. Hoped whatever demons Eli had been wrestling with half a decade ago had been long since exorcised. Because if not...

Things could get interesting.

As Eli took his seat, Silas leaned over, fixing her with dark, searching eyes. "Is everything alright?"

He nodded a furrowed brow and those searching eyes toward Eli, then swung back to Gina. Felt like Pendergast all over again, their former SAC (or special-agent-in-charge, for those not in the know).

"Yes. Fine," Elijah replied from the U-shaped table, slumping back into his dusty chair.

Gina nodded, shoving off from the workstation desk and joining her partner in another chair at his side. "We're good."

Truth be told, she wasn't sure about that. But she needed to show solidarity with her partner. These things had codes about them stretching back to time immemorial.

She could tell their boss wanted more—needed more after Eli's outburst—but Silas let it go. Was sure she'd hear more about it later, but for now the man was still on their side. For now…

But Gina knew better. Another moment, another outburst would lead to questions about his professional demeanor and mental capacity.

They always did from a world that didn't understand them.

Before anything else came of it, Elijah asked, "Why does this one matter?"

"I agree with Eli," Gina added. "Has the Order of Thaddeus ever investigated the deaths of priests before?"

Silas shook his head. "No, we haven't."

Now that was interesting.

Elijah sat straighter at that revelation. "Then why this one?"

The Order Master hesitated, the man's eyes flittering down and to the right. A tell, indicating he was searching for the right words. At the FBI, she had hammered and honed her ability to read people. To a T. Took effort and prayer to overcome gaze avoidance, like others, but she'd managed.

Although it's almost universally accepted that autistic peeps can't read emotion, the amount of scientific evidence to back it up is exactly bupkis. Not all autistic people are social nincompoops.

Put that in your neurotypical pipe and smoke it.

Silas snapped his eyes back to her and Elijah, answering, "Because that dead priest was also my childhood priest."

"Egads…" Gina said, bringing a hand to her mouth.

"And?" Elijah simply said. "Why does that concern us?"

Another hesitation, more eye movement down and to the right.

"And, well, he was also the reason my brother abandoned the faith."

"Sucks to be him," Elijah said.

"Eli…" Gina said, throwing him a frown.

Her partner sure hadn't changed much. Always the blunt one of the pair. Without fail. Got him into trouble a time or twelve. Too much trouble. Loved him to pieces, in the sort of brother-sister way. But she might have to play interference, like last time.

She offered, "Silas, do you mind sharing what happened?"

He ran a hand through his shaggy brown hair and took a seat in the opposite wing of the U-table.

"Among the two of us," Silas began, "Sebastian, my twin brother, had been the one most destined for a life in service of the Church. He should be the one sitting in this seat, not me. He was much more in tune with his spiritual side during our childhood than I ever was."

He leaned back and folded his arms, a smile playing across his face.

"I would sleep during Sunday morning Mass. Snores and snorts and all straight through the homily. Or I was too busy making faces at the parishioners behind us to get anything from it anyway. Sebastian though, he was the one taking notes and cross-checking what Father Rafferty said—that was our childhood priest. My brother dove deep into his sermons and what he had memorized from his Bible. And while I was off playing football or soccer or running track, there was my brother serving in the parish soup kitchen and as an altar boy at Saint Thomas Catholic Church in the heart of Falls Church, Virginia."

"Sounds like your model church boy," said Gina.

Her own mother would've been proud of the lad. Would've probably played matchmaker, too, if she were still alive. Could still hear Mama's complaint about Gina's ovaries not getting any younger ringing in her ears. Which she had thought an ironic jab coming from the woman who had always insisted she'd never let a man tie her to a four-poster bed and saddle her with a kid when the world was her oyster.

Supposed the absence of grandchildren made her own aging heart grow fonder for the domestic life, right up until her dying breath.

"So, your brother," Elijah said. "What happened?"

Silas shifted, leaning forward on the table. "From around fourteen or fifteen onward, I'd noticed a shift in Sebastian. It was subtle, and one only a close twin might recognize. Mom for sure would have, had she been alive."

"What happened to her?" Elijah asked.

"She passed during childbirth."

Gina's heart sank, the memory of her own mother's death smarting.

"Sorry to hear that," he said.

"Me too," Silas said. "Anyway, Dad hadn't noticed the changes either. Too focused on his military career saving the world."

Gina asked, "What changed in…Sebastian, is that right?"

"That's right. It was small things at first. A burst of anger here and combativeness there. Sebastian had always been the calm, quiet one of us Grey boys. I'd been the one born with the fiery temper, yet my brother just started going off on the smallest stuff. Then he'd started making excuses for not attending church activities. Stopped serving at the soup kitchen. Called in sick to the altar for several Sundays in a row until Dad forced him to go, even apologizing to Father Rafferty for shirking his responsibilities."

Silas took a breath, leaning back in his seat.

"Then there were his doubts, and his challenges to core Church teachings. From issues of science and the origins of the universe to women's rights and human sexuality. *The Church says it, that settles it,'* was our lay minister's response. Which lost mileage on Sebastian pretty quickly, leading to frustration and a fraying faith."

"Sounds like your run-of-the-mill teenager," Elijah said. "What does this have anything to do with our case?"

"Well, it wasn't until a few years ago that I learned why he'd lost interest in the Church, in Christianity itself."

"Why?"

"He—"

Silas's voice faltered. He swallowed hard and coughed, and Gina was sensitive to a rise in emotion at his eyes. Again, not all her kind were social nincompoops. The allistic world would be confounded by how socially aware she was.

"The reason why," Silas continued, "was that Sebastian had been abused. As a teenager."

That sinking feeling returned, a cold wave of dread washing through her. Didn't take a genius to know who he was talking about.

"The dead priest," she said.

Silas nodded. "It started when Sebastian was thirteen. When he was still serving as an altar boy. One Sunday morning, he was making preparations for the Mass. And—And the man came up behind him…"

He trailed off, a tear sliding down his cheek.

"Went on like that for a while." Clearing his throat, then wiping away the emotion, he continued, "I had no idea. Only found out about it on one SEPIO operation a few years. Tracking down the Holy Grail, of all things."

"Nope. Not a real thing," Elijah insisted.

"You're telling me. Anyway, had no idea—none! Never in a million years would I have thought my brother's changes had been because of such horrific abuse. So, after all those years, he left the Church, turning his back on God."

"Egads…" Gina whispered, wiping a tear of her own. "I suppose it's understandable."

Silence filled the vast room, the HVAC hum the only sound-track on the other side of the revelation.

Elijah finally said, "Not to poop on your family parade or anything, but what does this have to do with us?"

As much of a sob story as it was, Gina had to agree. "Why is it a Group X case?"

"Our first one at that?"

Silas explained, "Because it is unexplainable, that's why."

"In what way?" asked Elijah.

"If you'd read the investigative briefing…"

"Oh, right." He reached for the paper he had tossed earlier, giving it a once over.

And bolting to his feet.

"Oh my cheeps!"

"What?" asked Gina, snatching the paper from his hands.

"No known cause of death."

Silas nodded. "That's right. So far, anyway"

"Egads!" Gina exclaimed.

"You're telling me. An unholy violation is what it is. But that's not the kicker."

"Says here—"

Elijah snatched it back.

"Hey, I was reading that!" she protested, grabbing for it again while Elijah kept it out of reach.

"But I had it first!"

She sighed and crossed her arms. Elijah threw her a wry grin before returning to the sheet.

Couldn't help but suppress a smile, her heart warming to the idea of returning to their partnership again. Just like old times, it was. The pair of them fighting for the goods. Like the brother and sister both of them no longer had as only children—hers dead and Eli never having real ones of his own. The only two people in the world who got each other…

Elijah said, "Says here—"

"That's what I was saying…" Gina grumbled.

"—that this Father Rafferty character was found dead, but that…"

He stopped short, gasping with wide eyes.

"Is this right?" he asked, throwing Silas searching eyes.

"From what I understand, yes," Silas answered.

Gina sighed. "For the love…Is what right?"

She snatched the paper back then held it aloft after Elijah protested, giggling and telling him he deserved it.

He frowned and slumped back in his chair.

Yup, just like old times. They still had the chemistry. It was like they'd slid back into an old pair of shoes, the fit and comfort just as they had left it.

Gave her assurance she'd made the right decision after all. Because, unlike Elijah, getting a read on the Spirit had never been easy for her. Had even struggled of late to keep on believing. Sorry, Journey, but sometimes you can't hold on to that feeling—whether relational or religious—no matter how hard you try.

"Says here," Gina said, "that fingerprints were not found anywhere on the victim in question or at the crime scene."

Silas nodded, saying nothing more.

"Master Grey—" she started.

Before he put up a hand. "Silas is fine."

"Alright, Silas, you don't suspect your brother had anything to do with this, do you?"

He hesitated, taking a breath, then a beat, before standing.

"I don't know who is involved in this. I have to imagine the list could be long, given all that's been revealed in the past two decades about the Church."

"You mean pedophile priests?" Elijah said.

Gina threw him a frown. Ever the blunt one, he was.

Silas reddened but nodded before stepping down from the center platform. "As the saying goes, 'There's never just one cockroach in the kitchen.'"

Elijah hummed. "Warren Buffett. Interesting choice of phrase."

Gina said, "Was there any investigation into this Father Rafferty? Guessing you ran your brother's allegation up the ecclesial flagpole."

Silas threw up a nervous chuckle. "Not exactly…"

That caught her attention. "You never disclosed your brother's abuse?"

"Who was I supposed to tell?"

"The Pope, for one," Elijah said.

"I made some inquiries," Silas explained. "Let it be known to the Catholic Diocese of Arlington that they might have a problem on their hands. But without proof…without my brother's own testimony—"

He stopped for a breath, shifting on his feet before crossing his arms.

"There wasn't much I could do."

Another pause, another breath before he headed for the door.

"At any rate, Brittany Armstrong is the lead FBI investigator on this. Know her from way back. She even helped out on a SEPIO operation a few years ago."

"Know her?" Elijah snorted a laugh. "What, like Genesis 2 variety, when Adam *knew* his wife?"

He coughed and laughed. "Something like that."

"Really? I was just doing a funny…"

"Well, not in *that* sort of way. We dated a bit before—it doesn't matter!" Silas waved his arms before beelining it for the door. Except he forgot the shovel he was using to dig his hole. "She knows you're coming. If I were you, I'd get to it before the scene is locked down. Once the media gets wind of this, it might get dicey. Good luck."

With that, he left them with nothing more than the HVAC hum and their first case.

Elijah picked up the one-pager and scoffed before shoving it inside the manilla envelope. Holding it up, he said, "Can you believe this? One sheet of paper for a case file?"

Gina shrugged. "I don't know. Seems like a worthy challenge for us seasoned investigative agents. If you're up for it."

He bolted to his feet, shoving the envelope under his arm. "Onward and upward."

"That's the spirit!"

# CHAPTER 5

Elijah let Gina drive. Wasn't happy about it, not in the slightest. He didn't have an extra helmet for the beemer, and it seemed silly to take two vehicles to the crime scene, so he relented. But he didn't have to like it. And he didn't, never had.

Vans had always creeped him out. Reminded him of Child Protective Services. And subdivisions, which creeped him out more than vans. Both reminded him of his childhood, and being carted around from foster family to foster family, from subdivision to subdivision, never having a mom or dad or even siblings long enough to remember their last names.

And there he was, gripping the soft, supple armrest leather, palms slippery from perspiration.

Had a nice new car smell to it at least, a byproduct of the off-gassing chemical process attributable to the many plastics and adhesives used in a modern car's interior. The all-leather interior helped too, all of the scents combining in a balm to at least dampen the blunt force of those traumatic memories.

Gina also had a kicking sound system, that same soprano he'd heard when she rolled up really going at it now. Worried she'd burst some blood vessels in her brain, it was so high. Or he himself would burst some blood vessels in his brain, it was so high!

Wasn't jazz, but at least it wasn't any of that hippy top-40s nonsense. With all the sugary hooks about the emptiness of late-night hook-ups and frustrations with the local barista forgetting their extra shot of espresso. The head-pounding beats were the worst of it, sounding like the inside of a drying machine with a pile of shoes rumbling about. And what kind of name was Cardi B, anyway, or that Lady Gaga character with her twenty-inch stilettos and alien costumes? And who changes their name to Ye, anyhow, or Doja Cat?

Mama had always told him he was a middle-aged man stuck in a teenage body. Music was confirmation she was right.

Dad had been the one to introduce Elijah to all the great jazz artists. Obviously Miles Davis, John Coltrane, Theolonius Monk. Then Jimmy Smith, Art Blakey, Dexter Gordon. That last one was one of his faves, his *One Flight Up* a stroke of genius.

His pops had even bought him a vintage record player for Christmas one year from a neighborhood Salvation Army. Still had the gift, too, anchored between bookcases. One of those all-in-one wood contraptions with built-in speakers. Knew it wasn't high-fidelity listening, but it did the trick. Could more than afford an upgrade, but the honey wood cabinet held more than transistors and copper wires. It held memories. Of Dad and music, the two of them, listening to tunes and searching for hard-to-find vinyl at downtown hippy record stores before that was a thing.

About the only thing Elijah had left of the man.

And perhaps this case, the one about the dead priest sounding like the one that left him without a father.

Elijah shivered at the thought, but the good kind. Like when Miles Davis hit those haunting notes in "Flamenco" on his *Kind of Blue* album, a tingle winding up his spine and splitting into every one of his nerves, every single time. Or snacking on lemons, and the tart tang of its juices, with its wicked ph right up there with battery acid!

He smiled. Because where he had failed all those years ago working for the FBI to grasp some crumb of justice for what had befallen his father, now was his chance. Was the reason he'd gotten into the Bureau in the first place, the opportunity to track down his adoptive father's killer. To bring some level of justice to his crime, to right the world—his world.

Didn't work out that way, his SAC not appreciating his extracurricular activities avenging his father's murder, for one. And then his obsession over that one case that ended it all.

Maybe this would be different.

Gina turned off Interstate 66 and looped around the off-ramp on to Leesburg Pike. Passed the familiar furniture of suburban living. He snorted a laugh.

"What's so funny, bunny?" Gina said, her trademark rhyming-all-the-timing offering its own shiver of delight.

Had missed that the past few years. Hadn't known it until that moment. Was good to be back in the saddle with his old partner. Even if it was in the passenger's seat of a Honda Odyssey.

Elijah gestured out the front windshield. "All of this, that's what!"

Sitting at a stop light, she furrowed her brow and followed his gesture. "What, Mickey D's?"

"The Golden Arches, the Giant Food grocery store, the gas stations congregating like seagulls around some poor soul's food truck lunch."

The light turned green, and she revved up to speed. "What'd you expect? It's suburbia."

"Exactly! Creeps me out something fierce."

"I don't know. I sort of like the predictability of it all. Same stores, same layout, no need to overthink it all. Just sidle up to a Starbucks and order up a triple shot, eight-pump caramel macchiato with extra whip."

He grimaced at her. "Eww…" he said before returning to the suburban wasteland. "And look at this. The obligatory used car lots looking like sad stepchildren to their older brother actual car lots. A super sketchy massage parlor in an equally sketch strip mall. Wouldn't be caught dead darkening that door."

"True. Looks like you might wind up dead there."

"Exactly! Suburbs, I tell you. Creep me out something fierce."

She adjusted the volume to her radio, a tenor working up a Latin-induced lather. "Opera. Does a body good."

Rusted yellow cranes loomed above an intersection constructing the third floor of some condo for East Coast yuppies with little imagination. Much more preferred small-town living like he grew up with in Kenturkey. Even preferred urban living like the one he lived in back in Grand Rapids. Far more character and charm than what they were driving through.

Then he saw it.

"Pull over!" Elijah yelled, causing Gina to slam on the brakes and curse like the sailor he remembered her as from back in the day.

"Egads, man! Where's the hot potato?" she yelled, cars protesting with the East Coast manners he'd forgotten about since leaving DC half a decade ago.

He gestured out the window. "An Einstein Bros. Bagels. It's coffee break time."

"What?"

"At ten o'clock, every day, I have a raisin bagel with cream cheese. Plain, non-fat. And a cup of dark coffee."

She laughed. "Save it, flyboy. We've got to hop to it."

"Nope! We've got to stop. I'll jump if I have to."

And he was serious. He yanked at the door handle, but no go.

"Unlock the door. It's 10 o'clock. Every day I have a raisin bagel with cream cheese. Plain, non-fat. And a cup of dark coffee."

"For the love…" She pulled over and pulled through the

drive-thru. "But you owe me a triple shot, eight-pump caramel macchiato with extra whip."

Both were sorely disappointed.

The pimply faced college student rolled his eyes and sarcastically informed Gina they weren't Starbucks. She quickly informed him she'd take her business elsewhere. Forever. He shrugged.

Same pimply faced college student then informed Elijah all they had was some decaffeinated light roast slop. Something about supply chain issues. Coffee beans sitting in the Pacific Ocean on some barge floating outside the port of Los Angeles. Didn't know what in the slightest that had to do with the price of tea in China—or the absence of anything caffeinated in an Einstein Bros. Bagels shop in suburbia—but Elijah informed him he'd write corporate a heartfelt Dear John for such blasphemy. The dude shrugged again, but Elijah accepted the decaf light roast anyhow.

At least the bagel was hot and soft, the cream cheese plain and non-fat.

After settling for green tea, Gina rolled back onto West Broad Street. A few minutes later, she rolled into the downtown that was Falls Church proper, and found them stuck at a roadblock from hot Hades.

Elijah sat forward, amazed at the scene. "Oh my cheeps!"

She shut off the tenor. "You could say that again..."

Place was a regular Ringling Bros. and Barnum & Bailey circus!

Down the left road, a leafy, tree-lined street budding with new life that bespoke its name—Spring Street—the scene was straight out of something from his previous life. Dark sedans and SUVs marked by law enforcement departments from local to federal lined the road. Yellow police-line tape could be seen flapping in the morning breeze wrapped around massive trees towering above the crime scene.

And so much for the media. Everything from the local affiliates to the Most Trusted Name in News and that Fair and Balance outfit were anchored to the blacktop. Big boxy trucks, too, sporting satellite dishes and the faces of national news personalities slapped on their sides.

"Looks like our stop…" Gina offered, yanking the wheel toward destiny.

A rail-thin dude was leaning against a squad car, baby face pale and eyes far too close together to be of any use to any law enforcement agency. He pushed off on their arrival and put up a hand as Gina rolled down her window.

"Move it!" he ordered. "Street is closed."

"Nope," Elijah said. "We've got business."

Baby Face leaned a hand against the Honda. "What business?"

Gina answered, "We were asked by the FBI to help with the investigation."

The man shoved off and whipped out a small spiral notebook. "Which agency."

"Group X," Elijah answered.

Baby Face was back. "What's that?"

"Group X. Ask me again and I'll tell you the same."

That pale face reddened some, and its beady little eyes narrowed. "Never heard of it."

Gina explained, "We're an investigative group with the Order of Thaddeus."

"The Vatican," Elijah corrected. "So we've got diplomatic immunity."

She scoffed. "Tomato, potato. Either way, we're here for the thing up the road. Agent Brittany Armstrong asked us for help."

That seemed to finally work, Baby Face looking down the way and back again, straightening and nodding. "Go ahead."

Then he sauntered back to his perch, Elijah glimpsing a half-eaten donut and cup of coffee resting on the hood. A bit too cliché, but bet the man had a caffeinated dark roast coffee!

Gina pulled forward, saying, "How about you use the velvet hammer from your tool belt next time, alright?"

Elijah said nothing, looking outside and reaching inside his jacket for something to take away a rising sense of unease. A packet of salted sunflower seeds. The mild, nutty flavor with the firm but tender texture had somehow served as a release valve for rising stress. Something he'd discovered by accident in college. Never left home without no less than three packets.

He tore open one of the packets and poured a mouthful.

His partner parked her Honda behind a black Suburban. She turned to him as he munched.

"Look, Eli, I know it's been a few years since you've been in the saddle."

Elijah swallowed his mouthful hard. "I'm fine."

She smiled and tossed a stray lock of red hair behind an ear. "But you don't have to be. We're a pair. And as Solomon says in the Book of Ecclesiastes—"

"Solomon didn't write the Book of Ecclesiastes, Qoheleth did. He's different—"

"Shut it, Eli!"

He did. Sometimes she said that to him; sometimes he needed her to say that to him.

"Point is, the Good Book reminds us *Two are better than one, because they have a good reward for their toil.'*"

"'For if they fall,'" Elijah picked up quoting from chapter 4, "'*one will lift up the other.'* Look, I can quote the book too. What's the point?"

"The point is what you didn't quote, Mr. Old Testament scholar."

"Hebrew Scriptures, not the Old—"

"Eli…" Gina said, pointing a finger at him.

He sighed, running a hand through his thick hair. Sometimes he needed that too. Then continued quoting, "'*But woe to the one who is alone and falls and does not have another to help.'*"

"Exactly."

"What's your point?"

"My point is that you don't have to have all your chickens in a row."

"I think it's ducks in a row."

"I don't like ducks. I like chickens. And when someone is away from the field as long as you were, I'd expect them to be running around with its head lopped off."

He frowned. "Mixing metaphors a bit there, aren't you? But…" He looked outside at all those agents milling about, then back to Gina. His partner, his friend. "But I understand your meaning."

Gina put up her hand, palm flat and facing him. "So how about we let people like that poor baby-faced officer keep their heads and tackle this case together."

He put up his own hand next to hers, not touching it but close, and nodded.

"Deal."

The pair got out and headed for the large, imposing parish church building hidden behind towering oaks nestled in a quaint neighborhood. Turn-of-the-century homes—some brick, some not—with front porches that reminded Elijah of home surrounded the parish property.

A large L-shaped, red-brick school with white trim sat across the street from the stately ecclesial building of pale mismatched stones. Law enforcement vehicles were anchored to a generous parking lot, and bored law enforcement personnel meandered around searching for something to do.

A woman in your standard government-issued navy suit with white blouse was waving her arms before a group of five men standing at the base of concrete stairs in the same government-issued getup Elijah recalled from his own service. Sure didn't miss that costume, that's for sure!

Hair certainly wasn't government-issued, though. Blond hair cut pixie short. Could understand why Silas had dated the gal, but…Ugh.

"Never trust a woman with short hair..." he muttered on their approach.

"What was that?" Gina asked, playing with her own ginger locks. Which were much longer, thank Yeshua Almighty!

"Oh, nothing," he quickly said, neck reddening with embarrassment. Had always been one to speak his thoughts aloud. Got him into far too much trouble, more than he'd like to recall. Gina understood him and generally tolerated his bluntness, but he'd need to watch himself.

The woman who Elijah assumed was Agent Brittany Armstrong finished and the pair approached.

"Agent Armstrong," he called out, approaching the woman with hands in his pockets. It was better that way. Kept the possibility of handshakes to a minimum.

The woman turned toward them. "Yes, can I help you?"

"Actually, we're here to help you."

"I don't..."

Gina answered, "Silas Grey sent us."

"Ahh, right. The Navy SEALs for Jesus outfit."

Elijah said, "Sounds like the Order of Thaddeus gets that a lot."

"This is Elijah Fox," Gina explained. "I'm Georgina Anderson. But you can call me Gina."

"Well, I'm Brittany Armstrong, and you can call me Brit." She stuck out her hand, offering it as a greeting.

Elijah and Gina looked at it as one, eyes wide as if it were a live wire.

Neither of them handled physical contact well. Each for different reasons. But only Elijah had prepared for the inevitable with his hands in his pockets. Which he most certainly kept snug as a bug in a rug inside his pants.

An awkward silence fell across the trio before Brit sent that hand of hers to the back of that head of hers.

"I see you two aren't the hand-shaking type. Suppose we

should get to it." She motioned toward the church. "Come along, then. I'll show you around the crime scene."

She took off up the concrete stairs toward the open heavy walnut doors.

Elijah followed. "Into the portal we go…"

# CHAPTER 6

Gina followed Elijah up the concrete stairs past evergreen shrubs shaped like beach balls tossing up a piney hidey ho on their ascent.

A breeze whispering sweet, tangy nothings into her nose joined the shrubbery on an unseasonably warm breath from behind—cherry trees joined by apple pie from some dear mother's oven straight out of *Leave It to Beaver*. Not that she understood personally what that was like. June Cleaver was pure television fiction in Gina's world. Mama was more Marge Simpson or Peggy Bundy. Competent enough, but far from the pie-baking nurturing type.

The one thing they did share growing up, though, was a love for gardening. Their double-wide had the best darn looking landscape in all of the Presidential Estate trailer park! Mostly annual Kmart specials before the hedge funds got their grubby mitts on the joint and hollowed it out to nothing but studs. Hot pink petunias, white and purple calibrachoas, bright red geraniums, golden yellow marigolds that gave the sun a run for its money—you name it, Kmart had it, and the Anderson women planted it.

Ran their noses through the ringer, that's for darn tootin',

Gina inheriting her mama's bad nostrils. But they didn't care. Finding mental and emotional relief from feeling the cold, wet earth between her fingers and toes had done Gina a world of good, and it bonded daughter and mother together in a way the pair rarely experienced.

So every weekend, every spring and through the summer, the pair would make a Kmart run on Saturday mornings, bag of powdered donuts in tow, and spend the day planting and arranging the brightly colored flowers throughout their plot of rented land—in pots and flowerbeds, across the stony mobile home lot until every inch of the place was covered.

Then the flowers would die in fall and winter, and they'd have to repeat the process all over again the next year. Never got old.

Gina smiled at the memory, another gust of that cherry tree scent and its yellow pollen molecules getting shoved up her nose. Glad she gave each of her nostrils an extra squirt of Flonase that morning. They were going to need it with the relentless march of spring.

Continuing her march up the stairs, she noticed a white sign with black inlaid lettering sitting off to the side. It marked the church as St. Thomas Catholic Church. Mass was scheduled Saturday nights at 5 p.m. along with five services on Sunday: 7:30, 9, and 10:30 a.m., with another at noon and the evening Mass at 7 p.m. It also ran three times daily: 6:30 and 8:30 a.m., then noon. There was even a Spanish-only Mass service on Sundays at 2:30 in the afternoon.

Father Rafferty was a busy beaver. So was the church, having served the parish for 130 years, since 1892.

One of the massive walnut doors anchored between two spires soaring four stories stood open, a darkened void greeting them. The FBI agent disappeared inside, along with Elijah.

Into the portal was right…

A narthex was waiting on the other side, a generous antechamber painted white, with scuffed green-and-beige tiled floors straight from the '50s. Smelled like it too, wet wood and candle wax heavy, along with the sharp tang of cleaning agents. Pine-Sol floor cleaner and Holloway House Quick Shine, a multi-surface floor finish. Could place those cleaning smells anywhere, any time after how much she'd helped her mama with her janitorial jobs as a child.

The candle wax came from a black metal stand bearing near a hundred red votive holders absent any still-flickering tiny flames. The prayers of the saints gone quiet. If that ain't a metaphor for the modern state of things...

Some saint statue bore witness to the sight, an unknown wearing a brown robe and offering a loaf of bread to the faithful with outstretched hand. She wondered what he saw last night, what manner of wickedness he bore witness to in the absence of any prayers.

Which was an interesting sight. Never had seen a bank of prayer candles empty as long as she'd lived. Although...

On closer examination, one was still alive. Small and burnt down to the bottom. Perhaps the one candle was the killer's, lit to atone for his sin of commission. In her line of work, wouldn't put it past them.

The rest of the nave was about as uninspiring as the narthex. Same white walls vaulted high, supported by the same dark walnut wood beams as the door. Metal organ pipes stood ready for action in a wood structure above the entrance to the sanctuary at the back, along with a clock hung right where Father Rafferty could see it to ensure quick homilies and an on-time Mass. Same '50s-era green-and-beige tiles ran the length of the space about the size of an elementary gymnasium, lined by wooden pews of the same walnut wood, cushion-less seats polished over the years from the butts of the faithful squirming around under the watchful gaze of the priest.

The front chancel held the altar, white marble on a dais of the same stone. Behind it was a wooden structure jutting out from the back wall, where a gold crucifix hung anchored to the wood and a circular stained glass window hung above it all. A constellation of brilliant indigos and pinks and purples twinkled from the late-morning light.

Clearly, the Second Vatican Council did a number on this church.

Some have humorously called such meddlings with interior decorative choices 'wreckovations,' the ecclesial instructions from the 1960s influencing architectural design as much as liturgical worship. Stained glass windows were covered over by wood paneling. Interiors were whitewashed and the exterior was painted. Alter rails were removed on top of all the statues, except for Jesus. The Son of God was off limits. The Vatican II directives were meant to create *an atmosphere conducive to participation, worship, and prayer,* according to the official record.

From where Gina stood, they failed miserably. At least, according to one charismatic Catholic who preferred more pep in her liturgical step anyhow, but also valued the older forms of architecture that lifted their gaze beyond the mundane, beyond the metal and glass and white walls of modern living. At least they hadn't papered over the stained glass, the circular window bright now and casting faint colored light down on the altar below.

Smelled about not much different than the church she grew up in. Mold and mildew, old wood and stale Folgers. Funny how churches smelled the same, no matter the denomination. Old-school Catholic or charismatic Catholic, Lutheran or Episcopalian, Baptist or old-school Bible churches—didn't make a difference in the slightest.

Yellow police tape ringed that front section, and a pair of police officers stood guard. Brit led the way toward the front.

Gina's stomach sank at the thought. Surely the priest hadn't been killed at that sacred spot…

"By the way," the FBI agent said, "Thanks for—Hey, you're not allowed to do that!"

She was pointing an accusatory finger at Elijah, who was taking pictures with his phone.

"Yes, I am," he said, snapping away.

"No."

"Yuppers. First Amendment, and all."

"But this is a crime scene!" Brit continued her protest.

"And we're investigating it."

"At the FBI's request!"

"Exactly."

Another snap, then another before Elijah shoved the phone into his pocket with a grin.

Brit opened her mouth for another retort, but snapped it shut with a huff.

Gina completely understood the soul sister. When it came to Eli, sometimes it was best to walk away.

And she did, spinning back toward the front in a huff.

"Like I was saying," Brit continued, "thanks for joining us on this case. I hear you're both former Bureau."

Elijah followed. "That's right. And I heard you and Silas *knew* one another. Genesis 2 style."

She faltered her step in the middle of the aisle, then turned back with a raised eyebrow. "Excuse me?"

Gina laughed, then jammed an elbow in her partner's side.

Elijah yelped, but she interrupted any reply by explaining, "What my partner means is, Silas mentioned you two had a history."

"Of the romantic variety," Elijah added.

Brit scoffed and rolled her eyes. "If you call dating briefly back at Georgetown for all of two weeks romantic *history*, then yeah, we did. If memory serves me right, he ended it all with an email."

Gina twisted up her face. "Email?"

"Why not send a text?" asked Elijah.

Brit replied, "Hadn't been a thing yet, and serving notice through email wasn't supposed to be a thing."

"Except for immature twentysomethings, I suppose."

She smirked. "You can say that again."

"So…" Gina said. "The case."

"The case of the dead priest," Elijah said.

"Sounds like a *Murder She Wrote*."

Brit said, "Can't imagine Jessica Fletcher will be showing up to the confessional any time soon."

Gina threw confused, concerned eyes at Elijah. He matched them.

*"Confessional?"* they responded as one.

Elijah added, "As in, where the priest hears a parishioner's confession?"

"I'm not Catholic," Brit replied, "not religious of any sort, but I don't know of any other confessional, do you?"

"Egads…" Gina said, bringing a hand to her mouth. "What manner of wickedness have we gotten ourselves into?"

"Let's just say, I don't think anyone will be showing up to offer their confession any time soon with what we found."

"Can't imagine anyone will be hearing anyone's confession any time soon, either…"

She led them to the boxy wooden structure standing behind the altar. Gina eyed the golden crucifix affixed to its face, crossing herself on instinct.

Reaching one of the doors, Brit explained, "Rafferty was found inside with the door closed earlier this morning. But here's the kicker."

She paused, with a little too much dramatic flair for Gina's taste. Was never one to tolerate showboaters. Just get on with it and stick to the facts. Definitely a *Just the facts, ma'am* sort of ma'am. Without all the Dragnet chauvinism.

"And…" Elijah finally said, tapping his foot with the same impatience.

Brit crossed her arms, one end of her mouth curling upward with a measure of satisfaction Gina found unbecoming of law enforcement.

"And, it was locked."

Didn't expect that. Not in the slightest.

"Come again," Gina said.

Brit shrugged. "Just like I said. The confessional door was locked. And from the inside. Took a key to open it out here."

"That's generally how these things work," she said with a smirk, "but you're saying that Father Rafferty was found dead—murdered, even—behind a closed, locked door?"

"That's exactly what I'm saying."

"Any force of entry?"

"None."

Elijah added, "Silas said there weren't any prints found anywhere on Rafferty or the confessional, isn't that right?"

"Correct," Brit said.

"Which rules out any form of struggle," Gina surmised.

She nodded, saying nothing more.

"And no known cause of death?"

Elijah smirked. "That's what that blasted one-page case file said, anyway."

Brit answered, "Not unknown. Death was ruled by asphyxiation. We just don't know how it could have happened."

Gina was struggling to wrap her mind around this case. Elijah was loving it, the man starting to rock back and forth on the balls of his feet with the familiar unbounded energy she expected from her old partner.

"So, a locked-room mystery," Elijah said with the same air of satisfaction. "And a mysterious death."

"Something like that," Brit said. "It's all pretty unbelievable."

"*Inexplicitus*, actually," he corrected, grinning now and fingers running through their energized tick. "The reason the big guns were brought in."

"Sounds like I've got myself some new helpers."

"Most definitely."

Gina threw him a frown, knowing Elijah loved puzzles and was always giddy at the front end of a case. Couldn't help it.

Was just his manner about him, the man and his brain perfectly attuned to puzzle mysteries and loving the opportunity to work one out in that brain of his. Especially when it came to setting things to rights, bringing that brain to bear on criminal cases in order to bring a measure of justice to the world.

Still, wasn't at all thrilled their first Group X case was a dead priest. A murdered priest to boot! One who had apparently gotten frisky with the altar help. A bit too on the nose if you asked her.

She sighed. Her life had been reduced to sussing out perfectly coined clichés more tuned for bargain-bin Kindle thrillers than anything smacking of reality.

Such was her life, she supposed. What her life had been reduced to after following Elijah to this new gig.

That sign she saw out front coming up the stairs flashed in her mind's eye. A detail from the timing of the services.

Which didn't add up.

Gina said, "Excuse me, Agent Armstrong—"

"Brit is fine," the woman corrected.

"Brit, then, I'm confused. I saw on the sign out front that the confession schedule was on Saturday afternoons and evenings, from 3:30 to 4:30 and then again from 7:30 to 8 p.m."

Brit crossed her arms, furrowing her brow. "Alright."

"Oh my cheeps," Elijah said. "Today is Monday! Good call, Gina colada."

"I don't understand."

"Why was he hearing a confession on Sunday?"

"Good question."

"I'm sorry, but I'm confused." Brit said. "Do priests not hear confession on Sunday? Thought that was the whole purpose of the holy day."

Gina shook her head. "No, not really. The Eucharist is the climax of Sunday Mass, meant as a focal point of worship and receipt of God's grace through the Sacrament."

"OK…what's your point?"

"You said he wasn't noticed missing until this morning, when he didn't show for the morning service."

Brit nodded. "That's right."

"Which means he showed up for the five services—or perhaps six, if he spoke español—from the day before."

"The whole Sunday Mass taco," said Elijah.

Brit chuckled. "I think you mean enchilada, but I see—"

"Nope. Taco."

She sighed. "At any rate, I see what you're saying. Something happened between the end of the last Mass—which was?"

"Seven o'clock," Gina answered. "It runs an hour, so sometime after 8 p.m. And you said he was found this morning?"

Brit nodded. "By the...helper, or whatever."

Elijah corrected, "I think Lay Eucharistic Minister is the term you're searching for."

"Whatever. But that's a good catch. And not the only detail."

"What do you mean?" asked Gina.

"Well..." Brit stepped over to the still closed door. "See for yourself."

Slipping on a pair of baby blue crime-scene gloves, she grasped the burnished bronze handle, twisted it, and eased open the heavy walnut door.

Elijah gasped at what he saw. "Sweet mother of Melchizedek!"

Gina followed suit: "For the love..."

What they saw took this thing to a whole other level.

# CHAPTER 7

E lijah was like a kid in a candy store. No disrespect to the dearly departed, as much of a scoundrel as the pedophile priest was.

Or rather, *alleged* pedophile priest, in the parlance of litigious-averse journalists. How about wolf in sheep's clothing? That's certainly what he was. Jesus warned about them type.

Although, it wasn't like his own evangelical Protestant tradition escaped scrutiny under the microscope of wrongdoing. Plenty of patriarchal pastors who looked the other way while women were abused—spiritually, emotionally, sexually—with nary a word from the pulpit or from evangelical leaders about what the good Lord says on the subject.

But that was neither here nor there. Because all that mattered was what FBI Lady was about to reveal behind Door Number One.

Slipping on a pair of baby blue crime-scene gloves, she grasped the burnished bronze handle, twisted it, and eased open the heavy walnut door.

It threw up a mournful sigh, as if relenting at revealing what it was hiding within.

First thing that instantly flooded his senses was the scent of old wood whooshing by. It was a familiar scent that brought back all sorts of memories from his time stuck in that orphanage. The managers of the estate barely had enough money to feed and clothe their wards let alone fix leaky roofs that soaked floorboards and streaked cheap-o wood paneling during heavy rains. Wet wood and mildew were a constant during his childhood.

Except this wasn't the cheap-o paneling from the orphanage that stank of pee and mildew. Rather, it was the nice kind, sanded down and stained and shellacked with a craftsman's care. The kind that brings out all the grains and warm, earthy notes in the wood over time thanks to the donations of dutiful parishioners and Papa Pancho's purse.

The next thing that smacked his face was the scent of death. Another familiar scent that surfaced all sorts of memories.

Had been a long time since he'd smelled that one, a sharp tang comprised by over 480 different known chemical compounds when the human body decomposes—any body, really, from the birds that smacked into the large picture window at the orphanage, breaking their necks and then tumbling to their deaths below, to the squirrels a German Shepard tore to shreds at one foster house.

But that wasn't all. Couldn't place it entirely, but there was something else lingering.

Didn't matter a lick, though, because Elijah was too distracted by what his peepers were peeping than what his sniffer was sniffing.

Elijah gasped at what he saw. "Sweet mother of Melchizedek!"

Gina followed suit: "For the love…"

"I thought I already said that…"

Brit stood next to the door, eyeing the scene inside. "Don't know about you two, but this takes the cake as far as cases I've worked."

"Takes the cheesecake, that's for sure."

And he meant it, too. Because he hated cheesecake. And the

scene before him was like something out of a bakery case at that suburban restaurant chain he loathed with a similar name.

What stood before them took the whole taco of cases he had worked back in the day. Barely anything came close.

He whipped out his phone again to document more crazy, nabbing several more pictures.

An old man had been left right where he had been found. Presumably Father Rafferty. They had arrived at the scene early enough for the details of the crime to remain intact.

"He looks like the letter S," Gina said, hands at her hips with assessment. Her pose at any crime scene they had worked together. "A naked letter S, but the nineteenth number, nonetheless."

Elijah cocked his head. He sort of did.

Rafferty was stark naked, wearing nothing but his birthday suit. Naked as a bare-naked bear in a berry patch, he was! Skin pale and thin and saggy like the Salvation Army bathrobe five sizes too big he'd gotten for Christmas one year at the orphanage —the only thing he'd gotten for Christmas the entire time at the place. Veins were popping through, more on account of the man's years than anything. He looked like Gollum from his favorite film, the *Lord of the Rings*.

Elijah went for Rafferty's corpse to take a closer look.

When a loud throat-clearing was thrown up from the door.

He snapped his head toward FBI Lady holding up a pair of those blue latex gloves she was wearing.

Shoving his phone back into his pocket, he snatched them from her and slipped them on with a smack, then went inside the confessional for a closer look.

The old wood smell was more pronounced, as was the scent of death. Space was more generous than he would have thought. The size of his half bathroom, the walls entirely made of wood with a small window obscured by a weaving lattice pattern of delicate stained wood. Almost like a basket weave, with enough transparency for the voiced confession while obscuring the confessor's face. There was also a sliding window, but that was shut and looked secure. Suppose the criminal could have attacked Rafferty through that means. But it was latched, securely locked, and undisturbed. Again, from the inside.

The most curious thing of all, though, were Rafferty's clothes. His black vestments and clerical collar, worn by any minister of the Catholic cloth.

Yes, they weren't on the man; that much was a given. It wasn't so much where they weren't as where they *were*.

Which was lying on the floor beneath Father Rafferty. Not crumpled in a discarded pile, but folded in a neat stack. As if carefully, thoughtfully arranged. Almost as odd as the fact the priest carefully, thoughtfully disrobed before arranging himself like the letter S!

Alright, strike that. Not the most curious. But close.

The other weirdly curious part of it all was the man's posture. He was kneeling on the chair, legs folded underneath together; arms outstretched and stiff, head bowed and straight. Like the letter S, as Gina had observed.

Odd...

Elijah shuffled around the body for a better look, noting that the chair had been positioned at the center of the priest's side of the confessional booth. Gina joined him now on the other side of the priest, finishing up donning the same pair of gloves.

She noted, "Looks like rigor mortis has set in pretty well."

He nodded, saying nothing more. That it had.

Immediately upon death, the body's muscles relax, and it slowly stiffens over 24 to 48 hours due to the buildup of acid in the body's muscular tissue. It is through this stiffening process, and the presence or lack of body heat, that a rough estimate of the time of death can be ascertained.

In general, a warm-feeling body with no rigor present represents a death occurrence under three hours. If the body still feels warm and also stiff, death is pegged at three to eight hours earlier. A cold and stiff body passed eight to thirty-six hours earlier, while a body that is no longer stiff yet colder than his foster mama's stare died more than thirty-six hours.

Elijah was never a fan of using rigor mortis as a time of death indicator, because of the large spans of time indicating anywhere from a third of a day to a day and a half. Much more interested in precise timing, not the sort of windows that can vary by as much as twenty-four hours. That wasn't even taking into account all of the factors that can severely impact the onset and timeline of rigor mortis. Everything from temperature to the physical conditions of where the body was found. Even the level of activity before death and whether a victim had the flu or common cold can throw off the time of death.

"Cold and stiff," Gina announced.

Brit added, "Which certainly fits the time frame you indicated based on the Mass service. After 8 o'clock."

"When was he discovered?" Elijah asked, bending low and grimacing at the man's face, his putty cheeks gray and puffy, forehead creased with lines and mouth hanging open as if in a question.

"Just after nine."

"A pretty big window of opportunity, twelve hours or so."

"We'll know more when the coroner examines the body."

Elijah grunted an affirmation.

"Body doesn't look as though it was moved," he noted, "so the rigor process doesn't look like it was broken."

Gina pressed a finger against the man's back, the pale skin throwing up not a blanch. She moved down methodically toward his buttocks and then his legs, which looked like a bruised peach.

"Non-blanchable," she announced, the bruise fixed and unmoving. "So livor mortis has pretty well settled."

"Confirming the twelve-hour window," Elijah said. "A lot of spotting, as well."

"Indeed."

Livor mortis, or lividity, was the settling of blood in the body thanks to a little friend called gravity. It develops only a few hours after death and becomes non-fixed or blanchable within twelve hours. Not only does blood pool, small vessels throughout the body break down and throw up all sorts of Tardieu spots they're called, the round, dark purple spotting in places across the deceased.

As Gina demonstrated, investigators press their finger along the body and especially in areas where blood has pooled, which is a physical process based on the loss of blood pressure when the heart stops pumping blood through the body. Livor mortis readings carry the same difficulties as rigor mortis tests, but it's another way to determine time of death at the crime scene.

Non-blanchable means the lightening of the skin upon pressing your finger on an area doesn't occur as it does when you're alive, your finger pressure pushing the blood away from the area. Lack of color means lack of blood, until it comes rushing back when your finger pressure is removed. Pooled blood acts differently, remaining in place. If it's fixed, or non-blanchable, you've got a good half-day or more death on your hands.

Gina stood straight, staring off into the sanded, stained, shellacked confessional ceiling. "So, probably between 8 and 9 p.m then…"

"Sounds about right," Gina confirmed.

Brit added, "That's what we're working on as well."

Elijah looked at her. "You mentioned asphyxiation as cause of death."

"Preliminary cause of death, but that's what we think."

"I didn't see any ligature marks on the man's neck. No rope or cord, no hand marks indicating strangulation."

"One of my guys says his trachea was crushed…" She trailed off, taking a beat, then a breath before adding: "From the inside."

"*From the inside?*" the Group X pair exclaimed as one.

Brit nodded, leaning against the threshold and saying nothing more, but face saying all Elijah needed to know.

The agent didn't have the slightest clue what to make of it all. "Quite the locked-room mystery conundrum, this is," he said.

"Indeed," Gina said, shaking her head.

Brit asked, "What is this locked-room mystery nonsense you keep going on about?"

Elijah turned to her and slapped his hands together, slipping into professor mode. He loved it when he got the chance to flex his eidetic memory muscles.

"John Dickson Carr, in his classic novel *The Hollow Man*, wrote his protagonist, Dr. Fell, expounding upon the seven types of locked-room mysteries in an erudite lecture that continues to be, to this day, the foundational tropes for such modern yarns."

"The first being," Gina said, "the victim actually killed himself."

"Which could very well be the case here," Brit said.

Elijah shook his head. "Nope. Crushed windpipe, remember?"

She waved him onward. "Continue then."

"The second," he said, "is that the character's demise was the result of accidental death."

"Which means there was neither a murderer," Brit clarified, "from which the victim needed to escape, nor a murder. Unlikely in this case."

"Bingo. Then there's the overused trope that the lethal weapon was poison. Gas, some undetectable drug, and whatnot."

"Still a murder, but the murderer was not present when the victim died. Possible, but unlikely."

"Bingo. In the fourth locked-room mystery, the murdered person falls victim to a booby-trap."

"Which means, again," Gina explained, "the murderer wasn't present to commit the criminal act."

She made a dramatic show of leaning into the confessional

booth and glancing around the joint. "Can't imagine the place was booby-trapped."

"Fifth," Elijah went on, "the murderer impersonated the victim."

"How does that work?" asked Brit.

"As Dr. Fell explained, *'The victim, still thought to be alive, is already lying murdered inside a room, of which the door is under observation. The murderer, either dressed as his victim or mistaken from behind for the victim, hurries in at the door. He whirls round, gets rid of his disguise, and instantly comes out of the room as himself. The illusion is that he has merely passed the other man in coming out. In any event, he has an alibi; since, when the body is discovered later, the murder is presumed to have taken place some time after the impersonated victim entered the room.'"*

"Did you just quote that from memory?"

"Yuppers."

Gina explained, "He has an eidetic memory."

Brit frowned. "Show off. Alright, Sherlock, what's the next one?"

Sherlock. That was a new one. Not that he minded. Sort of wore the badge with honor. Better than freak, retard, or spooky —the nickname of choice at the Bureau. Spooky Eli.

Elijah explained, "The next method requires that the murder is accomplished from outside the room using a disappearing murder weapon."

Brit twisted up her face in confusion. "How do you disappear a murder weapon?"

Gina scoffed. "Don't tell me you've never run across an ice-knife or ice bullet!"

"That only happens in the movies."

"Which is the whole point. Bargain-bin Kindle mystery tropes!"

"Finally, as Dr. Fell lectured," Elijah said, wrapping up his own lecture, "the victim wasn't dead to begin with until the killer entered the room, along with police officers and other witnesses, at which time the killer executes the murder, making it seem like it happened earlier. It's a reversal of the fifth trope."

Brit put a hand to her temple. "You're making my head spin…What about the lock itself, or the hinges?"

"Dr. Fell has an answer for that, too."

The FBI agent put up a hand. "Save it, Sherlock. I've heard enough."

Gina leaned over to the woman. "I understand completely…"

Elijah threw her a frown but stood straight and smiled again, satisfied with his performance. While also intrigued about the mystery they had on their hands.

To think, their very first Group X case—a locked-room mystery! They hadn't even gotten one of them prize-winning fishes at the Farm. And now here one was, his first case on the job with the Church's investigative arm. Just his luck!

Brit sighed and crossed her arms, eyeing the body and the room. "So, which one of you locked-room mystery tropes does this fit?"

Elijah turned to her, grinning. "It's elementary, my dear Watson."

"It is?"

"Yuppers."

"And what, pray tell, is the answer to the mysterious riddle?"

"It's easy," Gina answered, grinning now herself.

Skipping a beat, the pair answered together: *"None of them."*

Brit scoffed, muttering a curse under her breath. "Remind me to send Silas a box of chocolates for lending me you two. Real help you two are. Just wait until you see the other side."

Elijah startled. "Other side?"

He looked at Gina, then raced to the other confessional booth compartment.

Come to Sherlock…

# CHAPTER 8

This case was too weird for words. And that was saying something, considering the level of crazy Gina had dealt with in her decade-long career with the FBI. Both she and her former-partner-now-partner Elijah, the pair of them stuffed down in the basement in J. Edgar Hoover Washington HQ dealing with the cases the Bureau didn't know what to do with.

The serial murderers and other locked-room mysteries with a paranormal twist to them. The cultic ritual abuse and para-normal cases of alien abduction that turned out to be said cultic ritual abuse. The street gangs and drug lords with superhuman strength destroying communities with their wars and wares. The bank heists and other hijackings that smacked of supernatural means. And that wasn't even touching on the run-of-the-mill kidnappings and ransoms, the assassination plots against politicians, the headline-making white-collar crimes that would put Enron to shame.

Then there was the one case that reminded her of this one. The one that had sent Elijah reeling and ended his career.

It happened on a breezy Saturday morning one January. Snow was thick and all whirly twirly. He was attending the morning Shabbat service at the worshipping community of Beth Yeshua in Northern Virginia. When this unique Christian community, the Messianic Jewish community of believers in Jesus as the Christ, the Messiah promised to the people of Israel, was ravaged by raw evil.

Given the day and age, the attack seemed like a too-on-the-nose cliché: A crazed Islamic man had come barging in wielding a machete. Had taken the worshipers completely by surprise, killing six of them before finally being overpowered. Including a child and their spiritual leader, Rabbi Michael.

Elijah took point on the investigation. Agent Pendergast, their special agent in charge, and even the FBI Director himself, had advised against it, given his closeness to it all. But he wouldn't have anything of it. He was relentless, tracking down every lead and networking with other Jewish communities in the surrounding area, even up and down the East Coast. Except, those leads didn't turn out the way he thought they would.

Turned out, it was just some loon off his meds who'd escaped a mental asylum up the road. But Elijah didn't buy it. Wouldn't buy it. Insisted it was a network of terrorists that would soon ravage other Jewish communities, Messianic or not. He became obsessed with his theories, surfacing evidence that was facile, making connections that weren't there, chasing down more leads that got him into trouble—especially with the media, who painted him as a Jewish zealot on a holy war against Islam itself. Aside from their obvious anti-Jewish bias, they sort of right.

It wasn't until Gina reached out to his mother in a protective last-ditch effort to save her partner that she understood the full scope of things. The personal backstory to the professional one unraveling before her eyes.

Elijah's own father had been gunned down during a Sunday morning service, taking down a number of congregants before being apprehended.

He had been a teenage boy, and the man had meant the

world to him. The father he literally never had, gunned down before his eyes.

When she confronted Elijah about it, asking if the one case was influencing the other, he exploded on her. Said there was no way the two were connected in his mind, because the one man was his father and he had no personal relationship with the other victims. Said one man used a machete, the other a Remington 1911 R1 handgun. Said the perp who killed his father was a lone-ranger white man who had killed his father in a drug-induced, schizophrenic, manic episode, someone who had showed up a time or two at his father's drug clinic and thought he was the devil himself. Said the perp who had sliced up his Shabbat service was an Islamic whack job who was part of a terrorist network hell-bent on exterminating his people.

Of course, that last part wasn't true, but he couldn't let it go. Wouldn't let it go. And when his superior told him to can the case and move on, Elijah had one of his meltdowns. The kind she herself had had a time or two growing up. The kind autistic people sometimes struggle to keep at bay, but nothing like what she'd witnessed.

For anyone with eyes to see and ears to hear, it was plain the explosive emotion was long overdue. Like a series of tremors before Mount St. Helen blew her lid. During a sit-down meeting with Pendergast, Eli had started rumbling; that's what they call it. Jumped up to his feet and paced the room and worked through his thumb-to-finger tick, raising his voice but more pleading his case. But then it shifted—his voice and movements. Until he lost it. Red-faced, spittle flying, cussing like a sailor, he was.

Understood completely what was happening, the inner emotion of losing control over something obsessed over—boiling into a fierce frenzy until he couldn't contain it any longer. A physical welling inside that needed to escape. Like a vomiting sensation that found relief when one expelled the contents of their stomach.

Our SAC labeled it a temper tantrum for not getting his way, which was completely not at all accurate. Elijah was overwhelmed by the loss of control. And really by the inability to solve the one case of a murdered religious leader he could reasonably solve, having transferred the psychological trauma of seeing his father gunned down to that other one, where that Christian minister was killed before his eyes. Any first-year psychology grad student could tell that.

But Elijah persisted with his plea while ramping up his meltdown, hyperventilating between screams until he was no longer able to communicate at all and security was called in.

The entire experience was dreadful, and Gina tried to explain it all to the SAC, but Pendergast wasn't having anything of it. Fired him on the spot and that was that.

And there they were with another case that smacked of those two other ones. Where a priest, a minister of the Church, regardless of how much of a scoundrel he was, had been killed in the middle of performing his ministerial duties. Just like his Rabbi, and then his father before him.

Gina wondered how Elijah was doing, how he was coping with the similarities. Knowing him, he was probably just fine. Had mastered the art of compartmentalization with surprising flair. Made sense, given his personal past with not only his father's death but also from the childhood trauma of being shuttled around from home to home and the horror stories she'd heard from his time in the orphanage.

Elijah seemed fine enough. Totally calm, cool, and collected. Giddy even, having jumped back in the saddle of a new case and slipped back into the echoes of a profession he was more than adept at. Much more than as a mere professor, his eidetic memory and puzzle-working brain a natural fit for this line of work.

And yet…

Gina threw up a prayer to the good Lord above anyway,

praying he would sustain her partner, her friend. And help them solve this bleepin' case too weird for words.

Elijah reached the confessional side of the booth first, throwing open the door and grimacing.

"*Oof!* Who forgot to flush!"

Gina joined him. And echoed his complaint. "*Oof* is right. Pee-ew!"

She held her arm at her nose and scrunched up her face. Smell was a cross between the contents of a toilet, as Elijah had so eloquently complained, and rotting beef set out in the summer heat. Reminded Gina of her mother's pet lizard that had crawled in the walls of their double-wide and keeled over. And the joint reeked of it!

It was also empty, but for a simple wood chair with a crimson cushion. No naked-as-a-jail-bird priest, that's for sure. The space was smaller too, giving the scent scant space to bloom, wherever it was coming from.

Elijah whipped out his phone again and snapped a few pictures, but gave up.

"As you can see," Brit said from behind. "Not much left behind."

"Nope. Crazy smell. That's more than enough." Elijah recoiled from the room, waving a hand in front of his face. "I can't even..."

Recalled something about his heightened olfactory causing him trouble, tweaking him in a way that certain sounds did for Gina. One of the many thorns in their side as autistic people, sensory overload, that often sent them reeling.

While he stumbled back, still swatting at the air and muttering complaints, Gina stepped inside to have a look around. Elijah helped himself to more picture taking. Brit was not amused, but she let it go.

Again, not much, other than the one chair, anchored to a wood floor with the same dark walnut wood making up the walls, and the basket-weave mesh at the confessional window.

Looked clean, as far as it was concerned. No puncture marks or slits of any kind. Same for the wall separating the priest's chamber from the confessor's. No marks, no nothing.

The chair, however…

She knelt down and chanced a sniff.

Confirmation.

"It's coming from the chair."

Elijah hustled back inside to have a look himself. Or a sniff, rather.

Chancing a smell, he knelt with twisted face and snorted a breath.

"Oh my cheeps, you're right!" He turned to her. "Good call, Gina colada."

She blushed, pushing her red locks behind her ears.

There was a commotion just outside. One of the uniformed officers needing a signature from Brit. She excused herself.

"Just the window I need…" Elijah yanked out a wadded napkin from his pocket with an Einstein Bros. Bagels logo and pressed it into the seat cushion.

Gina glanced outside and hissed, "What are you doing?"

"Collecting evidence."

"What evidence?"

He grinned. "Don't know till I have it analyzed, now do I."

She sighed. For the love…

"But that's the FBI's! We could get in a lot of trouble, mister."

He shrugged. "Only if we get caught."

There was a shuffle of feet outside, and Elijah hustled to slip the napkin into his pocket.

"Sorry about that." Brit appeared in the doorway and stepped closer. "What's that you found?"

Gina answered, "There's something about this chair that reeks to high heaven."

"You think it has something to do with the case?"

"Possibly. Since we don't have much to go on, any variable is worth looking into."

Brit eyed the thing and backed away, putting a hand to her own nose now. "I'll get one of my lab technicians to take a look."

Gina smirked. "Spoken like a true field agent."

"How soon?" asked Elijah, mouth working to suppress a grin.

"Well, it won't be today, I can tell you that."

"Suppose this isn't an episode of *NCIS* or *NYPD Blue*."

Brit raised a brow. "*NYPD Blue*? I think the '90s want their television fanboy back."

Gina snickered at the jab. She went to stand when she noticed something glinting in the corner from the light.

She reached for it with her gloved hand, then carefully picked it up.

A needle.

One of those hypodermic thingies the kind nurses use.

Or junkies…

"Found something," Gina announced, standing and walking out of the confessional.

She held it up for Elijah's and Brit's inspection.

Elijah smirked. "Looks like the Bureau missed something."

Brit frowned, taking the object from Gina and holding it up to the light.

"The church has a drug rehab program," she explained, taking out a plastic evidence bag from her back pocket. "Imagine riff raff from all walks of life come in and out of this confessional, but I'll add it to the pile of evidence to check out."

"Give it to us straight, FBI Lady," Elijah said. "What's the working theory you all have cooked up?"

Brit heaved a breath and ran a hand along her close-cropped blond hair, gesturing back around toward the altar. He led the way, with Gina close behind.

"Takes the right kind of person to kill a priest," the agent said. "That's for sure."

"Murder a priest," Elijah corrected.

"And in such a ghastly way."

Gina had to agree there. Only time she'd seen this level of ruthlessness was working a case with the DEA down along the US-Mexico border. Even then, no way would the cartels go after a priest like this.

"Let me ask you this," Elijah asked, "What do you make of the clothes?"

Brit snorted a laugh. "Which part? The fact he's not wearing any, or the fact they're neatly folded underneath his chair?"

"Both."

Gina shook her head. "One of the strangest parts of the scene, that's for sure."

Brit said, "Brings a whole new meaning to the term defrocked, doesn't it."

Now Gina snorted a laugh. "I'd say."

Then she gasped.

Defrocked. Good way to describe it. Right on the money, actually.

Someone—whoever he or she was, the one who had visited him last night—had not only humiliated Father Rafferty, laying him bare-naked bare before the world as the man had done countless times to others, stripping him of his dignity. The perp had gone through the trouble of removing his clothes.

Stripping him of his vestments, the clothes that marked Rafferty as a priest.

A man of God. A representative of Christ.

"That's it…" Gina whispered, the picture becoming clearer. Then louder: "He was defrocked!"

"Oh my cheeps, you're right!" Elijah shuffled back over to the priestly chamber of the confessional, nodding and bobbing on his feet now. "Bingo on that one."

Gina joined him. "Hit the motive on the head with that one, eh?"

"Motive?" Brit exclaimed. "What do you mean by that?"

"Yeah, motive," Elijah said. "You know, the third leg to the crime-case trifecta stool? Means, opportunity, *motive*."

Brit frowned. Looking at Gina, she jerked a thumb his way. "What is your partner going on about? What motive?"

Gina replied, "Didn't Master Grey tell you?"

She smirked. "*Master* Grey did not. What did Silas leave out that I should know about?"

"He had a thing for altar boys," Elijah said matter-of-factly.

"What?"

"That's right," Gina explained. "Apparently the man abused his brother for several years."

"Sebastian?" Brit put a hand to her head. "Yikes, I had no idea. This wasn't on any FBI report."

"And neither on any Catholic diocese radar. At least, as far as he knew."

"Which means the murderer could have been someone Rafferty recognized."

"Or knew personally," Gina said.

"Genesis 2 style…" Elijah added, rubbing his chin.

Silence fell between the trio, the grim scene and revelations a heavy blanket to bear.

"That should be enough to go on," Elijah announced, leaving the confessional scene and bending low under the yellow police tape.

Gina followed. Time to follow the lead. And a good one at that. A likely one that would do the Church nothing good.

"Wait a second," Brit protested. "Where are you going?"

Elijah spun around. "To look for answers."

"Where?"

"Isn't it obvious?"

She went to answer but snapped her mouth closed, her face twisted up in confusion.

Gina answered for him. "The Catholic Diocese of Arlington, where else?"

He grinned. "Bingo, Gina colada."

With that, he and Gina strode down the center aisle and out toward destiny.

Time to gather a list of suspects.

# CHAPTER 9

Chaos is not a happy camper. No, siree, he is not!

I should be, given what I orchestrated last night. The death of a priest is no small accomplishment. Especially the manner in which the man of the cloth had met his untimely end. Small potatoes for me and my crew, but to the rest of the world of mice and men, well, it was downright magic. Magic, I tell ya!

Yet, it was supposed to end there. Had been promised it would. Promised nobody would care about the death of a minister who played tiddlywinks with altar boys' marbles. And the details of the priest's demise, well, that should have left the Feds spinning in their government-issued suits and flipping their government-issued hair!

Except I had misunderestimated one pesky little detail of the world I inhabit. More a gangrenous sore on my backside than anything else. A cancer to all me and my crew have been working to accomplish.

A little outfit called the Order of Thaddeus.

Which showed up to the crime scene poking their schnozes in my business! Two numbskulls with a new outfit called Group X, according to my source.

Which changes everything. Changes every calculus for moving forward.

Of course, in my line of work I'd certainly heard tale of the Church's nanny around the water cooler from the brethren who'd gone up against them in one form or another. Heard tall tales of the religious order that wiped the Bride of Christ's backside and cleaned up its messes, burning its heretics at the stake and battling demons with all manner of muscular energy.

Literal and metaphorical…

Something familiar about them, too. Can't put my finger on it, but I feel we've met before. Not only professionally, but all personal like. Which is odd, since I dare say I haven't canoodled with children of the Name-Who-Shall-Remain-Nameless in eons! Quite literally, too…

Oh, bother. Who knows? Only question is: *What the Hades are they doing playing in my backyard?!*

Always been more of a global player, the Order of Thaddeus has been. Playing footsie with the Big Dogs and going on the defense against the forces doing its darndest to bring the Church to its knees.

That Nous outfit and the upstart Theoti one, the two of them contented with challenging the Church on the world stage, affecting global change and dismantling Christianity limb from limb.

Not me, see. I'm more of a street corner kind of player. Far more interested in the local opportunities. Like soccer moms and their rug rats, and middle-age middle managers with a paunch and no hair, and grannies with bad hips and too much time on their hands.

Hence my latest chess move, taking out a bishop before I went after the king.

And now some bloody Order of Thaddeus outfit, Group X or whatever, is showing up on my turf—two retards with sticks so far up their keisters they think they can take me on?

*CHAOS?!*

Two limp-wristed, lily-liver, chicken-hearted, lickspittles think they can prevail against me and my crew, against what we have designed for this world. They think they can save it—think they can redeem it, just like their dead god, with their ministry of reconciliation?!

I'm not even close to the finish line, nowhere near ready to toss in the towel and call it a day. Because that's where the Name-Who-Shall-Remain-Nameless got it wrong, see. The Nameless bleated about the gates of Hades not prevailing against the Church.

*Psht!* They got another thing coming when me and my crew are through, yessiree. They may have the keys to the Kingdom of Heaven, but I hold the keys to the Republic of Hades! Or at least a hall pass.

And those latest agents of the Church won't know what hit 'em!

Hey, that's a good idea…

They *won't* know what hit 'em. No way, no how.

In fact…

Ahh, yes. That's it. That will do. That will stop them in their tracks cold.

Stone cold dead.

Which will give me and my crew another window to unfold further turmoil in the Church and pandemonium in the streets.

After all, Chaos is my name.

And chaos is what I make.

# CHAPTER 10

While Brit led the way back outside, Elijah glanced around the nave and then narthex. He slid out his phone, took a few more pictures for good measure, then stuffed it back into his pocket. Before leaving, he took in the scenery a final time. The sights, sounds, smells—even tastes and feel of the place.

As a child, whether at the orphanage or shuttling about from foster home to foster home, he had learned to navigate his tenuous surroundings using his five senses. They were acutely attuned to his surroundings, in a way that often led to trouble. Sensory overload had always been a thing, but he had found ways to navigate it all.

That porta john smell still smarted his nostrils, the tang of urine doing the tango with that sour beef Gina mentioned still lacing the air. It was joined by the cloying incense those smells-and-bells type use in their worship services. But nothing else.

Obviously, there wasn't any lingering scent of gunpowder from a discharged weapon. Not only because a weapon didn't appear to be discharged in the commission of this crime. But, more importantly, there was no lingering scent of gunpowder from a discharged weapon! At least in modern weapons.

Elijah smirked to himself at the absurdity of modern, low-brow yarns that didn't know jack about firearms. No, the air doesn't smell of cordite, a ridiculously specific detail on the level of someone eating a handful of blueberries and it tasting like potassium! Just flat inaccurate and tedious.

Same for cordite, which has been rarely used in any weapon since like World War II! A smokeless propellant is modern gunpowder. It isn't even powdery, more like the little sprinkles you might find on a donut than anything else.

Back to the smell of the nave.

A bit of the pungent aroma of cleaner. Pine-Sol, maybe, or bleach. But he didn't smell any of it in the confessional, which means it wasn't used to wipe down the inside of prints. Yet there weren't any prints. Odd…

Everything else looked in order, felt in order. Other than the obvious out-of-place dead priest sitting prone on a confessional chair like the letter S.

No broken glass, no overturned pews indicating a fight, no shredded Bibles or lectionaries, no disturbance of any kind, matching the tidy scene inside the confessional, as well.

No cameras, either. At least none he could see in the interior, which was a bummer. Maybe the diocese had the foresight to at least give their parish church some security love on the outside.

Because without some sort of visual on the joint, some video lead that could send them in the right direction, they might very well be screwed.

The evidence was just too whacked out, too skimpy.

And yet…

Elijah clenched his fist. Had to solve this one, he just had to. It was all so ungodly, so wicked. Regardless how much of a scoundrel the victim had been, abusing teenage boys and all.

He'd resolved early in his career that unless justice was for all, justice was for none. So it didn't matter. Murder was murder was murder. And he'd spent his half-decade career with the FBI working from that core, centering mission.

Looked like the Church's cases weren't going to be any different.

Reaching the narthex, a coldness suddenly swept over him. Swore it was a breeze gusting in from outside, but the morning had been unseasonably warm. He spun around, searching for the HVAC source, but the parish church was too old and hadn't been modernized with the conveniences of forced air.

But chilled he was. So chilled, that his flesh started throwing up all sorts of goose pimples, the raised bumps rippling across his flesh beneath his shirt.

His mouth went dry and chalky at the feeling. An adrenaline ping coursed through his veins, sending his heart lurching forward and throwing up a coppery, metallic jolt to his tastebuds.

Then there was this pressure building and pressing in against his head—his very being—along with a churning, watery dread inside his stomach.

As if all that weren't enough, there was the sharp tang of the reptiles exhibit at the Smithsonian National Zoological Park over in the North-West end of Washington.

All of it—the chilled feeling, the chalky mouth and taste, the churning belly and pressure against his head, the smell of fried frog legs—smacked of one other time he'd had the same sensation. The first time that had led to more repeats of the same than he'd care to imagine.

It started at the orphanage. One of his floor mates, Tyler, had gone missing, and he and the other boys were volunteered to help look for the boy. They searched every room, even the basement, which was dark and dank and dungeony. Quite the feat for someone with an aversion for closed, dark spaces.

But off in one corner, behind a maze of boxes and cinder block foundation walls, was Tyler.

With five candles arranged into a five-point star.

He was sitting hunched over, muttering something lowly under his breath and working at something with his hands.

Wasn't clear what he was doing until Elijah inched closer, padding quietly a few feet from behind.

Then he saw it. A frog—or what he assumed to be a frog, for its head had been severed from its body. Ripped off, really, along with its four legs, and its bloated body had been torn open. Ribbons of guts, black and pale, spilled out from the cavity, the tangy scent of death clinging and cloying.

When he glimpsed the gruesome display in the flickering candlelight, Elijah had sucked in a startled breath. Which caused Tyler to arch his back and spin toward him.

He never forgot that face.

With its bulging eyes and vacant orbs of white, rolled back inside his head. With its nostrils flared and whistling from heaving breaths. With its bared teeth stained black by frog guts and shimmering in the light, strands of chewed flesh falling from the munching maw like maggots plopping down to the dirt floor.

But that wasn't all of it.

For in the bowels of that wicked place there was a darker wickedness that smacked of the cosmic powers of this present darkness, the spiritual forces of evil in the heavenly realms—a chill clawing through his skin right down to his bones, throwing up a blanket of goose flesh, and reaching down into his very soul. Not only at the sight of the grotesqueness, but the feeling that a Presence was standing by with watching wonder and demonic delight.

And there it was. The same sensation, only now experienced in the belly of a church.

That frigid breath, followed by goose flesh. The chalky mouth and coppery taste, followed by a dread churning in his stomach and a force pressing in against his head.

Didn't know what to make of it, not in the slightest. About the only thing he thought to do—knew to do—was to offer up a prayer for help.

*Lord Jesus Christ, son of God, make haste to help us…*

The words of a Jewish poem came to mind, easing the tension brewing in his very soul. From Psalm 91:

> *You who live in the shelter of the Most High,*
> *who abide in the shadow of the Almighty,*
> *will say to the Lord, "My refuge and my fortress;*
> *my God, in whom I trust."*
> *For he will deliver you from the snare of the fowler*
> *and from the deadly pestilence;*
> *he will cover you with his pinions,*
> *and under his wings you will find refuge;*
> *his faithfulness is a shield and buckler.*
> *You will not fear the terror of the night,*
> *or the arrow that flies by day,*
> *or the pestilence that stalks in darkness,*
> *or the destruction that wastes at noonday.*

"Amen," Elijah whispered, crossing himself on instinct.

Voices caught his attention. Raised and from behind.

He spun around, searching for the disturbance. It was coming from outside, Brit standing with Gina at the open front door waiting for him to follow, and a small group of men protesting about something from the sidewalk at the bottom of the concrete stairs.

Elijah made for them. Didn't even wait for permission. Destiny called. Perhaps someone there knew something that could start adding the pieces to that cotton pickin' one-pager.

Brit complained, "Hey, what are you—"

But he was gone in a flash from earshot.

Seven or eight men were gathered behind a portly man in a navy jacket with yellow FBI letters emblazoned across its back. One of his own. Or, rather, *former* own. The gathered were clearly riled up about something.

Working-class stiffs in mechanic jumpsuits smeared with black grease, some with hoodies with holes in their arms pulled low. Mostly white men with pale, hard age-lined and stress-lined mugs. A Latino man shifted with nervous energy near the back, a hood pulled low over a face marked by wicked ink whorls. He was joined by a back man in a Polo shirt and pleated Dockers craning for a look with a furrowed brow. The real kicker were the two white-collar, high-rise types: one in a charcoal suit with red checkered shirt and matching tie, another jacketless but dressed for a PowerPoint presentation just the same.

Elijah approached them, curious what they might know. If anything.

"Who are you, and what do you want?"

Mechanic Man threw him hard, dark eyes from a leathery face that meant business. A white name tag with red lettering hanging by fraying threads on one of those greasy navy mechanic jumpsuits said he was Jimmy.

"Wees guys'er here for da meetin'."

"What meeting?"

His face fell, eyes casting toward the ground while his foot kicked at a stone. Clearly embarrassed to voice the truth of it. He sniffed and looked up, those hard, dark eyes returning.

"What'r ya, a cop'er sumfin?"

"'Er sumfin."

A man with a loosened blue tie hanging against a clean white shirt approached.

"It's an NA meeting."

"Narcotics Anonymous?" asked Gina, joining Elijah at his side now.

Loosened Tie Man nodded. "That's right. Every Monday at 11 o'clock, before noon Mass."

Brit joined Gina. "I wasn't told about any NA meeting."

"Wellspring Ministry, it's called."

"Wellspring?" Gina asked.

"That's right, little missy," Mechanic Man said. "On account of chapter 4 of that Johnny Gospel."

"The Gospel of John," Elijah corrected.

"Same diff. Anyhoo, there was that little missy at the well who was thirstin' for her next sumfin-sumfin. When Jesus happened along and promised that she'd never thirst again if'n she asked him to pony up the satisfying water he offered."

"That's right," Loosened Tie Man added. "*'A spring of living water gushing up to eternal life'* as he put it, and all."

"Shouldn't it be Gushspring Ministry, then?" Elijah said.

The man furrowed his brow in confusion.

Gina elbowed him; he yelped. She asked, "And Father Rafferty ran this ministry?"

"He and some others, but he hosted the Falls Church chapter."

She eyed the crowd of men. "Quite the eclectic bunch. Looks like your average blue-collar working stiffs along with—" She stopped short, gesturing at the man's loosened tie.

The man glanced down with a weak smile. "Yes, well, drugs don't discriminate."

Three uniformed officers hustled over and informed the group all church functions had been canceled and they needed to leave the crime scene. Much to the protests of the gathered men.

The police escorted them away, the Group X pair looking on.

Gina said, "What are the odds the perp is among that lot?"

Elijah folded his arms. "Never trust a man with a loosened necktie…"

She scoffed. "Like you should never trust a woman with a pixie cut?"

"Bingo."

She hit his arm; he yelped. "You're wearing a tie!"

"Nope. Bow tie."

"For the love…"

Gina turned away and led them back to their awaiting chariot.

She said, "My money is on the scruffy fella. There was a look about him."

"Looks can be deceiving. Besides, shirts and ties cover a multitude of sins."

She chuckled. "Except that fella's tie was loosened."

"That's what I'm saying!"

"For the love…"

Gina unlocked the candy apple red Honda Odyssey with a chirp, and the pair climbed inside. Then she started the minivan, a grunting whine thrown up from the V6 that wasn't half-hearted at all, along with the squawks of that soprano. Might give his beemer motorcycle a run for its money with all those ponies.

Fat chance!

For once in his life, Elijah was thankful for opera. Thankful for the syrupy sounds of another soprano lulling his mind. The high and heady notes tasting in his ears like a good Côtes du Rhône red wine in his mouth—with its seductive blackcurrant, cherry, plum, and spicy flavors common to the Grenache grape at the heart of the silky smooth drink.

Yeah, like that.

Because after what they had witnessed at the crime scene… something about it all was needling his noggin something fierce. And while it was too early for a glass of the French wine—or, for that matter, a mojito—Gina's opera would have to do.

It started on his ascent up the stairs into the church, something about the place giving him the heebie-jeebies, a dozen butterflies doing the conga line in his stomach. Couldn't place it, and he thought it was his nerves flaring up after being off the crime-fighting job for so long. But then he saw him, the stark-naked priest looking like an S.

An S for sin, perhaps…

"What's shakin'—" Gina started.

"Fried bacon," Elijah said, his autopilot brain finishing her thought on cue.

She giggled. "Drats. Your memory is too sharp for your own good."

"Just my subconscious dredging up the memories of your coovey rhyming all the timing."

She giggled again. "Ahh, coovey. Your cool-plus-grovey neologism."

"Sounds like your own noggin's dredged up some memories of your own."

Gina made her way back onto West Broad Street and merged back onto Leesburg Pike, making for those perfectly suburban shops and restaurants. The rusted yellow crane swinging in the air still putting together that condo reminded him how much he'd missed small-town living.

Traffic was stop and go, with orange cones blocking one side of the two-lane road. And an aging, sagging Ford Escort from another lifetime ago forgot which pedal was its brakes and gas! It was so maddening Elijah wanted to jump out of the minivan and hoof it from there.

But he stayed put, kept his cool, and started up his finger tick to recenter him.

"Earth to Eli…" Gina said, snapping a finger.

"Right. What's shakin' fried bacon."

"Exactly. You've been quiet since we left the church."

He went to answer but was cut off by that feeling again. The one from the church. The bone-chill goose pimply flesh.

Except…

Now there was a shift. A feeling of bad-news-bears dread that sent him into action.

"*WATCH OUT!!*" Elijah screamed, not knowing what was coming except for the rising sense it was something wicked bad.

Gina braked hard, the Goodyears on the Honda Odyssey giving the soprano a run for her money. Squeals and squeaks and squawks were thrown from all four corners while the van screeched to a halt.

Right before the massive arm of the yellow crane

constructing that uninspiring condo came swooping down from the heavens with a dramatic *CRASH* that rattled the ground and shook the Honda.

Flattening the Escort like one of Grammy's pancakes.

# CHAPTER 11

Gina knew there were three kinds of people in the world. Three types conditioned by the automatic physiological reaction to an event that is perceived as stressful or frightening. What her type with psych degrees call the Fight-or-Flight Response, hammered and honed into our lizard brains over the eons fighting mastodons and saber-toothed tigers, not to mention fighting Mother Nature and ourselves.

It all starts with the amygdala sending a distress signal to the hypothalamus, activating the sympathetic nervous system. Which then pings the adrenal glands with a text message through the autonomic nerves—dumping epinephrine (aka adrenaline) into the bloodstream, activating an impulse to either flee or fight.

And that's when our three characters show up on the shiznit stage.

Freezers, callers, and runner-inners.

Freezers freeze when the shiznit hits the fan. Might be a third F word to the Fight-or-Flight Response, though when a mastodon was barreling down on your behind, didn't do much good to stay put! So, freezers are really fleers. In the face of disaster or stressful events, their brain pretty well flees, and they do bo-diddly.

Callers get on the horn and call for help. Whether the police or fire and rescue, or just dear ol' dad to help change a flat tire.

Then there are the runner-inners. Whether it's your average Joe Beat Cop chasing down a purse snatcher or your average Joe Six-Pack running back into their family split-level to save the family cat, they're the ordinary heroes who rise to the occasion to pull off the extraordinary by saving the day.

So, freezers, callers, and runner-inners. Three peeps that show their mugs to the scene of an epinephrine-inducing event.

Like when a crane topples five stories down to the world below from the heights of a new construction—smashing onto the roof of a Ford Escort!

Gina knew who she and Elijah were. They were former law enforcement. And law enforcement don't get where they are by fleeing. Or freezing and just phoning it in, for that matter.

Elijah threw his hands on his head. "Sweet mother of Melchizedek!"

"Egads!" Gina screamed. "You alright?"

"Better than the Escort." He swallowed hard, catching his breath. "And the passenger inside…"

Other drivers behind and on the other side of the road were opening their doors to rubberneck the mayhem. Some whipping out their cellphones and calling with activation (callers). Some standing with dumbfounded disbelief (freezers).

Gina was the first to throw off her seat belt and throw open the door, followed quickly by Elijah—the pair jumping out as one and their dual door-slamming throwing up an exclamation point at what kind of people they were.

Runner-inners, all the way.

Steam was roiling from the vehicle now, and two of the construction workers were running over to help assess the contents of the inside.

Which very well could have been their own inside.

Which begged the question…

"How did you know?" Gina asked.

"Huh?" Elijah asked dumbly.

Shutting her door and ready to hustle up Main Street (or whatever street was coursing through Falls Church) on toward destiny, she gestured toward the pancaked Ford Escort. "You screamed *'WATCH OUT!'* Like you knew something was coming. Like you knew th-th-*that* was coming!"

"Call it a feeling," Elijah said, shutting his door.

"Lucky feeling."

"Sensation more like it. A spiritual one. From the gut, welling within."

Her partner glanced all around—across the street at the massage parlor they'd passed earlier, the clear blue sky, up the height of the building under construction—everywhere but the Ford Escort.

She darted around the front end, not understanding what Eli was doing. Why wasn't he running toward the only thing that mattered?

The pancaked Escort!

Sirens were blaring from all around now, fire trucks and ambulances in the distance, but still far off.

But she wasn't concentrating on that. On those sounds and the other sensations—the people milling about, the warm breeze gusting through the suburban street, the scent of smoldering rubber and fabrics and plastics.

Negatory on all the above.

All that mattered was that word Eli had used. The one he'd used before, from their Bureau days.

*Sensation.* And a spiritual one at that.

Gina said, "You said sensation."

"Right." Elijah continued eyeing the structure, neck craning up the few stories before snapping around.

"Like a…a calling? From the Holy Spirit?"

Finally, he met her eyes. Wide and green and insistent. He

nodded, saying nothing more.

Screams snapped her attention back to the Escort, Gina glimpsing fingering orange and red flames reaching up and around from the undercarriage now.

Gina tugged at his sleeve. "Come on, Eli! We've got to help this poor person."

"No, don't you see!" he said, snapping his arm back, eyes wide and searching. "This was planned. Staged! For us!"

She twisted up her face. "What?"

He gestured wildly toward the Escort. "That was supposed to be us! They meant us to be pancaked!"

"Why? Who? What are you talking—"

Elijah quoted, "*'For our struggle is not against enemies of blood and flesh, but against—'*"

"*'—the rulers,'*" Gina picked up the quote from the Book of Ephesians with interruption, "*'against the authorities, against the cosmic powers of this present darkness—'*"

They finished the verse from chapter 6 as one: "*'against the spiritual forces of evil in the heavenly places.'*"

"This is that!" Elijah said, gesturing wildly at the scene unfolding before them, the construction men searching through the rubble and the two of them standing with gums flapping in the breeze. "Felt it. Know deep down something else is going on here. Something orchestrated, something trying to get us killed."

Gina threw her arms on her head, frustration mounting but also concern. For Elijah, and his state of mind. For what Elijah was suggesting, and what it meant for their investigation.

That the cosmic powers of this present darkness had tried to take them out by tipping over a construction crane—pancaking an innocent bystander to the cosmic struggle between the Church and the Enemy.

Instead of them…

She couldn't worry about that now, whether Eli was right on the money, or smoking something she could use right about then.

They were trained runner-inner pros. They had to do something before whoever was in that car passed from this life to the next.

She grabbed his arm and pulled him toward the Ford.

"Come on! We've got to help—"

Elijah yanked it back. "Nope. I need some air!"

Then he threw his arms on his head and started walking in circles, literally bouncing on his feet around and around. He did that sometimes.

Gina sighed, muttering to herself, "Please don't have a meltdown on me…"

Regretted it as soon as the words came out. Meltdowns were always misunderstood by an allistic world that thought they were simply temper tantrums, like Pendergast had accused Elijah back in the day. What he and the rest of humanity didn't understand was they were as necessary as air for her kind. Just like he'd said when he walked away, his watchword signaling—

Elijah suddenly seized her arm now.

She startled, glancing at it gripping her before looking at his face.

"Do you smell that?" he asked, eyes wide with panic.

Didn't have a clue what he was referring to, but Gina chanced a whiff anyway, heaving a lungful of air.

Right before she did smell…something.

"Something sweet," she said. "Like the smell of—"

She stopped short, her own eyes going wide now.

"Benzene," Elijah finished. "One of almost 150 chemicals in gasoline. The distinctive sweet smell from which increases octane levels and improves—"

"I don't care what it does! Where is it coming from?"

Gina gave a frantic search of the ground, Elijah joined her, both of their heads going this way and that until she thought they'd pop!

Then she saw it. A pool of clear liquid spreading beneath the tail end of the Escort like an overflowing toilet.

And winding their way!

She kicked at it, but only managed to soak her boots in the flammable liquid. It kept right on flowing.

Almost like it was making for Fuji!

And that wasn't even touching on the pool spreading beneath the fingering flames that threatened to blow the little slice of suburbia to kingdom come!

*Jesus, help...*

"Run!" Elijah shouted, waving his arms at the bystanders who were both rubbernecking and helping the Escort.

Gina shouted back, "But the Escort!"

"Nothing to do about that now. That thing is gonna blow." He glanced at it before backing up. "And us along with it. Come on!"

Elijah grabbed her arm and gently led her away from the scene. She took a step, stumbled with apprehension until the smell and sight and sound of the rising fire made her feet give way to resignation.

Gina turned tail and took off, the pair of them reaching the sidewalk—

Just as a massive explosion of fire and fury from behind sent them sailing into a grassy knoll like rag dolls.

Screams joined the mayhem, followed by another explosion that sent a hot, fiery, furious breath washing over their backs.

The pair struggled to their knees, winded and catching their breath. Gina had banged her head on a rock, and a nice-sized goose egg was forming. Eli had landed on his wrist wrong and complained it was sprained. But they'd both live. Both *had* lived to see another day, thank the good Lord above!

They rolled to their backsides.

And gasped as one.

The scene was like something out of a zombie apocalypse from some upstart video streaming service.

Bodies were sprawled unmoving across the pavement scorched by a river of flaming fires. Others were recovering from

NOT OF THIS WORLD   101

the sidelines, like Gina and Elijah, after having been blown back from the force of it all. The Escort was completely engulfed in flames. Magically, that yellow construction beam that had started all the chaos had blown clear off the roof of the Ford.

And landed on their own vehicle.

Its intended target, perhaps? Gina was beginning to seriously wonder about Eli's theory.

"Welp, there goes your new Honda, Gina colada," Elijah said, coughing and moaning.

"Hey, that rhymed," she said, eyes welling with emotion at the death and pain.

"All the time," he said without missing a beat.

And he was right.

Fuji was toast. Another Odyssey bit the dust.

Thanks to the cosmic powers of this present darkness?

Gina was beginning to wonder…

―――

The pair didn't wait around for the authorities. They had work to do, and the last thing they needed was to get sidetracked by paperwork.

Gina navigated them to a neighborhood park several blocks back. There, Elijah phoned in to Order HQ—not their digs beneath the Catholic basilica, but the mother ship beneath the Washington National Cathedral—and laid out what had just happened.

Silas Grey, their boss, wanted them back pronto, given what had happened, but Gina wasn't having anything of it, and neither was Eli. Took some doing, but the chief relented, connecting them with a helpful, petite woman (Zoe Corbino, if Gina recalled) who dispatched a pair of SEPIO agents with a new ride.

A brand-new black Mercedes G-Class SUV. Apparently, the Order's vehicle of choice. Not a fan, but it worked.

Eli sure wasn't thrilled. Hated cars in general, much more preferring his motorcycle. Especially hated foreign cars, and was loud about it. Which was ironic, considering his motorcycle of choice was a German-made ride, but whatever. He was a bundle of contradictions, and she rarely pointed it out to him.

He wouldn't touch the thing, so Gina drove. Before they left, Elijah handed off the napkin with the residue he'd swiped from the Rafferty crime scene to an Order agent and asked for an analysis. She hoped it was worth the trouble.

Leaving the scene, she offered up the prayer Jesus had given his followers to pray for such times as these:

> Our Father in heaven, hallowed be your name.
> Your kingdom come. Your will be done,
> on earth as it is in heaven.
> Give us this day our daily bread.
> And forgive us our debts, as we also have forgiven our
> debtors.
> And do not bring us to the time of trial,
> but rescue us from the evil one.
> For yours is the kingdom, and the power, and the glory,
> forever and ever.

"Amen," Gina said, finishing.

"Amen," Elijah echoed, crossing himself. "And rescue us from the Evil One is right. No way did that just happen to fall on the car literally feet from our own kissers!"

She turned to him. "You reckon?"

"You doubt it, after what we just went through?"

She sighed, leaning her head against her window as she drove. Just like old times, this was.

"Suppose you're right."

Elijah ran a hand through his hair. "What have we gotten ourselves into?"

"Only one way to find out…"

Gina turned off the highway onto North Glebe Road, heading south to the Catholic Diocese of Arlington offices.

It was another strip mall- and tree-lined road endemic of suburbia. An upper-crust suburbia, with three-story brick row houses and Ravi Kabob House joints and Harris Teeter supermarkets instead of cookie-cutter two-story vinyl-sided subdivisions and Cracker Barrels and Walmart Supercenters. But suburbia nonetheless.

She was more of a country girl herself. Although she never had lived in the country. Toledo, where she'd grown up, was one of several armpits of America, a former factory town full of Dollar Generals and KFCs and those double-wides she'd grown up in. Nothing like North Glebe.

Had always wanted to live on a farm and raise alpacas, actually. No, not llamas. Alpacas. Often confused with their South American camelid cousin, she much preferred their small size and sheep-like hair and small, blunt faces with those short, cute ears of theirs. That wasn't even touching on how much they respected fences and their intelligent, inquisitive minds. Then there was the profit margins for their fleece and hides.

Yessiree, country life had always intrigued Gina.

Especially because of the sensibilities of modern architects who didn't have a drop of class or character—the likes of which had built the ten-story concrete block that was their destination!

The cherry trees in full bloom helped—somewhat—but not enough to mask the eyesore. Which didn't even look like it was fully the Arlington Diocese HQ. Shared the space with a dentist office, a primary care outfit, and a realtor. The Church must be down on its luck to rent its diocese headquarters!

An apt metaphor for the state of Christianity generally…

"Egads…" Gina muttered as she pulled up to the squat parking ticket dispenser.

"Bingo," Elijah echoed. "Not what I'd expect from the Catholic Church."

She took her parking ticket and waited for the candy-cane

gate to lift. "Not an administrative arm of the Vatican, that's for sure."

"It's a concrete monstrosity, is what it is!"

The machine threw up a cranky beep, urging her to take her ticket.

Frowning, Gina yanked it and drove forward. "And the least the Church could do is give us free parking."

"We are their Navy SEALs for Jesus, after all."

A smattering of foreign and domestic rides were dutifully parked. The sight of a last-year Honda Odyssey, silver, made her tear up and recall what she'd lost. Again.

She slid their Mercedes into a Visitor Parking spot (Because, why not?), and the pair made their way through glass doors into a sad vestibule of black marble tiles (fake; can always tell it when they're fake) and walls shedding their paint like leprosy.

Praying to the good Lord above answers were awaiting them inside.

# CHAPTER 12

Elijah huffed and puffed as he took lead trudging up the stairs that hadn't seen a touch-up since they'd been built fifty years ago. Gina hated elevators. Fearful, really. And with all that had just gone down so far in their investigation, there was no way he was going to ask her to sacrifice her mental health just to lighten his own load.

So, trudge they did toward the ninth floor.

Along the way, he couldn't shake something from the crime scene. Something those men who had shown up for their noon-time recovery meeting had referenced. Chapter 4 of John's Gospel.

It was an incredibly meaningful passage to Elijah, on a number of levels. Reaching into his eidetic memory, he quoted it to himself as they climbed:

> *A Samaritan woman came to draw water, and Jesus said to her, "Give me a drink." (His disciples had gone to the city to buy food.) The Samaritan woman said to him, "How is it that you, a Jew, ask a drink of me, a woman of Samaria?" (Jews do not share things in common with Samaritans.)*

> Jesus answered her, "If you knew the gift of God, and
> who it is that is saying to you, 'Give me a drink,'
> you would have asked him, and he would have given
> you living water."
> The woman said to him, "Sir, you have no bucket, and
> the well is deep. Where do you get that living
> water? Are you greater than our ancestor Jacob,
> who gave us the well, and with his sons and his
> flocks drank from it?" Jesus said to her, "Everyone
> who drinks of this water will be thirsty again, but
> those who drink of the water that I will give them
> will never be thirsty. The water that I will give will
> become in them a spring of water gushing up to
> eternal life."
> The woman said to him, "Sir, give me this water, so that
> I may never be thirsty or have to keep coming here to
> draw water."

Elijah smiled at that line. *'The water that I will give will become in them a spring of water gushing up to eternal life.'*

Then still more, the woman's response: *'Sir, give me this water, so that I may never be thirsty…'*

Boy, could he understand her heart's desire. Her problem had been his problem when Jesus showed up in his own life through his forever family. His own longing for people to fill the god-shaped hole that had widened into a mawing grave over years of neglect had been satisfied by the One he had been searching for his whole life.

Rounding the stairs and continuing his hike up to the next level, Level 6, he recalled how the passage continued.

After Jesus asked the woman to *'Go, call your husband, and come back,'* the woman answered him, *'I have no husband.'* Of course, he knew that was the case and basically called her on it—saying she'd had five, and the man she was with wasn't even her own husband! Whether it was because she'd been used and abused and left as good as dead by those dead-beat men, or she was a loose woman herself, it wasn't clear.

What was clear was that there was something about these relationships—about relationships in general, even—that the woman used to satisfy her longings. Something there she thirsted for, and ran after to satiate her thirst, her desires—and it was never going to satisfy her.

Like any one of us when we're exposed for who we are and what we've done—or what's been done to us—our depths plumbed for what we search for to satisfy us and bring us meaning, she tried to change the subject, going on about how it was obvious Jesus was a prophet and weird historical references to the landscape and her people's worship practices.

But Jesus wasn't having anything of it. He leveraged her pivot to worship into a conversation about himself, saying: *'But the hour is coming, and is now here, when the true worshipers will worship the Father in spirit and truth, for the Father seeks such as these to worship him. God is spirit, and those who worship him must worship in spirit and truth.'*

The woman said she understood this, knowing that the Messiah was coming. Then Jesus dropped the little truth bomb on her: *'I am he, the one who is speaking to you,'* he said.

He smiled to himself. *'I am he, the one who is speaking to you.'*

The Messiah was who Elijah had been searching for his whole life. He understood he was Jewish; the kids teased him for it relentlessly, along with some foster parents who were even mildly anti-Semitic. And he understood Yahweh had pledged a Promised One who would someday put the world back together again. To put *him* back together again.

Long story short, his adoptive Baptist preacher dad helped him discover that Jesus was who he'd been searching for his whole life.

And there he was, reaching for the ninth level of a diocese within the Catholic Church. Go figure.

Boy, does Yeshua, Jesus Christ, have a sense of humor!

The knob was cold to the touch and definitely not code compliant. Elijah turned it then yanked the door open, holding it for his partner.

"After you," he said with a smile.

Smiling herself, Gina pushed a lock of ginger hair past an ear and strode into a tastefully assembled hallway. Surprising, given the '70s-era monstrosity they had trudged up for nine floors. Expected shag carpet the color of puke and rotten oranges, maybe matching striped wallpaper and some hippie love beads at the office doors.

Instead, walnut floors with a crimson runner edged by gold piping greeted them. Several doors of the same wood lining the hallway were securely shut. Console tables made of gold lined the walls, joined by crimson-padded chairs.

Oil paintings of past local priests and bishops, posing with half-serious faces in official vestments, peered at them from the wall with inquisition. Sort of creeped Elijah out walking past.

"Apparently," Gina said as they reached the office entrance, "the Catholic Diocese of Arlington didn't get the Second Vatican Council memo to ixnay the austentatiousay ecorday."

Elijah stopped short at the door and cocked his head. "Pig Latin for nix the austentatious decor. Amiright?"

She smirked and shoved past. "Show off…"

A gold placard violating the terms of Vatican II showed the suite to be 901, the office of the Episcopal Vicar for Clergy. Seemed like a reasonable starting place for the next leg of their investigation.

The room was spacious, carpeted in a deep blue Berber punctuated by yellow crowns. Plush couches of the same striped color scheme lined the walls painted lemon curd. Not his style, much more preferring dark, brooding, modern colors and angles, but it was tasteful enough. Supposed it matched the Vatican's personality, which is what mattered.

Smelled new, the carpet and paint and furniture. Some pungent potpourri joined it all. English garden, if he placed it.

Which was going to be a problem soon if they tarried too long. Strong aromas really weren't his thing.

A lone desk sat at the end with a wall of windows overlooking the street below humming with afternoon traffic and strip-mall shoppers. Typing at a laughably appropriate Compaq from last century was a short, squat woman wearing a floral moo moo and a mean bun that reminded him of the head guardian at his orphanage. Hunched and hurried in her work, she looked in her 70s.

Brought back searing memories from childhood, the guardian head having it out for him and letting him know with the back of her hand.

Elijah shivered at the sight, and the experiences that still haunted his dreams. But he pressed forward, padding across the plush carpet. A gold name plate identified her as Dorie Surgien.

He stopped short, smiling to himself and nearly laughing out loud.

Dorie Surgien. How perfect. Like that Dory fish character from one of his favorite movies, *Finding Nemo*, who was a Blue Tang variety. More specifically *paracanthurus hepatus*. Also known as a Palette Surgeonfish.

Shaking his head at the echo, he stepped up to the plate (or, in this case, the boxy old-world desk) and announced, "The Reverend Richard Rosner, please."

Dorie stopped typing and swiveled toward him, regarding him from behind rose-colored plastic reading glasses perched on a hooked nose. "And you are?"

"Elijah Fox. We need to see the Reverend Richard Rosner. Thanks, Dorie."

He smiled widely, trying not to laugh.

Her brow creased before she reached for a small binder that looked like a day planner, shoving her glasses back to her face.

"There isn't any Fox listed on his schedule," she said in an irritated rush.

His face fell. She wasn't living up to her name.

Gina explained, "Sort of an impromptu appointment."

The woman scoffed and pursed her lips with displeasure. "Regarding?"

"The Rafferty murder," Elijah said pointedly.

Her eyes flashed wide before narrowing. She took a beat, then a startled breath. Before he knew it, she was clutching her chest and grasping for breath.

Uh-oh...

Gina looked at Elijah, frowning with the same uh-oh wide eyes.

"I take it you didn't know," he said.

"What in heaven's name are you ta-ta-*talking* about?" Dorie stumbled, recovering her breath.

"Father Rafferty was found dead a few hours ago this morning."

Dorie reached for a box of tissues, plucking three before burrowing her face inside them.

Something in Elijah seized at the sight. Had never been comfortable with shows of emotion, even his own. Frankly, it wasn't in his constitution. An unfortunate, if not cliché, burden to bear. A thorn in his flesh, as the Apostle Paul had explained it in the Second Letter of Paul to the Corinthians. Described his own thorny burden, whatever it was, as *'a messenger of Satan to torment me.'* And while he said, *'Three times I appealed to the Lord about this, that it would leave me,'* instead the Lord said, *'My grace is sufficient for you, for power is made perfect in weakness.'*

Elijah had often viewed his autism in the same way, especially his emotional detachment from circumstances, from people even. Couldn't ever recall shedding a tear in his life. Even when his own adoptive father died in front of his very eyes. And there were times he hated himself for his differences, for the thorn that paralyzed him in moments like that when every neurally normal person would offer a comforting word or reassuring touch. Nope, not him. No words came, no impulse to reassure he was present.

Had pleaded with Yeshua to change him more times than he could remember. Pleaded that Jesus would make him whole, would put him back together again and repair his damaged mind and body. Because Lord knew that's how the rest of the world viewed him, as damaged goods. As disordered, as a problem.

But no bananas on that one. Yeshua instead used him in ways that confounded allistic people. His ability to detach from highly emotive situations had been a superpower that had served him well at the Bureau.

Lucky for him, and for Group X, Gina's emotional spidey senses were more tuned toward offering comfort. Probably her estrogen.

She edged around the desk and laid a hesitant hand on Dorie's shoulder while they bobbed up and down with muffled cries. The woman sat that way for several beats, and Gina kept patting her. Just enough to keep from reeling herself from physical touch, Elijah knowing she, like him, wasn't too keen on such things.

He worried the woman would keel over at the news of Rafferty himself keeling over. With her age and that ticker of hers somewhere inside that moo moo, he wouldn't be surprised.

Finally emerging, face beet red and shimmering wet in the sunlight, she heaved a choking breath and dabbed her eyes. "Are you the police or something?"

"Or something," Elijah said.

"We're investigators with the Order of Thaddeus," Gina explained, joining Elijah's side.

"Agents of the Vatican itself."

Not entirely true, but close enough. The Order was technically still connected to the Holy See, if only loosely. But Dorie didn't need to know that, and he imagined name-dropping the pontiff's outfit would do just the trick.

"Given the gravity of the crime," Gina went on, "we are

urgently in need of speaking with the Reverend regarding some sensitive matters about the case."

Dorie reached for the phone and pecked some keys, muttering, "What a lovely man he was. So gentle, so fatherly."

Elijah smirked. Try telling that to the boys he canoodled.

Didn't take long before a tall man with a football build came rushing out to meet them.

His comb-over had come undone at his sudden arrival, a whoosh from the door to his office messing with the tarpaulin of hair doing its best to give the man some dignity. "The pair from the Order of Thaddeus, I presume?"

There was a curious British lilt to the man's accent. Not purely, but accidentally. As if the man had practiced the inflection, or had been raised under its influence. Probably not truly from across the pond, but rather from New England. Probably raised in a prep school with a name like Yarmouth or Groton or Cardigan. Then studied at Dartmouth or Boston, even Yale or Harvard.

Elijah didn't like the man already.

He stuffed his hands in his pocket, asking, "And Reverend Richard Rosner, I presume?"

"Yes, yes, come along!" Rosner swept his long arm like a street sweeper toward his office, a pine candle telling Elijah to gird for more olfactory overload.

The man raced to the offending candle and snuffed it out, the faint scent of burning wick floating on a cool, air-conditioned breeze throughout the vast space. Reminded him of the Cambridge University library, the entire room wood-paneled in mahogany with the same kind of bookcases filled with aged tomes throwing up the dueling scents of pulpy paper and metallicy ink.

Rosner gestured to a collection of two overstuffed leather chairs and a couch. He slumped into the chair while Elijah and Gina took the couch, Elijah sitting closest to the man to be closest to the action.

"Right, shall we get on with it? What's this business with Father Rafferty?"

Elijah answered, "Given you're the Episcopal Vicar for Clergy, I presume you've heard of his untimely demise."

He swallowed hard and nodded. "Dreadful business, it is."

"We've just come from the crime scene," Gina added, "as investigators with the Order of Thaddeus."

He sat straighter with intrigue. "And?"

She walked through the highlights from the scene, the man visibly recoiling at the details.

"What we are wondering," Elijah said, taking over, "is if Rafferty was ever accused of any sexual misconduct."

A bit unorthodox, ripping the Band-Aid off, so to speak. But in his experience, catching informants off-guard was the best way to learn vital information germane to the case.

Especially the gruesome, inexplicable murder of a pedophile priest in a locked room.

Rosner's face remained impassioned, but he looked down and to the left. A tell that smacked of internal dialogue, as if he were having a conversation with himself about what to say.

Then he grinned and met Elijah's eyes. "You must understand, sir, that the internal goings on of the diocese aren't open for discussion."

"Nope. Those goings on, as you put it—" Hated that word (so pretentious and self-consciously elitist), but he mirrored it back anyway. "—are entirely open for discussion when a dead priest accused of sexual abuse is concerned. And murdered, no less."

Now he scoffed, rolling his eyes. "Accused? Who?"

Gina explained, "We have a credible accusation that was never disclosed."

"There you go. Never disclosed. We can't speak to nondisclosure."

"What about disclosure?" Elijah said, heat rising at his neck at the stonewalling.

"We can't speak to that either."

"Nope. Time to talk, Rev."

Rosner narrowed his eyes. "You don't have any jurisdiction in this matter."

"You don't know that!"

Neither did Elijah, but he didn't tell him that. Honestly, he didn't know what sort of jurisdiction Group X carried—both inside and outside the Church. Figured any investigative power they carried fell under basic citizen's arrest laws, carrying no more power than your run-of-the-mill bounty hunter or mall Rent-a-Cop.

But also, no less. And given they were investigating one of their own, one of the Vatican's own, which the Order was still connected with, even tangentially—in Elijah's mind that gave Group X at least the power of an ombudsman.

"Look, Reverend," Gina began, voice mellow and friendly, "our interest in this matter is your interest. We want whoever did this brought to justice. We also don't want any hidden motive biting the Church in the backside. We're not pointing fingers. We're not making accusations. We're only interested in solving this case."

Not bad, Gina colada. Offering a shared enemy and cause while pressing him for more. Clearly setting herself up for the good cop to his bad. Which Elijah didn't mind in the slightest.

Just like the old days…

Rosner sat back, crossing his arms and considering her argument. After a few beats passed, his shoulders slumped, and he heaved a breath. As if the weight of the diocesan world had just rolled off his back.

"Last year," he began, "the diocese settled several claims against Father Rafferty."

Elijah smirked. "Shoved them under the rug, you mean."

The man pursed his lips, casting his eyes to the floor in silence.

Gina asked, "Why was he never disposed of?"

Rosner shrugged. "Why were they all never disposed of?"

"Friends in high places?" answered Elijah.

Again, no answer. But answer enough.

Gina pressed, "Reverend, do you think any of these men might have had it out for Rafferty?"

Elijah added, "Might have been capable of murdering him?"

"Might have *wanted* to murder him?"

Rosner went to answer when a shrilly *bring-bring-bring* interrupted.

Gina withdrew her phone, reddening, then glanced at its face and showed it to Elijah.

He said, "It's HQ."

"Probably the chief checking in."

"Babysitting more like it…"

She answered it and put it on speaker.

"Hello, Silas, this is Gina. What—"

"Sorry to be disappointing you—" a very different man said. Sounded Asian. Indian, even. "But this is not being Silas."

"Who is this?" Elijah asked with a demanding edge.

"Abraham Patel."

"Patel? Sounds Indian."

"That is being correct!" Abraham said with enthusiasm.

"Hailing from Gujarati," Elijah continued, "if I'm not mistaken. The Indo-European language spoken in the western Indian state of Gujarat."

"Correct!"

"Hindi for *headman* or *village chief*."

"Correcto-mundo!"

Gina rolled her eyes at the show. "I'm sorry, but who are you and why are you calling? We're sort of in the middle of it, Mr. Patel."

"Abraham is being fine," the man said. "And, goodness me, where are my manners? I am being your new director of operational support."

"I didn't know we had a director of operational support."

116 J. A. BOUMA

Elijah said, "I didn't know we had any support."

"Silas was thinking," Abraham went on, "that it would be good if I were to be helping you along. After all, I am being a computer whiz!"

"An Indian computer whiz, how original," Elijah deadpanned.

Gina scoffed and recoiled, hitting Eli on the leg; he yelped. "You can't say that!"

"But it's true, isn't it?"

She rolled her eyes, and he got the hint. His mouth would get him into trouble one of these days...

"Abraham, glad to have you on board Team X," Gina said.

"Don't you mean Group X?" Elijah muttered.

"Not to be rude," she said, ignoring him, "but why are you calling?"

Abraham snorted a laugh. "Sorry about that. There is being news."

"Where?" Elijah asked.

"Well, on the news."

"So. What's it to us?"

"There is being another death. Two, actually."

"Priests?" Gina exclaimed.

"No, not Catholic," Abraham answered. "Protestant ministers."

Elijah looked at his partner. "Well, that takes the cheesecake."

# CHAPTER 13

Gina thanked Abraham for keeping them in the loop and ended the call.

Three ministers dead, presumably in the span of twenty-four hours? Eli was right.

Sure did take the cheesecake…

"Turn on the TV, will you?" Elijah gestured to a large flatscreen anchored on the other side of the room.

Rosner obliged, issuing a fancy-schmancy command for Alexa to turn the thing on and then turn it to CNN.

Who said the Church was behind the times?

The Most Trusted Name in News was just finishing a commercial for Viagra (that was still a thing?) and coming in for a wide shot of a brightly lit news studio. It was studded with America's colors and massive LCD panels. The main camera swooped in for a close-up of a dutiful-looking Kai Renolds, the mainstay broadcaster for the national cable news network. About as reliable as Fair and Balanced, but what's someone to do in a post-truth world filled with fake news and alternative facts?

So Gina sat tight, waiting for the next shoe to drop in their first Group X case that gave her more than a run for her money than even the FBI had. Which was saying something.

118 J. A. BOUMA

"If you're just joining us," the well-makuped anchor began, dark brown hair slicked back and glistening under too many klieg lights to count, face stoic with a set jaw and earnest eyes, "this is a CNN breaking news report with Mara Mitchell standing by. The third in a series of grizzly murders apparently targeting religious leaders in the last twenty-four hours is rocking our nation's capital. What's the news, Mara?"

As the picture faded to a nodding-head Mara Mitchell, Kai Renold's intrepid reporter sidekick, Gina chanced a glance at her own sidekick. Eli was sitting at the edge of his seat, back straight with both hands on his knees and eyes wide with transfixion on the screen.

One end of her mouth curled upward. A familiar pose that did her heart well. Boy, was it good to be back in the saddle of another case. Together...

"Isn't that right, Mara?" Kai said, shaking her back to the moment.

An equally well-makuped woman, hair blond and blown, lips glistening maroon, was standing on a street corner steps from what looked like a storefront. Perhaps the ministry where Father Rafferty served, Wellspring.

"That's right, Kai," Mara said, nodding her head toward the storefront and leading the camera on a journey down a stretch of DC sidewalk. "Ministers Jamar Atkins and Scott Stone were apparently murdered under very suspicious circumstances—"

An audible gasp from Richard Rosner thwarted Gina's concentration at the details of the new crimes.

The man was sitting himself ramrod straight, a bony hand covering his mouth and that comb-over drooping down across his face unnoticed.

"No, it can't be..." he said with a muffled whisper.

"Sorry to break it to you, pal," Elijah said, leaning over, "but if the Kai and Mara show have sunk their teeth into some news, it most certainly is."

Gina asked, "Do you know those men, Reverend?"

He looked at her and nodded, pushing his hair back into place. "Ministers at Kingdom Chapel AME and Harbor Hope Community Chapel, respectively."

"But AME is a black denomination. African Methodist Episcopal."

"And Harbor Hope Community," Elijah added, "sounds like some non-denominational upstart."

Rosner nodded. "You're correct on both counts."

Gina turned back to the television. "So, a Catholic priest, an African Methodist Episcopal minister, and an Evangelical pastor, murdered…"

Elijah snorted a laugh. "Sounds like the beginning of a bad joke."

"Indeed. But what does it mean?"

"It's obvious. We've got a serial killer on our hands."

And that was the argument being made by Mara Mitchell on a DC street. Along with another familiar face. Brit Armstrong was spilling the tea to rubbernecking Americans.

Elijah said, "Looks like the FBI is already all over this thing."

"Can you blame them? At least we've got an in with all the crazy."

"Sure thing. But FBI Lady better let us do our job."

Agent Armstrong ran through the highlights to the case—the who, what, where, and when details. The how was left out of the briefing; the why was yet to be determined.

With Mara's mic shoved in her face, the agent confirmed, "Jamar Atkins and Scott Stone, two DC ministers, were found dead this morning, each in their churches."

She continued, explaining to the broadcast audience that it was too soon to tell if the murders were linked. "However," Brit said, "given the nature of the two newest ones, and the peculiar connections to the earlier murder of Father Rafferty, it is the FBI's working assumption that these three murders are connected."

"Told you," Elijah said proudly, grinning from ear to ear. "Serial killer."

Gina nodded. Sure sounded that way.

Rosner threw up a moan from the chair while Brit continued her interview.

"This is just dreadful! Simply dreadful…" The Reverend buried his head in his hands, giving it a shake before reemerging for air. "Three board members, within twenty-four hours?"

Gina scrunched her brow. "Board members? Board of what?"

"Wellspring Ministry."

"Sweet mother of Melchizedek!" Elijah exclaimed.

Gina turned to him, eyes wide. "That was the NA meeting those men were attending when we left the first crime scene."

"Bingo."

"What are the odds three members of the cloth, serving in the same substance abuse recovery ministry, were murdered within hours of one another?"

"Not Vegas odds, that's for darn tootin'."

She turned back to the TV, mouth hung open in disbelief and mind reeling.

Mara retook the reins from Agent Armstrong, then handed it back to Kai Renolds. The perky broadcaster announced they had just witnessed a CNN Breaking News Event (which was pretty much anything they broadcasted these days) and they would return after another commercial break.

Rosner told Alexa to turn off the television, and the trio sat in silence.

"Maybe this isn't at all what we think it is," Eli finally said.

Gina took in a measured breath, nodding. Felt the exact same way. Felt like there was something else going on here. Something bigger than just a dead priest—even bigger than three dead ministers.

He turned to her, adding, "A truly *inexplicitus* case, if there ever was one."

Exactly what she was thinking. "Unexplainable indeed."

"Which begs the question."

She sighed. Hated those kinds of questions. The ones begging for answers were the worst, but she knew what he was driving at.

"Why," Gina answered.

"The big mo."

"Motive. On top of means and opportunity."

"The crime-case trifecta…" Elijah whispered, staring off.

Gina said to Rosner, "Reverend, do have any idea why these two men, on top of Father Rafferty, might have been murdered?"

The man's color had returned somewhat, but there was a sunken sense to his eyes. As if he had been walloped over the head. But no odd glancing or furtive eye movements, so that was something.

"None whatsoever. The three were impeccable ministers of the gospel who were the hands and feet of Jesus on DC streets."

Eli scoffed. "Aside from the canoodling priest…"

Rosner sighed. "Yes, well. That was a while ago. Inexcusable. But decades ago. The man had changed. Had a real heart for men and women down on their luck who had fallen into the narcotic snares of the Evil One. Same for Jamar and Scott."

"So, on the one hand," Elijah said, jumping to his feet and pacing the office, "we've got a dead priest with a known past, someone who settled several sexual abuse cases out of court. A good motive, if there ever was one, for exacting a pound of flesh for past sins."

Gina replied, "Except the other two ministers aren't involved in Rafferty's past sins."

"That we know of…"

Had to give him that. Unlikely, but alright. Something to check off the list.

She said to Rosner, "We're going to need the names of the men who settled earlier in the year."

The man's eyes went wide, and he opened his mouth. Thought he'd protest, but he held his tongue. Sounded like he was choking on it, too, but he snapped his mouth shut and simply nodded.

Eli pivoted on a heel and shuffled back their way. "On the other hand, we've got three ministers from three different wings of the Church's bench who served together helping people recover from drug addiction. With lots of jacked-up addicts roaming their halls."

"Not much of a motive," Gina said, "but certainly there was the opportunity to commit the crime."

"And means, whatever that might be."

"Reverend," she said to Rosner, "are you aware of any troublemakers roaming around Wellspring Ministry? Hobos and crackheads and the like."

The man sucked in a contemplative breath. "None come to mind, although my feet weren't on the ground like the other three. I'll look into it."

Elijah returned to the couch, leaning back and stretching his legs and putting his hands behind his head. "We've totally got a serial killer on our hands, I just know it."

"Except for one thing," said Gina.

He sat up with a frown. "What's that?"

"The locked confessional."

"Oh my cheeps, that's right!"

She added, "Although, we don't know yet what sort of mystery we have on our hands."

"Only one way to find out…"

Elijah stood; Gina joined him. She thanked the man for his time while Eli was already out the door. Rosner gave her the address to the other two churches and promised he would give her those victim names.

Didn't think they'd need them, the case looking like something else. Feeling like something else with these two other deaths. But a list of suspects was a good starting place for any case.

Soon the pair were trudging back down the nine flights of stairs down to the lobby below, then outside to their awaiting Order-issued Mercedes.

Gina brought the European beast to life and drove out onto Glebe Road toward the highway. They decided on Harbor Hope Community Chapel first, the storefront church in North East Washington.

"Didn't see that coming," Elijah said.

"Sure didn't," Gina agreed, speeding up the on-ramp and merging onto I-66.

"Three ministers murdered the same day. Now that's what I'm talking about!"

"Eli...don't gloat over three dead ministers."

"But this is what we lived for back at the Bureau! Jumping headlong into the unsolvable case. And serial killers always vexed the Farm. Vexed, I tell you. Vexed!"

Gina had to give it to him. "Sure sounds that way. But what do you reckon Agent Armstrong meant by *'peculiar connections'*?"

He gasped, snapping his head to her. "You don't think these others were naked as bears in a berry patch, do you?"

"And posed as the letter S?"

"For *sin*? Perhaps getting a little too fresh with the teenage help, or addicts needing help?"

Gina considered this. "S for *sin*. Is that what you think the serial killer is doing here? Stripping them—"

"Defrocking," Elijah corrected.

"Fine. Defrocking them of their ministerial creds?"

"Bingo."

"But you heard Rosner. There wasn't anything obviously untoward about them."

"Keyword being *obvious*."

"Yeah yeah yeah. Let's just wait until we get to the scene before making any judgments about the dearly departed."

Gina cranked another operatic number, grateful for the auditory massage to bring a level of peace and calm to her soul in the face of so much wickedness.

Half an hour later, she was sliding up to a police checkpoint with a grizzled officer and name-dropping Brit Armstrong along with the Vatican. Never hurt to slip their connection with the Holy See into a conversation with a law enforcement officer. Seemed to confuse him, the hard, wrinkled face gathering a few more lines in all the right places. But he waved them through anyhow. Imagined he'd heard it all with all those years on the force.

The second crime scene of the day was a far cry from the one from that morning. Definitely not tree-lined, definitely not your model posh suburban paradise.

In fact, there were no trees to be found! None of the aged oaks and flowering cherry trees of Northern Virginia. Just a depressing palette of silver and black, brown and beige thanks to several-story buildings of brick and steel. A mishmash of last-century and this-century apartments and corporate high-rises, boutique shops and bougie cafes.

At least it smelled decent, those cafes throwing up fried onions and garlic and sage, joined by roasting tomatoes and grilled meats and baking bread. And now voices rose from around, dialects from every continent reminding Gina she wasn't in Toledo anymore, the diverse DC cosmopolitan coming alive with the sounds of the nations.

Like every other city in 21st-century America, the neighborhood was gentrified, through and through. Except you can't always get what you want, thanks to the insights of that crooner Mick Jagger. Even with a sack of cash thrown at a neighborhood, you're going to have folks who don't get the memo that they're not wanted.

Alongside those towering buildings of steel and glass were makeshift tents of cardboard boxes and dirty sheets, joined by actual tents looking like they had been put together by third graders.

Gina parked in a no-parking zone a block from the yellow tape. Figured they were on official business, and the cops were

NOT OF THIS WORLD   125

too busy with a dead pastor to worry about an illegally parked Mercedes.

Although, it was DC. So who knew.

"There's our helpful FBI Lady," Elijah said, pointing at the woman with the blonde pixie cut.

She laughed as they walked. "Now she's helpful? So you can trust a woman with short hair?"

"Jury's still out on that."

On their approach, Brit finished with a pair of FBI agents and turned to them. "Figured you two would be dropping by soon."

Elijah smirked. "No thanks to Kai Renolds and Mara Mitchell."

"Would have been nice," Gina added, "getting a heads up from official channels than from CNN."

"Sorry about that," Brit acknowledged, "but we've had our hands full. Lots of moving parts—well, on the move."

"Three ministers murdered in a day. Suppose that's enough to ruin someone's day."

Elijah smirked. "Or three…"

Gina elbowed him; he yelped.

She asked, "How does this one compare to the first?"

Brit shrugged. "Take a look yourself."

# CHAPTER 14

Elijah couldn't believe his peepers.

Yet, instead of recoiling at yet another crime scene straight out of a Stephen King fever dream, he grinned and started to bounce back and forth on the balls of his feet.

It was too good to be true!

"Is this for real?" Gina asked, hand at her mouth and head shaking with disbelief.

"As real as rain," Brit replied.

"Right as rain," Elijah corrected.

"Huh?"

"It's right as rain. That's the expression."

She smirked. "Tough crowd…"

Regardless of her bungling the English idiom—which indeed originated in England, probably a variation on Charles Dickens's 'right as a trivet' from his Pickwick papers, though morphing into the more alliterative cousin as a pun riffing on the fact that, while the sun might come out for a little while, things will eventually return to a rainy British normal—regardless, FBI Lady's point was well taken.

While Elijah and Gina might be tempted to disregard the crime scene as an illusion, it was as real as rain.

And right as rain, the normal state of affairs for their day.

For their *inexplicitus* case.

Which needed some more documentation. He whipped out his phone and started snapping more pics. FBI Lady offered more huffs.

Hope Harbor Community Chapel was a far cry from the high-church ecclesial edifice they had left earlier that morning. No narthex with red votives holding unlit candles and a saintly statue. No highly vaulted ceilings or rows of walnut pews, polished to a shiny sheen by countless parishioner bottoms over the decades. No expertly crafted confessional booth beneath a magisterial stained glass window, a gold crucifix with a crucified Jesus peering down upon their investigative work. None of that. In its place was a crude ecclesial replica.

The storefront church was just that, a chapel carved from the side of the urban landscape and thrust inside the storefront of what could have passed for a high-end fashion boutique. It also looked like your run-of-the-mill, 21st-century Evangelical urban church plant that eschewed the trappings of religious architecture and iconography.

No vaulted ceilings or votive candles. No confessional booths or crucifixes. No incense and wet wood, either—although it smelled like fresh paint and small-batch roasted coffee, so at least they had that going for them. By Elijah's taste, it was about the only thing, though he could appreciate why some would find this sort of religious experience appealing. Not him, not by a long shot. But your average spiritual-but-not-religious twentysomething and recovering street druggie, maybe.

A wall of glass windows with the glass door flanked one side of the chapel, while the rest were exposed brick. Ceiling exposed and painted black, with floor lamps and theater lighting suspended from the ceiling, the room stretched the length and width of the block, the surprisingly high ceiling held by steel supports. Roomy, it was, with rows of cushioned chairs facing a stage at the far end. Some circular tables and chairs, even some couches, were arranged along the back near the entrance.

Not a cross or saintly statue to be found. Plenty of abstract wall art, though, hung around the joint, with a coffee bar nestled in the corner, a neon welcome sign hanging behind it dormant. Atop a small knee-high stage, a drum set stood and a keyboard, along with microphones and a few guitar stands.

And a body.

Familiar and foreboding.

Smack dab in the middle of the stage was a man. Naked as a bare-naked bear in a berry patch. However, whereas Father Rafferty's frock had been neatly folded under his chair, this fellow's clothes—Scott something-or-other—were lying in torn, tattered pieces. Shredded, even...

Almost like a machete had hacked them to pieces.

Those fateful events from the Saturday morning Shabbat service came rushing to the surface. A half-decade memory buried and forgotten, repressed and suppressed with the help of therapy and medication, bloomed in his brain—threatening to undo him, then and there.

Elijah braced against one of the cushioned chairs, the room blurring with darkness and stars. And there was a sudden heaviness in his chest. Falling upon him, in fact. All of him. From head to toe, as if he were being smothered by a weighted blanket.

"Do you need air?" someone sounded from his right.

Gina colada. Voicing his watchword signaling the onset of a meltdown.

Did he? Was that what was happening?

He wasn't sure.

No, he was. This was not that.

It was something else. Something entirely foreign. As if an echo of what had taken place in this room was bearing down upon him.

Just like in that orphanage basement so long ago...

He caught his breath and straightened. "I'm fine," he said

without making eye contact, then shoved his phone back into his pocket and strode down an aisle toward the front.

Brit was waiting for him and his partner, arms folded and regarding the body on the stage.

She said, "As you can see, we have a repeat from the morning. Or a copycat."

Elijah snorted a laugh. "Copycat? Yeah, right. No way this is not the same killer."

"Which means a serial killer," Gina said, voice laced with dread yet also chipper. As if mildly amused they were back in the saddle of their old pony, solving the FBI's unexplainable violent crimes.

He understood the feeling.

"I assume the door was locked," Elijah said.

Brit nodded. "That's right."

"Any other doors?"

"No. Just this one."

He shook his head. "That can't be fire-code compliant."

"I'll take it up with management."

"Can't. He's dead."

She sighed and rubbed her head. "Anyway, so far no prints have been lifted from the venue."

Gina responded, "You mean nothing discernable around the crime scene."

"No. I mean, there aren't any prints anywhere in the entire chapel, or whatever this is."

"What?" Elijah exclaimed, spinning around to take in the space. "You're saying, in a church visited by hundreds each week, there aren't any prints anywhere?"

"That's what I'm saying."

"Not the chairs or coffee bar. Not even the drums or microphones?"

"How is that possible?" Gina asked.

Brit shrugged. "You tell me. From what I hear, you're the experts at this sort of stuff."

Elijah turned back to the body. "*Inexplicitus* is right…"

He was just like the priest, only younger. Mid-thirties, by the look of it. Skin was drained of life, to be sure, but where the first victim had pasty white, lumpy, sagging skin, this pastor's was tanned and defined. Clearly worked out, this man a far more athletic fit. Hair was coiffed, too, slicked like some rock star. Dark and short at the sides, longer on the top and spread to the right. Clothes were a different sort as well. None of that priestly traditionalism, with the white clerical collar and plainspoken cassock. His were designer jeans and a T-shirt. Torn and tattered, but designer. Shows you what three-hundred clams gets you in the end.

But what did it all mean?

The dead pastor, naked and prone, just like the priest. Except, where Rafferty's clothes had been folded neatly under his chair, these were slashed to ribbons. Mutilated, even.

"Wait a minute…"

He stepped closer to the man, past the first row and right up to the stage.

"Oh my cheeps!"

Out came his phone again with more snapping. Brit didn't bother protesting this time around.

"What do you have?" asked Gina as she joined him. Then: "Egads!"

Egads was right.

There were jagged cuts all along his body. Rough and imprecise with crusted blood.

Brit said, "We haven't been able to find the device that did this. No knife or other weapon."

Elijah asked, "Was it the cause of death?"

She shook her head.

"Asphyxiation."

"Like the priest," Gina added.

Now a nod from FBI Lady, nothing more.

He sucked in a breath and pursed his lips. Weirder than words, this case was…

"For your information," Brit went on, startling Elijah from his contemplation, "Jamar Atkins, the black minister from the African Methodist Episcopal Church on the other side of town was found in the exact same posture."

"Naked and prone?" he asked.

"Naked and prone."

"No fingerprints, on a stage, in a locked room?"

"Right on the fingerprints and locked room, wrong on the stage. He was in his office."

Elijah cocked his head. "Like I said. Serial killer."

The FBI agent frowned and nodded, saying nothing more.

"Now this is different," Gina said.

He turned her way. "What is different?"

She gestured at the still-seated, prone man. "What do you see?"

"A naked dead man?" Elijah said with furrowed brow, not getting her meaning.

She folded her arms and frowned. "Thanks, captain obvious. No, I'm talking about his position! Especially in relation to Father Rafferty. Think about that crime scene and then this one. What's different?"

He joined her, folding his own arms and cocking his head, squinting as he took in the scene. Took a beat, then another.

Until he had it.

"The letter…" he muttered.

"The letter?" Brit asked. "What letter?"

"The letter Z! Good one, Gina colada."

"I don't under—"

"Back at the confessional," Elijah explained, "Gina noted how the priest had been positioned in the shape of the letter S."

"We surmised," Gina added, "that it meant *sin*. S for sin."

"Bingo."

"Unless it was a Z all along," Brit said.

"Sweet mother of Melchizedek," Elijah exclaimed. "I think you're right!"

He took off toward the top of the stage, running along the back wall and looking out into the sanctuary. Or rather, the storefront assembly of cushioned chairs.

"From this perspective, Pastor Stone looks like an S. Just like Father Rafferty."

Gina said, "But not from the perspective of the assailant."

"Bingo!"

"Same for the confessional booth at Saint Thomas."

Elijah started pacing, his limbs feeling tingly with unbounded energy from the thrill of the mystery.

He said, "We already know we had a locked room mystery on our hands at the Catholic church. The priest was killed inside a locked room. And, by all appearances, the assailant had done his assailing from the confessional side of the booth."

Gina cleared her throat. "*His* assailant?"

He slapped his forehead with the palm of his hand. "Or her, I suppose. Always an egalitarian when it comes to murder."

"There you go."

Brit snorted a laugh. "Yeah, but how?"

"Not sure." Elijah stopped short and pivoted toward her. "Yet."

Then he resumed his pacing.

Gina joined in: "But if the man was positioned on the chair from the assailant's point of view, then the letter would be a Z from his or her perspective."

"Bingo."

Brit knelt down beside the body. "What do you make of this?"

Elijah went to her and peered over her shoulder, startling at the sight. Hadn't seen it the first time.

An *NIV Study Bible* was lying face-up on the floor in front of the man, wrapped in a burgundy brown bonded leather cover. The hotdog of leather, as he recalled reading once. Not the soft, supple kind of cowhide or even goatskin, but a mishmash of the leftovers mixed together like Oscar Mayer wieners, then bound around God's Word.

It was also something far more personal to Elijah.

That Bible was Dad's go-to Bible. Still had it tucked away in his bedroom bookshelf. An older version, from the 1984 translation, but now his go-to Bible when he needed a dose of insight into God's Word.

A shiver ratcheted up his spine at the sight. First the tattered clothes, shredded by something reminiscent of the attack on his Rabbi at Beth Messiah. Now this, a similar Bible to Dad's lying face-up before a dead man?

Too weird for words.

And personal…

Elijah swallowed hard, his mouth like sandpaper and vinegar, laced with the metallic tang of adrenaline. Time to stand against the darkness.

"What do we know?" he asked.

Brit replied, "Victim is Scott Stone, pastor of Harbor Life Community Chapel—"

"And board member of Wellspring Ministry."

"What's that?"

"A collaborative outreach to drug addicts run by Father Rafferty, Scott Stone, and Jamar Atkins."

"The third vic?" Brit said with a start, standing and crossing her arms. "That's news."

"That's why we get paid the big bucks," Elijah deadpanned, kneeling down to take a look at the Bible.

The pages were clearly well-worn, wrinkled from years of use and hours of study, with several passages underlined in a black ballpoint pen and highlighted with various neon colors. Never understood why anyone would use a Bic, let alone dirty up a book with highlighters, let alone a Bible! Straight blue gel pen for him, but to each their own. He did respect the man's marginals, though. And boy, were there marginals! The margins were filled with scrawled notes—for personal application, original word studies, theological insight. Up and down the two open pages, along both sides and around the header and footer.

Felt bad now for being so judgmental and snooty about the man's church and ministry. Pastor Stone was an obvious student of the Word who took his Bible reading seriously, and he imagined his outreach to druggies and all other manner of urban dwellers as well.

Elijah inhaled a sudden breath, his mouth growing dryer and pulse racing.

"Oh my cheeps!"

He went to pick up the Bible but stayed his hand, knowing better than to mess with a crime scene, even if it were a Bible.

Gina knelt next to him. "What do you have?"

He pointed to one passage, highlighted in orange and circled with Bic black, pondering its meaning in silence.

She hummed with recognition. "Jesus' healing of the Gerasene demoniac. A familiar enough passage from Mark's Gospel."

"Bingo…"

"For the religiously uninitiated," Brit said from behind, arms folded, "how about you enlighten me?"

Elijah stood. "After rowing across the Sea of Galilee, Jesus and his disciples arrived in the region of Gerasenes. A man possessed by a demon met them."

She startled, her arms slumping with surprise. "A demon?"

"Well, several of them, given its self-identification as Legion and depending on your translation of the original Greek."

He returned to the NIV Bible. "Here, let me…" Stooping back down to the well-worn text, he read aloud from chapter 5:

---

They went across the lake to the region of the Gerasenes. When Jesus got out of the boat, a man with an impure spirit came from the tombs to meet him. This man lived in the tombs, and no one could bind him anymore, not even with a chain. For he had often been chained hand and foot, but he tore the chains apart and broke the irons on his feet. No one was strong enough to subdue him. Night and day among the tombs and in the hills he would cry out and cut himself with stones.

When he saw Jesus from a distance, he ran and fell on his knees in front of him. He shouted at the top of his voice, "What do you want with me, Jesus, Son of the Most High God? In God's name don't torture me!" For Jesus had said to him, "Come out of this man, you impure spirit!"

Then Jesus asked him, "What is your name?"

"My name is Legion," he replied, "for we are many." And he begged Jesus again and again not to send them out of the area.

A large herd of pigs was feeding on the nearby hillside. The demons begged Jesus, "Send us among the pigs; allow us to go into them." He gave them permission, and the impure spirits came out and went into the pigs. The herd, about two thousand in number, rushed down the steep bank into the lake and were drowned.

---

Brit shrugged. "Interesting reading material. Not all that surprising, given we are standing inside a church." She regarded the place, frowning. "Sort of…"

"*'No one was strong enough to subdue him,'*" Gina intoned quietly, regarding the body with a hand over her mouth. "*'Night and day among the tombs and in the hills he would cry out and cut himself with stones.'*"

Took a beat until it dawned on Elijah.

"Cuts?" Brit said. "Like on the body?"

"Sweet mother of Melchizedek…" he whispered, then

glanced at Gina. "This strikes at something from our days at the Bureau, doesn't it?"

"I don't know…" Gina said, taking a breath. "There is a darkness to it, an edge of the supernatural beyond the wickedness of murder itself."

The trio stood in silence for the longest time, the scene making not a lick of sense.

"I need to get inside!" someone pleaded from behind with a raised voice.

Then again, more insistent, enraged even: *"Let me through!"*

Elijah spun around toward the voice. He spotted flailing arms trying to muscle their way through two burly police officers blocking the entrance. Couldn't tell who, but looked important.

So he made for the commotion.

Hoping for answers to an *inexplicitus* case straight from hot Hades itself.

# CHAPTER 15

"'N o one was strong enough to subdue him,'" Gina repeated to herself, continuing to regard the body with a hand over her mouth. "'Night and day among the tombs and in the hills he would cry out and cut himself with stones.'"

A chill ratcheted up and down her spine at the verse, as well as the memories from her work with the FBI investigating cases of the paranormal variety. The supernatural kind straight from the Unseen Realm.

She recalled one such case, one of their first. A serial killer working along the Vegas Strip picking off prostitutes one by one until thirteen had gone missing, and then later found torn apart. Only stopped when the psycho had finally been captured thanks to her and Eli's sleuthing.

The psycho had been found living in a ramshackle tent of boxes in Woodland Cemetery in North Las Vegas. Much like the Gerasene Demoniac.

The verses from Mark 5 rose to the surface again: *This man lived in the tombs, and no one could bind him anymore, not even with a chain. For he had often been chained hand and foot, but he tore the chains apart and broke the irons on his feet. No one was strong enough to subdue him.'*

No one could subdue was right! Took five burly officers to finally bring the perp under control, along with several yards of heavy chains. Even then, he nearly escaped from custody after tearing off those chains! Took a strong sedative and cords of galvanized steel cables to bring him under control.

The psycho had exhibited some sort of superhuman strength. Just like this man in Mark's Gospel. Gina could hardly believe it when it all went down, chalking it all up to illicit drug use infusing him with the abilities, cocaine or ecstasy. But none of that had been later found in his bloodstream. Elijah had chalked it up to demonic possession, which she found hard to believe.

Not that she didn't believe in that sort of thing. She had been raised a charismatic Catholic, after all, where the supernatural was viewed as a more common, pedestrian occurrence, and such possession was certainly a reality. The Church had rites for that sort of thing.

Problem was, she had never seen anything of the sort up close and personal. Had rejected it, even, thanks to Mama, who blamed all her troubles on demons hiding behind every rock. But after what they had seen, and everything else they had witnessed, she was a firm believer in the Unseen Realm—and all that it held for the *seen* world.

Like a dead pastor cut up like the Gerasene Demoniac.

Looked just like the man of the cloth back in Northern Virginia. Naked, prone, propped like a Z on a chair, or an S or whatever. Clothes were tattered this time, so that was new. And there was a ring of white gold on his left hand, another difference.

And yet...

What did it all mean?

"I need to get inside!" someone pleaded from behind with a raised voice.

Then again, more insistent, enraged even: *"Let me through!"*

NOT OF THIS WORLD   139

Eli spun toward the voice, then Gina.

A striking Latin woman with full, flowing black hair wearing a pink and orange floral dress was trying to muscle her way into the building. Couldn't place her age, but she looked in her mid-30s, and she sure packed a punch.

*"Déjame entrar!"* she insisted again as two burly uniformed officers held her at bay, commanding her to calm down and step back.

Brit rushed to the disturbance, barking her own set of orders.

Elijah turned to Gina with a smile. "This looks promising."

"Sure does."

She took off with Eli close behind.

"Ma'am, calm down," Brit said, standing straight with outstretched arms waving up and down. "This is a crime scene! You're not allowed inside. You have to step back."

"Who is inside?" the mystery woman said with wide eyes, clawing toward the air beyond the door's threshold. *"Es mijo?* Is it my son?"

Elijah smirked. "Fat chance, señora. The dead guy is definitely a gringo."

*"Muerto?"* she exclaimed before lunging back toward the inside chapel, screaming and muttering more Spanish.

He turned to Gina. "Was it something I said?"

She smirked. "You think?"

The two officers did everything they could to hold her at bay, but she was a fighter. She managed to break free, stumbling a few steps before taking a halting, bracing step at the sight within.

There was a pause, then a sudden intake of air—startled and disbelieving.

Then she let loose.

The mystery woman shrieked before collapsing to her knees in a crying fit, her body folding in on itself and face burying into small hands, her Latin locks falling around her like a cocoon.

The officers looked like deer in headlights, the burly men looking unsure of themselves in the face of the weeping woman.

Brit took a step between her and the crime scene. Was never a good idea to let a foreign subject onto the premises, given the contaminants they can introduce. But clearly the woman knew Pastor Stone, so Gina imagined the FBI agent wanted a word.

Who…now that was the question.

She knelt beside the woman, who was still weeping and muttering Spanish. Didn't touch her; didn't want to and didn't dare while she was in that state. But she ventured into an impromptu interrogation anyway.

"Ma'am, can I get a name?" Gina asked.

Start with something small, something easy to answer, then build from there. Primes the suspect to offer answers—especially when the questions aren't so small and easy later on. Interrogation 101 that had served her well the past decade.

The question seemed to reset the mystery woman. She came up for air, unfolding her body and spreading her hair back. Black mascara ran down from the corners of her eyes across defined cheekbones, and bloodshot brown eyes fixed themselves at the center stage. Leading to another bout of racking cries and heaving breaths that shuddered through her small frame.

Telling her there was something more going on here than a parishioner mourning the loss of her pastor. The way she was carrying on—it was like she was his wife. But that didn't seem right.

"What's your name, sweet girl?" Gina tried again.

She sniffed and batted trembling hands at her eyes, making the mascara a blackened, smudgy mess now. "Carmen Santiago."

"For real?" Elijah said. "And where in the world, pray tell, have you been?"

Gina threw him a frown, catching his attempt at humor with the reference to the 90s PBS television show. She took minor pleasure from the fact she could still read him, still got his corny humor. The pair had always been on the same wavelength back in the day; were still on the same wavelength.

But now was not the time for Eli Time, as she'd referred to his antics back then.

And she let him know, clearing her throat and drilling him with neither-the-time-nor-the-place eyes. He picked up what she was putting down and folded his arms with a huffing nod.

Brit turned to one of the officers. "Harvey, do we have a cup of coffee to spare?"

He nodded. "Coming right up."

The FBI agent suggested they talk outside, get some fresh air and all. Carmen sniffled and nodded, accepting Brit's hand and rising back to her feet. Elijah continued snapping those pictures of his.

She led the woman through the entrance to a sidewalk bench behind the police line that had seen better days. Thick, chipping green paint revealed several more layers of brown and yellow and blue beneath. The backside was spray painted by graffiti that had been uselessly scrubbed by city worker bees, then tagged all over again in whorls and odd shapes and letters. Almost like it was someone's turf.

The sky had turned dark and cloudy, and a whipping breeze gusted through the street, the balmy warm morning turning south with a cold front. About the way their first case had gone, too. Such was life in the investigative saddle.

Carmen slumped at one end of the bench. Gina sat next to her while Elijah and Brit stood.

"Was Pastor Stone your minister?" Gina began. Sort of an obvious question, but always best to start with small and easy.

The woman nodded, saying nothing more.

"Why were you coming to the chapel, it's Monday?"

"Work," she simply said with a sniffle.

"What kind of work?"

Harvey appeared with a cup of Joe and handed it off to the

woman. She took it with a weak smile and promptly skimmed a slurping sip off the top.

Like nails on a chalkboard, it was. Sounds were a thing for Gina, like she knew smells were for Eli. Too many of a certain kind, and they would overwhelm her, sending her heart rate soaring and pulse pounding in her head, a skittering scratching feeling skating across her skin until she felt like she would scream from the sensory overwhelm.

But she let it go. She was good, so far...

"Ms. Santiago," Brit said, "what kind of work did you do for Harbor Life Community Chapel?"

Annoyed Gina that FBI Lady was taking over after the groundwork she was laying. Especially annoyed her she couldn't be bothered to let the lady enjoy a few sips of coffee after seeing her minister naked as a jaybird in the middle of her church—her place of employ, no less. Was more a tea gal herself, but still. Not the velvet glove approach she was used to.

"I direct the recovery services at Wellspring Ministry," Carmen answered, taking another sip. Her shoulders slumped, and she seemed to be breathing better now. Whether from the caffeine jolt or the initial shock wearing off, it wasn't clear.

"Working alongside Pastor Stone?"

She grabbed for a ring on her right ring finger, nodding and saying nothing more. A white gold piece of jewelry with sleek curves and contours, accented by brilliant diamonds sparkling in the dimming sunshine. And stamped by T & CO. Any girly girl like Gina would instantly recognize those letters.

Tiffany and Company.

Pretty fancy for a church secretary.

"You said *mijo*," Elijah said, picking up the interrogation baton, "indicating your son."

Carmen slid the ring back into place and dabbed at her right eye, nodding and sniffling. "*Sí, Pablo es mi hijo.* He is my son."

"And you thought he had killed Pastor Stone?"

Carmen's eyes flew open. "*De qué estás hablando?*"

"What I'm talking about is, you heard on CNN that a Harbor Hope pastor had been murdered and you came running, thinking you'd find Pablito cuffed and being read his rights."

"No, no, that isn't it at all!"

Brit pressed, "Then why did you come here for him at Harbor Hope Community Chapel?"

This had gone from small and easy to big and hairy in no time flat! And Gina didn't like it one bit. Was more a good cop sort of interrogator, which made her and Eli such a good pair.

Looked like Brit and Elijah were cut from the same bad-cop cloth.

Carmen hesitated, swallowing with hesitation and looking down at the cracked cement marked by old gum and spent cigarettes.

Took a beat, then a breath before she answered: "Pablo was part of Scott's NA program."

Scott. Not Pastor Stone. The two must have been close. Which made sense, given their mutual ministry to the city's underbelly.

The agent asked, "Narcotics Anonymous, you mean?"

"I thought he might have been here," she went on, dabbing her eyes.

"Why is that?"

"It's group day today."

"During school?"

"He and some other students get release time." More dabbing, followed by sniffling. "When I saw the police and yellow tape, I thought the worst. That something had happened to him."

Gina asked, "Why was he part of the pastor's recovery program?"

"Pablito got caught up in drugs after my husband and I divorced a few years ago. He took it hard, then took to one of the local gangs. Before I knew it, I'd lost my baby to…"

She trailed off, her eyes gushing with emotion and lip quivering.

Recovering, Carmen continued, "One thing led to another, and we started attending Harbor Hope. Pablo immediately took to Scott, who has been like a second father to *mijo*. Such a kind and caring man, sweet and sensitive. The only one who was able to get through to my Pablito. First, it was pickup games down at the park. Basketball, one on one. Then after school homework and the recovery group for teens where Pablito thrived."

A wide grin replaced the quivering lip, and her face brightened, all emotion vanishing.

"He was the reason my little boy got clean."

"Little boy?" Elijah exclaimed. "How old is he?"

"Sixteen."

"No way you have a sixteen-year-old. How old are you?"

Gina cleared her throat. "Eli…"

He turned to her. "What? She doesn't look a day over 29."

"I'm a few years past 29, actually," Carmen answered.

"Oh my cheeps!"

Even Gina startled at that revelation.

The woman cast her eyes to the floor. "I had Pablo young."

"I suppose so…" she said.

Elijah asked, "You said you were the director of Wellspring Ministry."

Carmen nodded. "*Sí.* When I saw what Scott was doing, and after my own son found healing and rescue from addiction, I joined as director of the program."

Made sense to Gina. What mother wouldn't want to join the mission of a program that saved her very own flesh and blood?

"At the time, I was a social worker with the District. We were getting nowhere with the proliferation of drugs, but Scott…"

There was the wide grin again, that bright face. And now she was playing with that piece of Tiffany bling.

"*Él es un mago…*"

"You mean he *was* a magician," said Elijah.

Carmen's face fell, and that emotion returned to her eyes.

Brit took over: "What kind of drugs was Pablo into, and the others that Pastor Stone and you counseled?"

"Mostly methamphetamines. Most of the guys coming through here are hooked on meth, or a *muy loco mezcla.*"

"Translation please?"

"She means," Elijah answered, "a super crazy mixture or concoction of drugs."

"That is being right. Some crazy stuff has been making its way into the city. Was breaking Scott apart, too, seeing how it had been destroying men and woman alike. Teenagers like *mijo Pablo*, even. He had such big plans to help rid the streets of that stuff…"

There were those fingers again, twisting and turning that Tiffany ring something fierce. Right before the woman choked back a rise of emotion, her eyes closing tight and spilling tears down her cheeks. Then she doubled over again, pressing her face into her hands, her body convulsing.

Which seemed…off. Could understand the response from losing a coworker. But this seemed deeper. More than the kind one sheds for a dead colleague, murdered or not.

Something had been needling Gina the whole conversation. Something off, not right. Something Carmen was holding back.

More a feeling than anything, in the gut. But there was one tell Carmen kept returning to that told her the gut feeling was far more probable than merely possible.

So, while the woman was down for the count, her head buried in her hands and hair shaking along with her body with every sob, Gina went for it. Not her normal interrogator MO. Again, was more a good-cop than bad-cop interrogator. But given the gravity and nature of their first Group X case, she needed to switch things up.

She asked, "How long were you having an affair with Pastor Stone?"

There was a moment when Gina regretted the question. Just a split second, the time and space between the final consonant and what happened next making her doubt her intuitions. If she was wrong, it'd be game over, and the woman would be burned.

But if she were right...it could mean a break in the *inexplicitus* case from Mars.

Moment of truth.

There was a sudden intake of breath and a choking sound, as if the woman were swallowing her own tongue. Then she stiffened, shooting back against the wooden bench like a sprung cadaver from a coffin with eyes as big as her mama's tea saucer collection.

And looking every bit as white as the priest from earlier that day.

Gotcha...

# CHAPTER 16

"You were having an affair with him, weren't you—with Scott?" his partner went on.

Elijah was taken aback by the question. Almost as much as Carmen Santiago was, the poor thing snapping up to attention and drained of color, eyes as wide as his vintage vinyl and mouth swallowing for relief.

All dead giveaways that Gina colada had hit pay dirt.

A wicked wind whipped through the street. Colder, smelling of the static charge of an impending thunderstorm. Time sort of sat still as he and Gina and FBI Lady waited for Carmen to answer, channeling Barbara Walters's infamous interview style. Nothing like silence and stares to get an interviewee to spill the tea.

And spill she did.

Carmen bowed her head and said quietly, "It started a year ago, a few months after I joined Wellspring. Scott had been so good to Pablo, to me, showering him with attention and care, helping him navigate his addiction—"

The woman stopped short, choking down a muffled cry. Or maybe choking on her confession. It wasn't clear.

"Anyway, one thing led to another, and…"

She trailed off, the obvious left unsaid.

Elijah smirked. "Delila to his Sampson, were you?"

Carmen glanced up from the sidewalk before returning her gaze to the broken, dirty cement—along with her color, a lovely shade of crimson.

"The reason I ask," Gina said, pressing the woman, "is that I would imagine you're pretty familiar with Pastor Stone's schedule, his comings and goings. In my experience, the side dish is often more knowledgeable than the spouse when it comes to their lover."

The woman pulled her arms in close around her chest in a guarded posture, continuing to avoid eye contact. But she nodded, explaining, "We worked closely together, if that's what you mean."

"I suppose canoodling does take 'work,'" Elijah said, making air quotes.

Gina threw him eyes that said neither the time nor the place; she had to do that sometimes.

He shrugged and let her do her thing.

Brit threw Elijah a frown herself before asking, "Was there anyone who would have wanted to hurt the minister?"

Elijah asked, "What about his wife? Maybe she found out about the affair and went all *Desperate Housewives*, gangstas in paradise style."

Carmen shook her head. "She's not like that."

"Anyone else?" Gina pressed.

"Not that I can think of."

FBI Lady asked, "What about one of the addicts in the recovery program, parishioners even?"

"Everybody loved Scott. Especially the men he served—and women, but very few. It was mostly men who came through these doors seeking relief."

"And you directed that relief," Elijah said, "the ministry?"

"The programming, the day-to-day operations, yes. Overseeing the volunteers and coordinating Scott's NA meeting schedule. And quite the schedule it was!"

"In what way?"

"It's like I was telling you before, there is some *muy loco mezcla* flowing through these streets—and people's veins."

Carmen jerked a thumb toward the collection of tents Elijah had spotted on arrival.

He said, "The super crazy drugs you were talking about earlier?"

"*Sí.* Super crazy drugs is right."

"How so?" Brit asked.

Carmen sat straighter and crossed a leg, pulling her dress down tight across her bare legs. She was looking them in the eyes now, engaged with the conversation in a way she hadn't since showing up.

She said, "You know the problem with habits, with addiction?"

Gina shook her head. "No, what's that?"

"Once they're entrenched, once they are part of a person, they're difficult to change. If they weren't, more Americans would have quit smoking in the 1960s after the Surgeon General's report outlining its risks. But no, they kept right at it because nicotine had changed their brain chemistry and you couldn't spit without landing on a pack of Camels. Cigarettes were everywhere."

Elijah said. "Nope. Smoking rates have been declining for years."

Carmen looked at him. "*Exactamente, muchacho.*"

"What changed?" asked Gina.

"Friction."

"Friction?"

"Society made it harder and limited access to supply. No more vending machines, banned in restaurants, and whatnot. Trouble is, the opposite has happened with meth. Meth is everywhere! There's an availability to it that's just not the case with other drugs, like heroin or crack."

"So it's an epidemic, then?" Gina asked. "Like the opioid crisis?"

"*Sí, epidemia.* What we are seeing on the streets with meth also grew with the rise of opioids. Which is interesting, because historically meth and opioid users have been totally separate groups. Different cultures, different effects on the brain. But as I have conferred with others in similar programs across the country, they are seeing a massive rise in the spread of meth, and opioid addicts have been shifting to the stuff as well."

Elijah asked, "And dying of overdoses, I bet?"

Carmen shook her head. "With meth, you don't overdose or die. You decay. And now these new traffickers are creating a ready market of mentally ill Americans. I don't even know if I would call it meth anymore. The brain goes bonkers on this stuff! Now people in their 30s and 40s with no prior history of mental illness are going mad, with massive amounts of schizophrenia and bipolar disorders."

That seemed relevant. Maybe one of Wellspring's patrons went cuckoo for Cocoa Puffs on Father Rafferty and Pastor Stone.

Elijah snickered to himself. Stone. An unfortunate last name for someone ministering to druggies.

Carmen went on, "It has only gotten worse in recent months with this new junk on the streets."

"The *muy loco mezcla*?" he said.

She nodded.

"What's different about it?"

"On crack, they'd be OK," Carmen explained. "But with this new meth, they just deteriorate into mental illness faster than I've ever seen with any other drug. Now, if they're not raging and agitated, they can be completely non-communicative. And the problem is, treatment relies on your ability to have a connec-

NOT OF THIS WORLD   151

tion with someone to pull them through to the other side. Now, there's just no way into that person."

Gina perked up now, sitting straighter with interest. Made sense, given her academic background in psychology and experience with the Bureau. Elijah also stood with interest, but for different reasons.

The man who shot his father had been a raving lunatic when he burst into their country church that Sunday morning. Jacked up on smack (a syringe-worth of heroin had zapped the man's brain, converted to morphine and binding rapidly to his opioid receptors) and sending him into a frenzy. Went and shot the man who'd been his NA sponsor. Dad. Later came out the murderous psycho had had a relapse, then snapped.

"Explain what you mean by that," Gina said, snapping him from his memory. "You're speaking of some sort of psychosis, related to this new strand of drugs?"

"*Sí*. You'd be astonished by how many severely mentally ill people are out there, especially among the homeless outreach of Wellspring. Now everyone is on it, and it's causing long-term psychosis similar to schizophrenia, within hours of people using. Everything from psychotic symptoms, hallucinations, delusions. And it lingers even after they stop using. It's horrible, totally dehumanizing."

"Fascinating…"

Elijah homed in on that word, *dehumanizing*. Recalled how his father had explained his heart for the people who had fallen sway under the powers of addiction and substances, how they had dehumanized people, stripping them of their humanity and binding them in shackles that stifled and deadened the image of God within each person. Demonic, he had called it, given how targeted drug addiction is to destroying Yahweh's Image Bearers.

Recalled the tenderness of his father, likening it to Jesus' own compassion for the crowds of harassed and helpless Image Bearers. Matthew 9:36 came to mind: *'When he saw the crowds, he had compassion for them, because they were harassed and helpless, like sheep without a shepherd.'*

Elijah's throat constricted, oddly with emotion at the memory of his father and his heart of compassion fresh on the heels of this case.

"Harassed and helpless, they are," Carmen said, snapping him back to the moment again with surprise at the connection.

"What did you say?" he asked.

She looked up at him. "Harassed and helpless. That's how Scott had described the people he cared for."

"Insightful…"

"DC hadn't seen much meth until a few years ago. Then people were showing up who were just grossly psychotic. The last few years have given us a crisis in our local mental-health hospitals, in the District and also in Northern Virginia and Maryland. Now those who are truly mentally ill can't get care because they're filled with people who are on meth."

"Tell us about these users," Brit said. "Their symptoms and experiences."

Gina nodded. "Especially as it relates to this new crazy concoction, as you described it."

Carmen shifted, crossing her other leg now. "With the old meth stuff, if a user didn't relapse, the symptoms could fade once they purged the drug out of their system. This new meth, though, is a whole other ball of ugly. They grow antisocial and all but mute. They even have to relearn how to speak. I know one guy in our Wellspring program who took a year and a half to recover from the brain damage it did to him. Couldn't hardly form sentences, couldn't laugh or smile. They can't think."

She paused, shaking her head with a sigh.

"I've been part of drug recover for nearly a decade. First for the District, then at Wellspring. At first, we could handle the meth addicts who got their drugs from local shake-and-bake manufacturers."

"Shake-and-bake?" said Elijah.

"Small-batch cooks using Sudafed producing just a few grams of the drug at a time. Back in the day, those meth users were gaunt and picked at their skin. But they were animated and lucid, full of memories, and they still had personalities when they showed up for help. Now it's all *muy loco*. The new stuff has stripped them of human energy, of their humanity! It's like their brains can't fire, like there's nothing left to fire."

Brit looked at Gina before settling on Elijah. "I'm not on the drug enforcement side of the FBI, but I have a colleague in the Northern Virginia Field Office who has explained some of what he has been seeing."

Elijah shifted. "Which is?"

"Something about a shift in the drug supply from plant-based drugs like marijuana and coke and heroin to synthetic drugs that can be manufactured anywhere, anytime, for cheap. The dealers are constantly seeking more potent and addictive varieties to pawn off on their clientele, which is readily available and seems to be growing."

"Why? Who would want this stuff?"

"It's not who you might think."

Carmen snorted a laugh. "You can say that again. Not just your basket of deplorables, to coin one politician. But your average middle-class middle manager and even Wall Street white-color type. The new *muy loco mezcla*, as I've been calling it, is really a metaphor for our age—with how isolated we are and free from normal social and ethical standards, with paranoia and delusion, with communities falling apart and fracturing. The drug isn't just responsible for these broader social problems. It's a symptom of them, while contributing to them."

"And Pastor Stone," Gina said, "was on the front lines trying to make a difference."

Elijah said, "Along with Father Rafferty."

"And Jamar Atkins," added Brit.

"*Sí.* Along with a few others."

"Who?"

"Ronny Parks, pastor of Renovate Community Church."

Elijah smirked. "Sounds like some fancy-shmancy megachurch."

"*Sí*, it is. In Northern Virginia. He's been away for a few days on business but should be back."

"Maybe I'll give him a call," Brit said. "Could be trouble coming his way."

Gina added, "If there isn't any already."

"Like I warned ya," Elijah said. "Serial killer."

Brit left that one alone, asking instead: "Anyone you can think of who would have wanted to harm these men?"

Carmen put a hand to her mouth and closed her eyes, stifling a sob and shaking her head. Looked spent from the interrogation, which was pretty tame, all things considering.

Brit nodded at Elijah and Gina. "Thank you for your time, Ms. Santiago. We'll stay in touch if we need anything further for our investigation."

She led the pair back to the threshold of the entrance into Harbor Hope Community Chapel. Inside, the body still sat prone, in the shape of an S. Or Z, or whatever it was. Two other agents were taking notes and photographs now. Another dusted for prints while a fourth examined the cadaver.

Elijah shook his head. What a way to go. And after canoodling with his secretary, or director, or whatever.

Brit leaned against the building and folded her arms. "So, what do you two think?"

Gina stared off toward the crime scene inside and shook her head. "Two bodies—"

"Three," Elijah corrected with interruption. "Don't forget the AME minister."

"Jamar Atkins," said Brit.

"That's right," Gina said. "So, three bodies, all found in the same odd posture."

Elijah added. "Don't forget the locked room."

She nodded. "With the only seemingly obvious connection

between them being Wellspring Ministry, a recovery outreach to drug addicts."

Folding his arms, he shook his head. "Sure does take the cheesecake."

Brit furrowed her brow. "You mean, takes the cake."

"Nope. Cheesecake."

A silence settled between the trio, the sounds of the city and rumblings of the crime scene investigators the only soundtrack. Rain joined them now, the cool droplets smacking to the ground and offering a natural endpoint.

Brit looked into the sky and brushed the droplets off her government-issued navy suit. "I better check in with my team, see if anything else has been discovered in my absence. You two should get out of the rain. Looks like it'll be a doozie."

She hustled back inside for safety, then turned back with her hand at her head like a phone. "Call me if you discover anything further. You have my number."

"We'll keep watching CNN for more clues," Elijah shouted back.

The rain picked up its pace now, and the pair hustled back to their Mercedes. Surprisingly, there wasn't a ticket plastered to the windshield for illegally parking. A first for DC's finest.

Sliding inside, Elijah shut his door and asked, "How did you know?"

Gina roared the SUV to life. "Know what?"

"About the affair?"

She shrugged. "Woman's intuition."

Elijah scoffed. "That's some intuition."

"And the ring."

"Ring?"

She held up her right hand and grabbed her ring finger. "A fine piece of Tiffany and Company. White gold and diamonds. Much too fancy for a director of a recovery ministry."

"And expensive."

"Figured it had to be a gift from someone. With the way she

kept grabbing for it every time either I mentioned the pastor's name or she talked about Scott—"

"You figured she was his chickadee on the side."

Gina nodded.

Shaking his head, Elijah chuckled. "Have to hand it to you. Didn't spot that one worth a lick if it were to save my life."

She smiled. "Like I said, woman's intuition."

Elijah smirked. "I guess so. But now what? So we got the lowdown on Pastor Scott and his chickadee side dish, as you said."

"And don't forget a deep-dive into addiction recovery."

"But that's about it. We're no closer to solving this dang case than we were when Master Grey handed it to us this morning."

"You know what this calls for, don't you?"

Elijah thought a beat, then grinned. "Steak and eggs!"

"You know it!"

He slapped his hands together and rubbed them, mouth already salivating and stomach doing a somersault with hungry anticipation.

Cracker Barrel, here we come!

# CHAPTER 17

I spy something with my little eye, something that walks and talks and pokes its schnoz where it don't belong.

And is big trouble, mister.

Two somethings, actually...

A brown-haired doofus with his red-haired bimbo sidekick. Or is it the other way around? The broad certainly seems to hold her own against the patriarchy, probably wearing the pants in the relationship. Good for her!

And yet...

My face is burning with the fire and fury of a thousand suns, I am so hopping mad.

Hopping mad, I tell you. Hopping!

Twice in one day. First at that pedophile den of iniquity in Virginia, and now at the epicenter of all that is crass and consumeristic about those insufferable Christians?

The epicenter of what threatens all that I have built over the past few decades...

This is not the way it was supposed to go down.

I gave explicit orders to eliminate the threat and dispose of the evidence, ridding the world—my world!—of the threat to my operation.

Gone. Forgotten.

Dead.

Those were my explicit orders. Which were really orders straight from the top of the food chain. That crooner was right: Everybody's gotta serve somebody.

Even little devils like me…

I grin, the fact of the matter truer than what that doofus and his bimbo could even fathom.

Then my smile fades, the heat returning to my face and a rage boiling deep within. Because Marduk and Shiva did it wrong.

I scoff. Marduk and Shiva. Their names taste sour in my mouth, the pretentiousness of their monikers on par with their insufferable arrogance that is only outmatched by their incompetence! Why they couldn't have chosen simple names is beyond me.

Marduk, ancient god of Babylon? What a showboat he is. And what's with donning a name like Shiva, after a god straight from the armpit of the world? I get it means destroyer in the language of northern India, so at least he has that going for him. Certainly fits the bill, given what he is tasked with. But why not just go with that, Destroyer? That I could respect. Instead, he went all fancy-pants. Another showboat that got his goat.

Take Chaos for instance. It's simple. To the point. No airs about it. Gets the job done. And entirely apropos for the services I offer.

But no! They had to reach back into history and appropriate what wasn't theirs.

Again, on some level, I could respect it. Names for our kind have always been important. It's what gives us our powers.

Like Chaos. Creator of tumult and turmoil, discord and disarray.

Despair, even…

Which was why I was tapped by the muckety-mucks up the

food chain. The one in particular who has been most conscious of the World—and those who roam upon its soil.

But, alas, *nom de plumes* are not on the agenda. Failure is.

And those insufferable investigators with the Church sussing out why their precious servants of the Name-Who-Shall-Remain-Nameless are turning up deader than doornails.

If only they knew…

My grin returns, and a certain delight begins to rise.

Right before it crashes down to Earth below.

Because those knuckleheads, Marduk and Shiva, got creative. Or perhaps those they've partnered with did, a certain flare for the phantasmagoric and gory something of a hallmark of their kind.

Regardless, they screwed up. They got caught. And given what we're up against, we might have a major problem on our hands. With a level of exposure that could put it all at risk.

A thought suddenly blooms within. Something far more problematic. Something far more personal.

I may very well get exposed…

And Wormwood will not be happy, whenever he returns from roaming to and fro across Earth. Never did say when he'd be back. But knowing him, it will be at the most inopportune time.

I just hope I have results by the time he comes calling.

Because if not…

Not good Chaos. Not good at all.

Something must be done. Because they are closer than ever at solving their sweet little mystery. Even the locked-room part of it.

Especially the locked-room part of it.

Which would bring it all to an end. Shed light on the bigger picture, even.

And we all know how much I and my fellow colleagues love light…

Time is running out. I must take matters into my own hands.

And I know just what the doc has ordered for such a time as this.

Because I know who they are, what makes them tick.

One of them, anyway…

I mull it over. Consider, intuiting, discerning the best path forward.

Yes.

That will work perfectly.

After all, I am Chaos.

Creator of tumult and turmoil. Discord and disarray.

And despair…

Might as well flex my wings and take flight. Put my years of experience to work. Because as those insufferable, mousy lemmings roaming the earth often quip: If you want something done right, you've got to do it yourself.

And I know just the ticket.

# CHAPTER 18

t was really coming down now. Raining cats and kittens to
beat the band, the day turning on a dime. Which was an apt
metaphor for how their Group X case had gone from the
get-go.

First a run-of-the-mill murder case of a dead priest, in a
locked room, accused of canoodling with the altar-boy help.

Yep. Mundane to crazy to weird in no time flat. Like the
sunny day turning into sour rain.

Thunder rumbled overhead, putting an exclamation point on
that one.

And sending Elijah for the supple armrests of their Mercedes
privilege, the soft leather under his fingertips grounding him
even as the skies grumbled in his ears and rattled his chest with
doom.

Had always struggled with thunderstorms. Probably because
half the time the orphanage electricity would cut to nothing
when one of them came rolling through. Plunging the sarcoph-
agus into darkness, but for the few working lanterns they had
available and any candles they could muster—and forcing him
to fend for himself against the older boys who had it out for him.

About the only thing that kept Elijah from reeling in the

passenger's seat was the promise of steak and eggs from his favorite restaurant. A chain joint bearing fond memories from the near and distant past.

Dad had introduced him to Cracker Barrel the day after he'd arrived in his forever home. In Kenturkey, there were about as many of them joints as there were churches. Which was saying something in a part of America that was still 76% percent Christian—with half of them Evangelical Protestant. So churches were a thing. And it was the South, so Cracker Barrels were a thing too.

Kid in a candy store, Elijah was, when he and his new dad and mom rolled up to the restaurant. The Southern chain sported a gift store with a bit too much kitsch for his taste now, but back in the day it was like Disney—with all the radio-controlled cars and board games, the stuffed animals and T-shirts with funny slogans he could ever want. And candy. Lots and lots of candy. Had hardly seen so much candy in all his life. And Dad let him take as much of it home as he wanted after filling up on steak and eggs.

First thing Elijah did when he joined the FBI and partnered with Gina was look for a Cracker Barrel. The joint had become their standard place to powwow—which he knew wasn't really a kosher thing to say anymore, given the colonialistic appropriation of the term for white-man board meetings and middle-management water cooler meetups, but whatever. They'd solved more cases at those tables meeting over plates of pancakes and cheesy eggs, bacon and steak, fried apples and grits than any of their former colleagues had in official Bureau powwows packed into fluorescent-lit conference rooms with burnt Folgers and Krispy Kreme donuts.

Given all the crazy the past day, a powwow at Cracker Barrel was exactly what the doc ordered to connect all the dots that needed connecting.

Rain was still doing its thing while a soprano was reaching for the upper register of what Elijah thought possible, and aurally appropriate. But he sat back with a satisfied grin as Gina pulled into the Cracker Barrel parking lot, sandwiching their Mercedes between a rusting Chevy pickup and an aging, sagging Crown Vic, both from another century that felt right.

Climbing out, the scent of burning wood hung heavy, along with grilled meat and something sugary. Stomach rumbled something fierce on their march across the parking lot and his head felt faint now with hunger. They took a table along the back wall and within darting distance of an emergency exit.

Because if he'd learned anything while at the FBI, it was to be within eyeshot of an emergency exit. Never knew when the shiznit would hit the fan, and a quick escape you would need.

Their waitress was a frazzled middle-aged woman wearing a blue pin-stripe shirt and brown apron who looked like she enjoyed the joint's all-day breakfast perk a little too much. Name tag read *Gladys*. Seemed right.

The woman took their orders.

Tea and Mama's Pancake Breakfast for Gina, complete with three buttermilk pancakes, scrambled eggs, and thick slicked bacon. The Cracker Barrel's Country Boy Breakfast was up Elijah's alley, with a sirloin steak he had to cajole into getting moo-ready rare on top of three scrambled eggs smothered in cheddar along with fried apples, hash brown casserole, grits, and biscuits and gravy, along with the best cup of Joe this side of the Mississippi. Figured he earned the meal after the morning they'd had—they both did.

The food fit the decor, a collection of Americana kitsch that bespoke a good-'ol-days vibe that never really existed. A bright red metal Coca-Cola sign marked by rusted age hung on a wall above their table, surrounded by black-and-white framed pictures of the Dust Bowl era. A roaring fire crackled and popped in a large stone fireplace down the way, a buck with a large rack anchored above along with a flintlock rifle under-neath. The open floor plan was filled with tables and filling with diners for their Cracker Barrel dinner, their conversations mixing together in a vortex that threatened to swallow his ears.

Elijah rested his elbows on the table, fresh cleaner still left over wetting his shirt. He frowned, but at least cleanliness was their policy. He started playing with a triangle peg game. Loved that as a child. He'd whip Dad every time.

"This place still gives me the heebie-jeebies," Gina said, looking around.

Elijah gasped, dropping the red golf tee peg. "Sweet mother of Melchizedek! For heaven's sake, why?"

She shrugged, eyes still darting about. "Probably because it reminds me of home. Mama was a hoarder. Filled our double-wide with all sorts of stuff from way back when. Antiques, she called them. Swore up and down they'd be worth a pretty penny someday. A bunch of useless junk is what it was."

He frowned, feeling bad and reddening with self-consciousness about the restaurant choice.

"Sorry I suggested we come here all those years. Didn't realize that's what the place meant to you."

"*Psht.* No worries. Besides, it was good therapy, having to face down my childhood demons. And I did it for you."

Elijah perked up at that. The idea she did it for him hit him squarely between the eyes. And something about the way she said it, voice soft and silky, and the way her eyes and mouth lit up ran heat up his neck.

Gina's phone pinged with an incoming email. She glanced at it and smirked. "Looks like our new pal Rosner has had a change of heart. Sent over the list of men from the settlement."

"Sweetness! Maybe send that over to Abraham and see if he can find anything out."

"Sure thing, chicken wing."

Gladys shuffled over with interruption bearing their drinks. An off-white diner mug brimming with brew and another of the same for Gina, only with Lipton. The waitress said their food would be out shortly; his stomach thanked her.

But, given the undercurrent of it all—the horrific nature of the crimes straight from a Stephen King fever dream, the supernatural feel of it all straight from a Chris Carter fever dream—Elijah also didn't bank on steak and eggs doing the entire job.

He knew that if they were to make any headway into this Group X case straight from hot Hades, he would need Yeshua's help, would need the wisdom of Jesus Christ. After all, as Proverbs 3 exhorts: *'Trust in the Lord with all your heart, and do not rely on your own insight. In all your ways acknowledge him and he will make straight your paths.'*

So, while some country crooner did his thing from the speakers overhead, he offered the Lord a prayer based on *The Book of Common Prayer* he'd memorized:

> *O God, by whom the meek are guided in judgment, and*
> *light riseth up in darkness for the godly: Grant us,*
> *in all our doubts and uncertainties, the grace to ask*
> *what thou wouldest have us to do, that the Spirit of*
> *wisdom may save us from all false choices, and that*
> *in thy light we may see light, and in thy straight*
> *path may not stumble; through Jesus Christ our*
> *Lord. Amen.*

Muttering an "Amen," he crossed himself.

Now he was ready. Should have done that earlier, but he was so caught up in starting his new gig and the joy of a new case that it slipped his mind.

Something he'd fix moving forward.

Food arrived and they attacked their meal. Steak was moo perfect! Red and bloody, warm and juicy. Same for the apples. The eggs were perfectly scrambled and smothered in cheddar, and the biscuits were buttered and piping hot.

Between the prayer and the food, now they were ready to debrief.

Swallowing a bite of pancakes, Gina asked, "So, what do we know?"

Elijah washed down a mouthful of grits. "Three dead ministers, naked and shaped like an S, or Z, inside a locked room. Death by suffocation, apparently, with no obvious means or method. Bupkis on opportunity and motive, as well."

He sliced through his steak, crimson juice seeping out across the plate and staining his biscuit, then shoved it in his mouth. The taste of heaven right there. A bit peppery and very raw.

"The big mystery for me," Gina said, "is motive."

"The locked room takes the cheesecake, too."

"Yeah, but that's secondary to the Big Why. That was always the Bureau way."

"Don't I know it. Pendergast drilled that one into us, didn't he?"

"Sure did. Suppose he did us one solid in all those years working under his watchful eye."

"Suppose…" Elijah trailed off, the memory of his firing smarting, but he let it go.

"What I don't understand is," Gina went on, "why off a priest?"

"And an Evangelical pastor and AME minister."

"Takes some pretty big cojones to go down that path. Even if you're not religious, you at least know you don't off a minister."

Chewing his steak, he washed down the bite with coffee. "Yeah, bad juju, no matter how you shake it."

"From what it seems, the only reason why the other board member—what's his name?"

"Parks. Pastor Ronny Parks, from some megachurch in Northern Virginia."

"Right. Renovate Community Church. Away the week on business. Expected back sometime today."

"Lucky break." Biting into that blood-soaked biscuit, Elijah asked, "So, what do you figure?"

Gina leaned back with her mug and took a sip, squinting far

off with a familiar face. Her thinking face. She swished the tea around in her mouth before swallowing and eyes went wide.

She sat forward and said, "Has to be something about their shared ministry."

"Wellspring, the narcotics recovery outfit?"

"Absotootalutely."

"Some addict strung out on that *muy loco mezcla*, the crazy drugs Carmen said had been coming into the city of late."

"Maybe…" Gina sat back again, face pinched in contemplation.

"There's always the abuse connection, one of the guys who settled coming back to settle the score with Rafferty from back in his teenage days."

"Then what about the others, Stone and Atkins?"

"Touché. Suppose we'll have to wait on Abraham for confirmation anyway."

Elijah finished his steak, humming with pleasure and feeling stuffed. Seemed like they were on the right track, the drug angle. But means and opportunity were sketchy.

Swallowing, he said, "You've got a problem, sister magister."

Her face relaxed. "What's that?"

"How does one strung-out junkie take out three members of the cloth within twenty-four hours? Maybe less, more like twelve?"

She hummed. "Good point. Maybe it was a pair of them. Or a trio."

"Three drugged-out junkies coordinating a hit on three ministers of their narcotics recovery ministry? From what Carmen said, peeps on that *muy loco mezcla* drugs could barely tie their shoes, let alone coordinate a serial killing spree."

Gina frowned. "Yeah, I suppose you're right. Doesn't seem plausible."

"Nope."

"Maybe we should take a gander at those illegal photos you took."

He scoffed. "Illegal schmegal! I was merely exercising my First Amendment right to freedom of speech."

"Yeah yeah yeah. Save it for Judge Judy."

Elijah slid his phone from his pants pocket. The face-recognition feature that gave him the heebie-jeebies, smacking of an Orwell fever dream, brought the phone to life, and he opened the photos app. With the flick of his thumb, he scrolled back to Saint Thomas Catholic Church and ran through the images.

There were shots of the bank of votive candles with the single flickering flame; the nave interior in all its boring, bland glory; the walnut confessional booth behind the altar gift wrapped in yellow police-line tape. Then the inside of the confessional with the body, and several shots of the poor dead priest: his backside and underside and topside and front side. There was the confessor's booth, empty except for the chair with that wicked reptile smell that still lingered in his memory.

Elijah said, "See anything we don't already know?"

"Nothing but nothing," Gina complained in a huff.

"About the long and short of it."

Same for Harbor Hope Community Chapel. Images of the outside wrapped in more yellow tape, followed by interior shots and the on-stage body of Pastor Stone. Definitely looked like a Z this time looking at the images he took rolling up the aisle toward the victim. Then more of the same body shots: backside, underside, topside, front side. None of it yielded anything they didn't know.

Elijah kept scrolling, flicking through the opened *NIV Study Bible*, some voyeuristic images of poor Carmen Santiago crying on the floor, some outside shots of FBI agents, graffiti at the back of the green bench, Carmen sitting in her flowery dress, more shots of the FBI and a few parting shots of the chapel.

Gina sighed. "Anything?"

"Nothing but nothing."

"You can say that again."

Elijah shut the phone off and slid it into his pocket again, running the images through his noggin and the details of the case.

And coming up dry.

Heat ran up the back of his neck at the reality they had come up against a brick wall.

*He* had come up against a brick wall! Felt like a dumbass for it, too.

Didn't know if it was being off the beat for half a decade, his investigator chops a bit rusty, or it was the locked-room mysterious nature of the case itself. Regardless, a sudden feeling of shame and inferiority began to wash over him.

Suffocating, drowning.

He should be able to solve this thing—locked-room mystery or not! Even without motive, means, or opportunity nailed down. Those three stooges had never stopped Elijah before. Had always been able to use his eidetic memory and analytical skills to work through the details of a crime to bring a resolution.

Always!

But now…

Panic began needling his mind at the distinct possibility of failure. His heart rate and lungs matched the blooming anxiety. He needed air, but they didn't have time for a meltdown. So he reached for his coffee instead.

Leaning back in his chair, he grabbed his mug with a shaky hand and took a sip—and grimaced, spitting it back out into his mug.

*Blech!*

Coffee had gone warm. Not cold, just not hot. His mouth had a certain tolerance for liquid temperatures. And this Joe had crossed the Rubicon into Nastyville.

He twisted around looking for their waitress.

Gina snapped her fingers. "Eli, can we focus?"

"Where's Gladys?" he snapped back.

"Don't know. But I was saying—"

"My coffee's gone lukewarm."

"So what?"

"Can't drink it. Tastes like vinegar. I need a refill before we can go on."

"I'm sure she'll be back for a refill soon. Can we get back to—"

"Nope. Can't drink it. Tastes like vinegar. I need a refill before we can go on."

"For the love..."

Elijah twisted to look for Gladys again—

When his mug exploded, sending Cracker Barrel's finest spraying across his face and shirt and ruining the remains of his breakfast.

Good thing their frazzled waitress was late on that refill. Otherwise his face would have been scorched with third-degree burns.

But he had bigger problems than a ruined shirt and breakfast.

Because sending a *rat-a-tat* spray their way was some dude in fatigues with a black balaclava over his head.

And wielding a menacing assault rifle.

If he wasn't mistaken, a Colt XM-177E2. Rare and discontinued in 1969, but packed a wicked punch.

Which meant no uncertain doom...

# CHAPTER 19

Gina was about to finish off her final piece of bacon, saving the salty, fatty wiggly end piece for last—her most favoritest part of the whole slaughtered piglet—when cold liquid slapped her in the face.

The nasty kind, too. Tasting all bitter and sour and very, very much like *coffee*!

Eww! Hated, hated that brown brew with a passion that burned bright and strong. Only thing she could stomach was the Starbucks frou-frou kind. Her triple shot, eight-pump caramel macchiato with extra whip. Which was more a milkshake than coffee in her book.

No, no, no. Tea for her, all the way (had her mama to thank for that). And mostly the black kind. Red Rose brand. Usually not the herbal stuff—mint, peach, rose petals—though sometimes she dabbled in those flights of hot-beverage fancy. Definitely not, not, not Earl Grey, though, flavored with those hippy oils of bergamot that tasted like Grammy's unwashed armpits. No way, Freddy.

What had flown into her mouth wasn't that. Not Red Rose, not the Lipton that barely passed tea muster. She couldn't make sense of it, neither hide nor tail of it.

But then a curious thing happened between the split seconds she felt and tasted the cooled coffee against her face and in her mouth.

Shards of hard ceramic fell across her half-eaten plate of pancakes. Looked like the white chocolate chips Mama would use for special Saturday morning breakfasts. Except these were tinkling across her syrup right after some rattling sounded from across the room.

Made not a lick of sense!

Was that Eli's coffee mug? Exploding in his hand? But why?

Again, made not a lick of sense!

But then the other thing happened. The one she was more concerned with in that moment than the tang of black coffee slapping her in the face.

All that mattered was the salty, fatty, wiggly piece of bacon she'd saved as her swan-song bite.

She was so startled by what she felt in her mouth and on her face that the livid *rat-a-tat-tats* didn't register as gunfire. Sounded more like plates crashing to the floor, which was the only thing that made sense in her subconscious while she was paying attention to the only thing that mattered.

The fact she dropped her fatty, salty goodness in her surprise, the wiggly last piece falling to her lap before bouncing to the floor!

Besides, why the hey-ho day would an assault rifle be *rat-a-tat-tating* inside of a Cracker Barrel in Nowheresville, Virginia?

No siree, had to be a stack of plates tumbling to the hard floor. All that mattered was retrieving that final bite. After all, it was bacon. And when it came to bacon, the five-second rule extended to ten.

"For the love…" she muttered with complaint, ignoring both the sounds and sensations in her frustration.

She'd be darned if that salty, fatty, wiggly piece of bacon got away from her.

Bending over to retrieve her precious last bite, the wall just above her head exploded—*one-two-three-four-five* bullets shredding the olden-days pictures and sending shards of picture-frame glass dancing across her back. A few nicked her neck, sending sharp needles clawing into her skin.

Supposed it was better than the alternative: the *rat-a-tat-tat* blast of an assault rifle shredding her body!

As soon as Gina hit the deck—and retrieved that piece of salty, fatty, wiggly last-bite bacon—panicked screams and shouted curses clued her conscious brain into what was what.

Some lunatic was tearing through a Cracker Barrel in Nowheresville, Virginia!

"Sweet mother of Melchizedek!" Elijah shouted, her partner joining her on the floor and whipping out a concealed Glock Gen 5 handgun from beneath his shirt. Doubted he had a concealed carry permit for the Commonwealth of Virginia, and doubted worth a lick that Eli had followed section 18.2-308.02 of the Code of Virginia for an application. But that was neither here nor there.

What was, was the fact some lunatic was tearing through a Cracker Barrel in Nowheresville, Virginia!

Although, now that she thought of it in between another round of *rat-a-tat-tat* rifle shots and freaked-out patron screams, reciprocity was probably allowed by their DC carry permit. Which wasn't really a permit anyway, since their Vatican credentials, by nature of their connection to the Order of Thaddeus, gave them federal diplomatic rights and immunity in such scenarios.

Gina smacked her hand against her head spinning away from her like a runaway freight train.

Focus, you idiot!

Regardless—she followed Eli's lead and yanked out her own black piece from her days at the FBI, both of their days. The Bureau's 9mm service weapon of choice.

Went to offer a reply when another gout of liquid slapped her in the face.

174 J. A. BOUMA

This time warm, this time sticky.

And red, the crimson wetness streaking across her white blouse.

A body slumped to the floor across the aisle, the head shredded like a smashed pumpkin, blood and matter spread across the floor. Like someone had dropped a pot of chilli, the thing tipping over and spreading in a smear.

This was not happening! Not in a Cracker Barrel in Nowheresville, Virginia!

And not to her.

She was an analyst, for the sake of all that was holy and right in the world. Had barely seen a lick of action at the FBI. Was the only reason she'd managed to hold on for dear life over the decade she'd been with the Bureau. Desk work suited her far more than field work. Had only fired her Glock Gen 5 during her yearly firearms testing. Definitely never at any human!

Was a secret she held close to her chest, one she hadn't told Silas Grey when he asked her to join Group X. He'd said she had the right mixture of academic acumen (given her graduate degree in psychology), kinetic chops (given her experience with law enforcement), and heart for the spiritual (given her Christian faith and expertise in the supernatural).

Didn't have the heart to tell him she was about as useful as a *Call of Duty* gamer when it came to the kinetic part of the job. Had wanted to serve the Church in that way investigating the mysteries of the Unseen Realm threatening the faith. Had wanted to join forces with her old partner in picking back up where they had left off investigating the cray-cray x-files that still kept her up at night.

Never, no never in all her five hundred twenty-five thousand six hundred yearly minutes with the Farm had she shot at someone, let alone been shot at! Ditto for getting into a firefight that sprayed blood and brains across her face!

And now look at her.

Kneeling on the dirty, grimy floor slick with grease and mud, now joined by blood and brains.

And the body of a middle-aged woman wearing a blue pin-stripe shirt and brown apron.

Wait…

The body of a middle-aged woman wearing a blue pin-stripe shirt and brown apron!

Something in the back of her lizard brain put two and two together, coming to a horrifying number-four conclusion that put an exclamation point on all the horror.

Gladys, their waitress.

A Bunn coffee pot sat shattered next to her in a pool of hot, steaming brown liquid that confirmed it.

Eli's refill.

Darkness and stars bloomed in her head, and she could hardly breathe. Felt like she was sucking air through a coffee stir stick, it was so bad. Heart was strumming a mean beat, too, her ticker galloping something fierce. Thought she was having a heart attack, it was so wretched.

Not heart attack.

Panic attack.

No, not now…

Reaching into the inner recesses of her brain, she latched onto the one thing that got her through those sorts of moments. The same ones that had bloomed in various ways through her childhood watching her mother waste away at the hands of drugs, experiencing the abuse of her boyfriends that had come in and out, mourning her sister's death.

Psalm 23.

Had wanted instead to latch onto the opening to Psalm 22, speaking the very words that Jesus himself spoke during his hour of dereliction: *'My God, my God, why have you forsaken me? Why are you so far from helping me, from the words of my groanings?'*

But she didn't.

Instead, even as bullets sailed above her with menacing

intent, strafing across the wall above and sending the Coca-Cola sign clattering to the floor with several bullet holes, she closed her eyes and quoted the ancient words that had guided countless believers through darkness.

Even while some lunatic tore through a Cracker Barrel in Nowheresville, Virginia!

*'The Lord is my shepherd, I lack nothing. He makes me lie down in green pastures, he leads me beside quiet waters, he refreshes my soul.'*

"Gina colada," a voice rang out above the din, but she paid it no mind. Couldn't. Was paralyzed with overwhelm. Had to keep from spiraling into the abyss.

*'He guides me along the right paths for his name's sake. Even though I walk through the darkest valley, I will fear no evil, for you are with me; your rod and your staff, they comfort me.'*

Something suddenly lifted as she silently voiced those words, even as the world outside her lizard brain rang with *rat-a-tat-tat* chaos.

Her heart rate slowed, her chest expanded with breath. Clarity replaced confusion and a shimmering Presence was near.

Just like all those other times she had voiced those words about the Divine Shepherd.

*'You prepare a table before me in the presence of my enemies. You anoint my head with oil; my cup overflows. Surely your goodness and love will follow me all the days of my life, and I will dwell in the house of the Lord forever.'*

Finishing, Gina smiled and took a breath. *Amen.*

"Gina!" someone shouted again, and now shaking both of her shoulders.

"What?" she screamed, snapping her eyes wide and searching with panic.

The world suddenly sharpened into high-definition color and full-on, five-point-one surround sound.

More menacing *rat-a-tat-tats* rang, followed by panicked screams and agonizing groans in the middle of a Cracker Barrel whose walls and olden-days kitsch had been chewed up and spit out like it was nobody's business. The wide, open-floor plan was littered with overturned tables and shattered dishes, half-eaten sandwiches and mashed potatoes and crumbly cornbread spread across the floor.

Along with bodies, a dozen or so.

Hunched and huddled beneath right-sided tables and behind overturned ones. Bloodied and bullet-ridden ones sprawled across the floor or slumped in chairs.

And Eli on his knees with his right palm facing her. He'd never touched her like that before, shaking her shoulders or anything else. Neither of them had, so it must have been the emergency.

She immediately put her own left palm up to his. Something they had devised as a way to connect back in the day that skirted their mutual aversion to physical touch.

A *pop-pop-pop* sounded from across the room, jolting her back to the urgency of the hour and sending her hands for her head.

Then another: *pop-pop-pop.*

Gina rose to her knees to find a burly man in mud brown Carhartt overalls and a blue checkered flannel shirt standing at one end and taking aim with a handgun rivaling their own.

God bless the Commonwealth of Virginia's conceal carried laws!

But it did no good. They really were stuck in a Stephen King fever dream, the hostile unstoppable.

As if possessed by a Power straight from the Unseen Realm…

What came next confirmed it.

A sudden sound—haunting, moaning, shuddering—sprang from the lunatic's kisser.

Like a grizzly bear strangling a sheep. A roary, snorty, skittering screech reverberating from the depths of hell itself!

Gina wanted nothing more than to go back to that analyst's desk in Quantico. With her Red Rose black tea and piney candle and slippers. Burrowed down deep under a mound of paperwork. Avoiding the chaos, avoiding the sheer horrifying demonic display as she knelt trembling on the floor.

Avoiding this—lunatic tearing through a Cracker Barrel in Nowheresville, Virginia!

But she couldn't. She wouldn't. Didn't really have a choice in the matter anyway.

Because the lunatic in fatigues and black ski mask sent up a spraying hose of bullets, catching a granny in a lace dress and her book club sisters in matching attire in their kissers before shattering a bay of windows and landing on the large man.

Put him down like a dog, the hero shuddering with wide arms as blood bloomed from his wounds before slumping against a table and clattering down to the floor.

But it was just the window they needed.

Just the window *she* needed to shut this circus down.

Only had a few seconds.

So she took them.

Springing to her feet, Gina put all those years testing with the Bureau's Firearms Training Unit to work.

Taking aim, she widened her stance and held her Glock aloft on stiff arms.

Just as the perp raised his own assault rifle.

As if sensing her preparation for the inevitable.

He swung the weapon in slow-mo. A Colt XM-177E2 assault rifle.

Rare and discontinued back in the late '60s. One attached to a curious memory from an operation from years ago.

Didn't have time to dwell on the details of the moment.

All that mattered was the shot.

And there it was.

*Pop-pop-pop.*

One shot, one kill, had been the FBI Firearms Training Unit's motto. She took three, and every single one connected in spades.

First the head, then the neck, then the middle of the chest.

Brain, carotid artery, and heart.

Blood bloomed, but nothing else.

He slumped to the floor without another *rat-a-tat-tat*, without further bloodshed.

Just like that. It was over. Much different than in those streamer shows.

Gina released a breath she didn't know she was holding. Then heaved one she needed.

"Whoa," Elijah said, staggering.

She looked at him dumbly, still shocked by the encounter and uncertain what he was registering.

His eyes were wide and mouth held open as if in a question.

"Did you feel that Gina colada?" Elijah asked.

"Feel what?"

He swallowed and shook his head. "Never mind. Nice shot, by the way. You alright?"

She turned back to the perp—lying still, thank the good Lord above—swallowing hard and nodding. "Never shot a man before."

"Always time for a first. Preferably not in a Cracker Barrel, but you can't always choose the hour of your heroics."

She slipped her Glock back in her boot. "I guess not…"

Elijah held his weapon firm and padded forward, nodding toward the downed hostile.

She followed, saying, "We better get out of here if we don't want any issues with law enforcement."

They reached the body, and Eli knelt down. "First things first…"

Taking a sweeping glance and looking satisfied they were dealing with a lone ranger, he stuffed his own Glock at his back under his shirt and reached for the black mask.

Yanking it off revealed a man with a hard face. Eyes were wide and brown, black and blue inky whorls extending to the sides of the face in some weird tattoo. Mouth was hanging open, as if disbelieving his death, and ringed by a black-hair goatee. Looked Latino, or Latinx as those pretentious upper-middle class white people insist on naming a people who don't care a lick about their self-identification. Why is it people are always trying to define the other? Lord knew she and Elijah understood that better than most, neuronormative people insisting their autism was something to be overcome.

But wait…

He also looked familiar.

"I know that face," Gina said from behind. "Those whorls, that tattoo ink!"

Elijah glanced up at her. "From the crowd outside Saint Thomas. The NA group."

She sucked in a measured breath, nodding and saying nothing more.

This perp had been at the beginning of it all.

Shaking the revelation away, he kept at it, ruffling through the man for anything else to make sense of this new crazy. Yanking back a sleeve revealed another peculiar tat on his forearm. Some weird crossish thing, a circle ringing the top stem and dotted by four tiny crosses in the center with flaring lines like the sun at the top.

Gina glanced up and around to assess the crime scene.

And startled.

Literally, the only place in all the joint that was blasted away was the way they came.

Aside from the shattered window, not a bullet or strafing scar on any other wall except for theirs, above their table.

It was as if they were the target.

The only target…

"Wait just a hot anchovy…" Elijah said.

Gina glanced his way. "What do you have?"

He whipped out his phone and scrolled through his pictures. Then gasped and held up the phone at her.

Gina was confused. "That's the bench where we had our chit-chat with Carmen."

He giggled. "Carmen Santiago." Another giggle before he pressed a finger against the phone. "There."

"Where?"

"There."

Gina frowned. "Where there?"

"The back of the bench."

She squinted, leaning toward the device and taking a beat before a sharp intake of breath.

"Egads. The tattoo!"

"Bingo."

"I thought that bench had been tagged. By someone who was marking their turf, even."

"Only question is, who? And what is this insignia?"

"And why did they just try and take us out?"

Nodding, Elijah returned to the device, whispering, "This could be the whole taco right here."

Gina agreed. She also feared what it meant.

For their case.

For them.

# CHAPTER 20

Gina exited off I-66, the main East-West artery running into DC, and onto Prince William Parkway. The rain eased some under a ceiling of charcoal clouds, its darkness compounded by the setting sun.

They had been driving without aim or direction the past hour after fleeing the scene of the Cracker Barrel crime. No way would they get stuck answering questions for hours—days, weeks—on end while they had a case to solve.

An *inexplicitus* case that grew unexplainable by the hour.

Gina colada was right on the *Price is Right* money: the tatted Latino perp was gunning for them. Was a Holy Spirit miracle the man hadn't succeeded in tearing through their heads. The only fallout for them was Elijah's coffee-stained shirt and a few cuts Gina had suffered from the shredded glass pictures above.

Not so much for the others. The four grannies, the family of four, Carhartt Dude who made a heroic effort at taking out the perp but tripped on the layup.

Not so much for Gladys…

Elijah vowed to track down her next of kin and offer a nice tip for her services. Even if she had been a little slow on the coffee refill.

After they fled, Gina had wanted to check in with Order HQ to let their boss, Silas Grey, know about the development. Still stuck in Bureau standard operating procedure, she was. Elijah could care less about SOPs, whether the FBI's or the Order of Thaddeus's. Those just led to paperwork and powwows that rarely led to answers.

He had a different idea.

Instead, he called up their new friend, FBI Lady. She'd mentioned a contact in the Northern Virginia FBI Field Office. Someone with their narcotics division. Had a hunch he might have the 411 on the drugs angle, as well as what had gone down at Cracker Barrel. Because in fleeing the crime scene and driving around like chickens with their feet cut off, there was something about that assault rifle that rang true. The rare, discontinued Colt XM-177E2. Gina mentioned it, too. A case they'd worked on long ago that had been tied to a string of unsolved murders in El Paso, Texas.

But that wasn't all of it.

Because right after Balaclava Dude went down for the count after Gina's excellent kill shot, there'd been a disturbance in the force. Almost like a shock wave had ricocheted out from the man after his brain stem was severed by that well-placed bullet.

He'd felt the vestiges of such a Force in each of the crime scenes, the traces of an unseen...something—a bone-chilling coldness, a rancid smell, a putrid Presence.

From the Unseen Realm...

A chill ratcheted up and down his spine at the thought.

Had always been a spiritually sensitive kid. Perhaps his time at the orphanage had hammered and honed his spidey senses (after all, Spiderman was his favorite comic book hero). Through the years, those senses had served him well, helping him stay out of trouble and generally walking the straight and narrow. Could have been from his innate desire to please, but it was more than that. The Spirit of God himself seemed to be upon him in a special way, cluing him into another dimension with an awareness that was as mystical and creepy as it was real and helpful.

Sure had served him a time or twelve during his years with the Bureau as well, his sensitivity to the working of the Unseen Realm breaking into their mundane world through violent acts of wickedness and evil.

Like what had hit him in Cracker Barrel when that psycho had been killed. As if something that had possessed the man had been flushed from him when his life ended.

Didn't quite know what to make of it, one more rando piece to the *inexplicitus* puzzle straight from hot Hades to add to the pile. Just hoped FBI Lady and her contact with the drug enforcement task force offered some more clarity.

That's where they were heading now, the rain picking up its pace again as they pulled into a side road that led to the Northern Virginia FBI Field Office in Manassas.

Gina suddenly braked hard and pulled off into a strip mall parking lot for a fitness center that was empty but for two cars. The pimply faced college student manning the ID check-in counter and his body builder buddy. A racket, those joints were. A perfectly designed business model that preyed on the hopes and dreams of weak-willed humans with a built-in monthly revenue stream. He'd gone into the wrong business.

"Something the matter?" Elijah asked.

"After everything that went down, I think we should pray before we debrief."

"Nope. Already did. Back at Cracker Barrel."

She frowned. "Without me?"

"Well, yes...But I suppose a second helping of the spiritual practice wouldn't hurt."

"Ooh, I've got one!"

Gina bowed her head and intoned:

*Direct us, O Lord, in all our doings with thy most gracious favor, and further us with thy continual*

*help; that in all our works begun, continued, and
ended in thee, we may glorify thy holy Name, and
finally, by thy mercy, obtain everlasting life; through
Jesus Christ our Lord. Amen.*

"That's familiar. But…isn't that *The Book of Common Prayer*?"

"Sure thing, chicken wing."

He laughed, delighted with her rhyming all the timing.

"Didn't think a Catholic like yourself was allowed to offer a Protestant prayer."

Gina shrugged. "A prayer is a prayer is a prayer, in my book."

"Touché. But don't you mean prayer book?"

"That too."

"I've got another one myself."

"Might as well stock up on our prayers. With what we're up against, we can use all the spiritual protection we can get."

Elijah agreed and closed his eyes. "Almighty God," he prayed, "deliver you from the powers of darkness and evil, and lead you into the light and obedience of the kingdom of his Son Jesus Christ our Lord. From all evil and wickedness; from sin, from the works and assaults of the devil; from your wrath and everlasting condemnation—good Lord, deliver us."

"Good Lord, deliver us," Gina repeated.

"From all disordered and sinful affections; and from all the deceits of the world, the flesh, and the devil—good Lord, deliver us."

Again from Gina: "Good Lord, deliver us."

"O Lord God," Elijah continued, "grant your people grace to withstand the temptations of the world, the flesh, and the devil, and with pure hearts and minds to follow you, the only God; through Jesus Christ our Lord, who lives and reigns with you and the Holy Spirit, one God, now and forever. Amen."

"Amen," Gina repeated, crossing herself.

Elijah clapped his hands together. "Now we're ready."

She pulled back out onto the side road that led toward destiny.

Bright white lights illuminated a driveway entrance into a nondescript four-story building off University Boulevard that looked more like an office park for start-ups than a bureaucratic bunker for spooks and g-men. Another vehicle was idling at the security checkpoint, with a woman standing next to the driver's side door chatting with a guard.

Brit Armstrong.

A man wearing black and bearing an assault rifle slung across his chest walked up to them as Gina pulled their Mercedes G-Class in behind FBI Lady's perfectly coined cliché Chevy Suburban. Black, of course. Another officer roamed around the SUV's perimeter with a bomb-sniffing German Shepherd.

Hated them type. Too many teeth and too much testosterone. Jack Russells all the way. Wondered how Dexter was doing. Hmm… Hope she hadn't torn his leather couch to shreds!

Gina rolled down her window. "Nice to see a familiar face."

Brit sauntered their way and leaned against the car door. "And nice to see you both still intact. Can't say I approve of you fleeing the scene of the crime. But given the stakes, I think we can make an exception. My guy Joe Cosgrove is waiting inside. Ready?"

Gina answered, "Sure thing—"

"Chicken wing," Elijah finished, followed by a Gina giggle.

Brit raised a brow. "Alrighty then. Let's get to it."

She climbed back into her Suburban and led them through the driveway, pulling around into a visitor's spot near the entrance. Swiping her ID badge at the door, she unlocked it and instructed them to sign in with an attendant at the front desk in a vestibule that soared the full four floors. A fountain bubbled away surrounded by a few trees and other foliage. The man in black manning the desk, feet propped up and reading a comic book, barely gave them a passing glance.

Elijah smirked. Good to know the Feds were still recruiting the brightest and best and most vigilant.

Brit went to the elevators, but Elijah stopped her.

"I prefer the stairs," he said.

"Why?" She punched the 2nd Floor button anyway and threw him a furrowed brow.

Glancing Gina's way, he found her twisting her ginger locks, then plucking a single strand of hair. A tick when she was anxious. Knew she wouldn't be a fan, and wouldn't say anything to draw attention to herself, so he took one for the team.

"A severe phobia that'll leave me in a catatonic fettle position in the corner."

Brit straightened at that, then nodded, saying nothing more.

"Thanks," Gina whispered, as FBI Lady led them across the vestibule.

"No prob, Bob."

Bypassing a door that led to one wing in favor of another one, Brit again used her badge to gain entrance before ushering them inside a long hallway. Utilitarian, government-issued walls lit by dimmed recessed lighting that reminded Elijah of his days with the FBI led them down a wing that smelled of alcohol and sanitized air. They passed a set of windows peering into a lab that looked like a coroner's office. Creepy. At the other end, they shoved through a door that led to a stairwell taking them up to the second floor.

The door led into a large open-floor office area with low-rise cubicles and fluorescent lighting that shouldn't be OSHA approved. Hated the way its white lighting made him look pastier than he really was. At least it was empty. Too late in the day for government-issued lemmings in dark suites and white shirts clacking away at computers and yakking away on phones. So at least they had that going for them. An orange glow spilled into the room from the corner down the way, as well as the faint smell of tobacco.

FBI Lady made for the back corner.

Elijah's mouth salivated for his own pipe. When all this was over, he'd break out his best bowl and fill it with slowly steamed burley, then fill his mouth with the warm, sweet flavor and his nostrils with the vanilla aroma of his favorite Cavendish tobacco blend.

They rounded the corner to find the source of the glow: a messy room stacked high with folders spilling papers, a green floor lamp leaning in the corner, and a wiry, bespeckle man in a tweed jacket that definitely wasn't government-issued. Round glasses framed a round face. His feet were propped on his desk, puffing away.

Brit cleared her throat, sending the man scrambling from his desk and fumbling with his half-bent Dublin pipe. Which sent burnt tobacco and live embers tumbling across the papers strewn about his desk.

"Crapola!" the man exclaimed, jumping from his chair and swatting furiously at his papers.

Elijah smirked. "Nice pipe."

He looked up while continuing to damp down any chance of a fire. "Who are you?"

"The cavalry," Brit said from the door, arms folded and leaning against the threshold.

The man stiffened, and he chuckled nervously. "Uh, hey, Brit. Didn't expect you so soon."

"You know, I could have your hide for smoking in a government facility. What would Keener say?"

His face fell, and he went whiter than he already was. "Uh, nothing good."

"Got that right. Which is why you're going to help me with that thing I called about." She gestured to Elijah and Gina. "Gina Anderson and Elijah Fox, former FBI down at Quantico. This is Joe Cosgrove."

Cosgrove nodded and made a hat-tipping motion to one that

definitely wasn't holding his long gray hair in place. Looked like a drowned muskrat, it was so greasy and unkempt.

"Elijah Fox…" he said, leaning back and staring at the ceiling. "You wouldn't happen to be Spooky Eli, would you?"

Heat ran up Elijah's neck, and he could feel Gina glancing his way with sympathy. The name still smarted after all these years. Not only because it was said in jest at his work on the more paranormal, supernatural cases, but also because of his peculiarities. Autistic people were spooky in his colleagues' minds. At least *that* autistic person.

"Bingo," he simply said, taking a seat in one of two empty chairs in front of Cosgrove's desk. Sad and well-worn vinyl things that were definitely government-issued.

"Make yourself at home…" the agent muttered, coming around to clear the other one of stacked papers and folders.

Brit offered the other one to Gina; she took it. Cosgrove returned to his seat, frowning at his spent pipe and planting his feet back on his desk.

"What can I do you for?" he asked.

Elijah took a breath, praying to Yeshua Almighty above he could do something for them. Like explain what the hot Hades was happening!

Because if not…well—if not, they might very well be screwed.

# CHAPTER 21

Gina took a deep breath, steadying herself from being back inside the Farm after what went down last year.

And instantly regretted it.

The wretched scent of burnt tobacco sent her reeling. Hated the smell with a passion that burned bright and strong. Reminded her of a string of her mama's lovers who came through their double-wide like cattle to a feeding trough. More like to the slaughter, as was the case with Mama. And every last one of them stank to high heaven.

Of tobacco.

She shoved the memory aside, repeating a line from Psalm 23 from earlier: *'Surely goodness and mercy shall follow me all the days of my life, and I shall dwell in the house of the Lord my whole life long.'*

The good Lord above had certainly made good and that promise, a through line darting from that double-wide in Toledo to an FBI field office in Manassas, Virginia.

Who would've thunk it?

Elijah said, "What can you tell us about the new junk that's been hitting the streets—the crazy meth mixture? Sounds pretty brutal."

Gina snapped back to the moment, suppressing a smile.

Always the no-nonsense one of the pair, getting right down to business. She liked that about him.

The agent named Cosgrove snorted a laugh and adjusted his glasses. "Yeah, it's brutal alright."

Gina said, "Tell us what you know."

The agent put his hands behind his head, his tweed jacket opening to reveal stained pits.

She turned up a corner of her lip. Eww...

"I joined the DEA seventeen years ago," he explained. "Recruited from one of those Big Pharma outfits to understand the thinking and methods of black-market chemists, their work regularly plopping on my desk to sample. A few years later, the FBI recruited me for their own drug enforcement task force."

Elijah smirked. "A little pissing contest between Uncle Sam's agencies, was it?"

He laughed. "So you understand then. Soon, I started globe-trotting to labs seized around the world. Meth was the drug-of-choice I analyzed most. Guess where most large quantities were trafficked?"

"Mexico?" Gina asked, the memory of that Latino hombre smarting.

"Exactamundo."

She glanced at Elijah; he nodded with pursed lips, his jaw muscles clenched tight.

She understood the feeling, given their ordeal.

Cosgrove continued, "Traffickers industrialized their production and dragged it across the border into the Southwest. Now, the stuff I analyzed back then was made from ephedrine, the common ingredient found in decongestants."

"Derived from the ephedra plant," Elijah said, "and first altered to synthesize crystal methamphetamine in 1919 by a Japanese researcher. He called it *hiropon*, a word combining the Japanese terms for *fatigue* and *fly away*, and it was given to soldiers to increase their alertness."

He chuckled and looked to Brit. "Wow, he's good."

She shrugged and said nothing. But the agent was right. He was, that whip-smart eidetic memory of his saving them a time or twelve.

"In the early 1980s," the agent went on, "the criminal underworld rediscovered the ephedrine method for making meth by pulling the active ingredient from the over-the-counter decongestant Sudafed."

Gina said, "And this new…junk, as Eli said—this is that?"

"No, it ain't. What we've been seeing hitting the streets isn't made from ephedrine, which is hard to come by as both the U.S. and Mexico clamped down on it decades ago."

"What is it?"

"P2P."

"P2P? Sounds like a Star Wars droid."

"Phenyl-2-propanone," Elijah answered. "The other way to make methamphetamine."

"Exactamundo," Cosgrove said. "It had been used by biker gangs like the Hell's Angels in the '80s, but it was small-time trade. Essentially, it's a clear liquid chemical made from common, cheap, and toxic chemicals. Cyanide, lye, mercury, sulfuric acid, hydrochloric acid, nitrostyrene. Stuff any schmuck can get their hands on in legal ways from a wide array of industries, and used in a dozen or more combinations to get the end result. Only problem is, it's super complicated and volatile to make."

Brit asked now, "What's so complicated about it?"

"Part of the problem with the P2P method is that the end result births two kinds of methamphetamine. D-methamphetamine, which is the stuff that makes you high, and l-methamphetamine, which just makes your heart race but does diddly squat to your brain."

Gina said, "In other words, product waste."

"Exactamundo. Meth cooks want to get rid of as much of the l-meth as possible, except separating the two is tricky business. A skill set way beyond most trailer-park chemists. Without that separation, though, you get an inferior product to ephedrine-based meth."

Elijah said, "Guessing all you get is a hammering heart without the trippy high."

"Exactamundo again, partner."

"So, what's this new stuff?"

"Mostly d-meth. Someone's removed most of the l-meth."

Gina asked, "And that's unusual?"

"Look, I've taken down labs in several continents," Cosgrove said, "And no one in the criminal underworld that I've ever seen has figured out how to separate d-meth from l-meth on such a large scale."

"Until now."

Cosgrove nodded. "The last few years, at least."

He reached for his pipe, as if to relight it and puff it back to life, but glanced at Brit and frowned. He folded his hands instead.

Clearing his throat, he explained, "When I first encountered it back in '06, it hit me that these drugs made in labs weren't subject to weather and seasons, to soil and rain. It was all about chemical availability. This new method, combined with the world's chemical markets accessed through Mexican shipping ports—well, traffickers could do whatever the hell they wanted, ramping up production of P2P meth in basically limitless quantities. No way could I have anticipated just how widely this new crop of meth epidemic would reach nearly two decades later."

He leaned back and smiled, staring off into the ceiling as if reliving a memory.

"One of my first busts," he went on, "had been surveying a pair that burned down their lab a decade ago. A cross-border operation with Mexico that showed how industrial meth production had gone. Lots of other labs had been popping up in Mexico thanks to the influx of substantial capital and almost zero concern for law enforcement. They used expensive equipment and stored large inventories of chemicals for processing, netting 240 pounds per batch."

"That a lot?" asked Elijah.

"Heck yeah! Standing at the edge of the smokey, ashy remains of the lab and shielding my nose from the stench of it all, I felt I was glimpsing a new drug world. What was striking is what we weren't seeing."

Gina asked, "What was that?"

"No ephedrine. The joint was exclusively set up to make P2P meth. Not only that, it wasn't holed up in some mountain or out on a ranch in butt-freakin-nowhere. It was just 15 miles south of Guadalajara, one of Mexico's largest cities, and right near the city's international airport. The labs just exploded! Not like, exploded exploded."

"Geometrically, you mean."

"Exactamundo. Throw a stone in a five-square-kilometer area outside Sinaloa's capital city of Culiacán and you'd hit 20 labs. No exaggeration. Expand that to 15 kilometers and there were more than a hundred. And now—" He whistled and shook his head. "Now, the confederations of meth suppliers are this loose ecosystem of independent brokers, truckers, packagers, pilots, shrimp-boat captains, mechanics, and tire-shop owners. In the United States, you've got meat-plant workers, money-wiring services, restaurants, farm foremen, drivers, safe houses, and used-car lots in the ecosystem. All of it's just spread out—from Mexico to Miami, up the East Coast and on through the Midwest to Cali."

Gina said, "Sounds like you've got your work cut out for you."

Cosgrove nodded. "Exactamundo. Take Louisville, Kentucky."

Elijah perked up at the mention of the Bluegrass State. Kenturkey, as he called it, was the home state of his forever family. She also recalled how his father had led a recovery ministry much like Wellspring—ending in an almost mirror tragedy.

She hoped the connection didn't send him into a panic...

"Before 2016," the agent explained, "the place had an insignificant meth market, where a pound sold for $14,000. But with the explosion of supply and demand, it's fallen to less than a tenth of that. The market is utterly transformed, drawing more dealers who have cobbled together their own supply networks. To compete, these dealers offer free delivery, fully loaded with liquid meth for immediate consumption."

Elijah snorted a laugh. "Like UberEats, ehh?"

"Good way of putting it."

Gina asked, "But how could this have happened so quickly, and so invisible it seems?"

Elijah nodded. "So that even you, a government agent, were caught off guard?"

Cosgrove leaned forward, propping his elbows on his desk and folding his hands into a tent. "One probable reason is the U.S. government was so focused on the opioid epidemic for so long, which was itself ignored for so long. Think of what all the headlines the last several years have been about."

Gina said, "Pain-pill and heroin overdoses."

"Then fentanyl overdoses. And money chases the headlines in my line of work. Then there's the fact meth doesn't kill people like it does opioids, or at least at the same rates. Which defies the first law of journalism that gives us all those headlines."

"Which is?"

"If it bleeds, it leads," Elijah replied.

"Exactamundo. With deaths, and lots of them, you've got head-lines, yes, but also memorials. Chances to remember the deceased's better days. No such luck with meth addicts, who are a constant, raw, living face of addiction. People don't want to touch that stuff. Not the media, not politicians, not even recovery counselors."

Gina said, "Except Rafferty, Stone, and Atkins."

Cosgrove squinted at her. "Who're they?"

Brit answered, "Three ministers leading the drug recovery ministry I told you about."

"Ahh, yes. Right right right. Well, at any rate, with no central villain in the P2P-meth story—no Big Pharma, no Big Cartel—there's no single entity to target. Either with blame or legal recourse. So the meth issue is sort of swept under the rug or enveloped in the blobby War on Drugs. Add to that a reluctance to speak about homeless drug use, for fear that the downtrodden will be blamed for their troubles, and you've got a recipe for disaster. From the government to non-profits, the media to the medical industry."

"Except now," Gina said, "drug dealers are targeting ministers."

Cosgrove threw his head back and laughed. "Not likely, sister. This isn't a *Breaking Bad* spin-off series."

Heat raced up her neck at the slight. She'd certainly handled her fair share of Jack the Lads who thought they knew better than their female agent counterparts. Had been one of a handful of women in Quantico at the turn of the century. So she'd been up this creek before. Still chapped her backside to cross it again, but at least it didn't bother her now.

Much...

Sitting straighter, Elijah insisted, "Nope. You're wrong. They did attack those ministers and then us—" He gestured between him and Gina. "—who are investigating them."

Another giggle slipped through the agent's mouth. Cosgrove folded his hands on his desk now. "And how, pray tell, do you know that?"

"Because a man with a tattoo matching tagging graffiti we found at the crime scene tried to mow us down, El Chapo style."

"I think you mean Al Capone."

"Nope. El Chapo. The man was Latino and wielding a Colt XM-177E2 assault rifle. A super-rare weapon I recall from a task force Gina and I worked on with the DEA a decade ago. Some small-time drug runners who we thought would lead us to the big cheese that never panned out."

Cosgrove sat straighter at that revelation. "Tattoo, you say…"

Elijah nodded, whipping out his phone and activating it to the photos app. Finding the image, he wheeled it around for the agent's viewing.

He took it, adjusted his glasses, squinted toward the device.

Then dropped it with a shudder.

"No. Freakin'. Way…"

Brit stepped forward, leaning over the desk between Elijah and Gina. "No freaking what way?"

Cosgrove asked, "You found this at the crime scene of one of your vics?"

Elijah nodded. "On the backside of a bench outside the narcotics recovery ministry. Then again, on a Latino who tried to mow us down El—"

"Right right right. El Chapo style."

"Yuppers. But what does it mean?"

He gave Brit a glance that asked if it was alright to spill the tea. She nodded, and he did.

Cosgrove said, "It belongs to an outfit called Santa Muerte."

"Santa Muerte?" asked Gina, dread starting to bloom in both her brain and belly.

"Santa Muerte?" Brit echoed.

"Is there an echo in here?" Elijah said. "Death Saint, right?"

Cosgrove nodded. "Or Holy Death."

"What is it?" asked Brit.

"A ritualistic cult linked with gang *narcocultura*. Specifically, Los Zorros."

Gina startled. "Los Zorros?"

Elijah snickered. "Like that pulp fiction character?"

The agent nodded. "Inspired by it, apparently."

Had certainly encountered them during her tenure with the FBI. Not directly, but that case with Eli he mentioned from early in their career helping out the DEA, and then water-cooler chatter.

So, to hear that name now, in connection with their own case —their first Group X case...

Egads. The revelation changed everything! Now they had a link between a drug cartel and their dead ministers.

They had a suspect. Motive, means, and opportunity were still question marks, but they'd get there. And she guessed soon.

"Zorros means *foxes* in Spanish," Cosgrove explained, "The original founder was Alberto Manuel de la Vega."

"How original," Elijah sneered. "Just like the masked vigilante, Don Diego de la Vega."

Gina said, "They're a criminal syndicate operating from the United Mexican States, isn't that right? Regarded as one of the most dangerous of Mexico's drug cartels."

The agent said lowly, "Exactamundo. And known for engaging in brutally violent tactics that shock and awe those they wish to intimidate and punish, including—"

"Beheadings, torture, and indiscriminate murder, right? I recall reading about a case from 2011. The San Fernando massacre, where 193 people were killed by Los Zorros drug cartel at some ranch."

"You're pretty quick on the draw, little sister."

Elijah said, "What about this ritualistic cult business, and linked with gang *narcocultura*?"

Cosgrove answered, "Most of the attention from the U.S. with regards to the cartels and gangs has been about their illicit narcotics and other criminal economic activities. Far less has focused on some of the darker spiritualistic parts of the drug wars."

Gina flashed wide eye at Elijah; he matched them.

Darker spiritualistic parts? This could get twisty real quick...

"Go on," Elijah said.

"One component entails the rise of the cartel and gang *narcocultura* drug culture variant of the Cult of Santa Muerte."

"Holy Death."

Cosgrove added, "This variant of the cult promotes greater levels of criminality than the more mainstream and older forms of Santa Muerte worship. Sometimes it can be so extreme that it condones morally corrupt behaviors—what many people would consider as resulting from an evil value system that rewards personal gain above all else, promoting the intentional pain and suffering of others, and, even, viewing killing as a pleasurable activity."

The agent paused, taking a breath and looking down at his desk. Didn't seem like so much deciding whether or not to tell as genuinely catching his breath at the revelation.

Most unnerving…

He continued, "Enough ritualistic behaviors, including killings, have occurred in Mexico to leave open the possibility that a spiritual insurgency component of the narcotics war now exists."

"Spiritual insurgency…" Elijah muttered, throwing another glance her way.

Gina nodded, definitely picking up what he was putting down. This might be exactly what they were looking for to blow the case wide open. The cipher to the riddle that had been vexing them from that morning.

"Evidence suggests," Cosgrove explained, "that the numbers of defections to the cults that worship a perverted Christian god and the various unsanctioned saints have grown for years. For U.S. law enforcement agencies, the rise of a criminalized and dark variant of Santa Muerte worship holds many negative implications. Of greatest concern, the inspired and ritualistic killings associated with this cult could cross the border and take place in the United States."

Gina perked up at that. "Ritualistic killings? Such as priests and pastors?"

Elijah nodded. "Have to imagine when a priest is killed, it sends a pretty strong message."

"Yeah, like, 'If I'm able to kill a priest, I can kill anyone.'"

"Bingo."

She turned to Cosgrove and wanted an answer from the horse's mouth. "Do you think this death cult could be our prep?"

Cosgrove opened his mouth to answer, but threw Brit searching eyes instead. He took a breath, then a beat. "Can we talk outside?"

He leaped to his feet and shuffled to the open door, motioning for his fellow agent to follow. She threw Gina and Elijah a shrug and joined him in the hallway, the two shuffling down a way.

"How rude," Elijah said.

"But predictable," Gina said with a sigh. "Dude doesn't trust us with his precious inside baseball info."

"Now what?"

One thing was darn tootin'. She was over this Jack the Lad and his coyness. So, she sprang to her feet and shuffled around to the man's desk.

"We improvise, that's what."

Sliding into Cosgrove's chair, she wheeled it to a Hewlett Packard desktop still partying like it was 1999.

Elijah joined her as she started clattering away on the keyboard.

"Gina colada…" he said lowly, "what are you doing?"

Entering in a username and passcode, she smiled with satisfaction.

Success.

# CHAPTER 22

For most of Elijah's life, he was what you call a rule follower. Perhaps that was because of the dear ol' orphanage guardians and the back of their hands against his head when he broke the letter, jot, and tittle of the law. Perhaps it was because of his personal constitution.

That changed at some point while getting tangled in the FBI's bureaucratic red tape. All that mattered to him was justice, setting the world right. That's what motivated him day in and day out working long hours that sacrificed any sort of social life.

Not Uncle Sam. All he seemed to care about was the right colored TPS report attached to the right supporting documents. Same for Gina, a by-the-books girl for the half decade he'd worked with her.

But now—to see her breaking and entering into a secure federal computer…Well, that took the red velvet cake.

Not cheesecake. Because in this case, it was fine by him!

"Gina colada…" he said sidling up to her, "what are you doing?"

"Getting answers, that's what."

"I see that, but how?" He squinted, leaning in and furrowing his brow. "And who's Tom Winter?"

She shrugged. "An old flame."

"The guy from IT, with the mullet and weak chin that would put Dana Carvey to shame?"

"Stop judging and start helping, would you?"

"You do realize this breaks like seventy-nine sections of the U.S. Code, don't you? 18 U.S. Code, section 1752, clearly states—"

"Never quote the U.S. Code to me when we're in the middle of an investigation."

"Just saying, it might behoove us to take a breath and—"

"Got it!"

Elijah slapped her back. "Thata girl. What'd you find?"

She pointed at the screen. "The lowdown on our Latino muchachos. Take a gander."

He did, reading up on the history of the drug cartel. Quite the history, too:

---

Historically, Los Zorros is rooted in the late 1990s when the Sinaloa Cartel sought enforcement capabilities to control a portion of the burgeoning cocaine-trafficking market through Mexico. Recruited by Sinaloa Cartel kingpin Alberto Manuel de la Vega as his personal security detail to protect his own cartel leadership position, the original Los Zorros were a fifty-member team of deserters from the Mexican Special Forces.

Having received training in commando and urban warfare from Israeli and U.S. Special Forces, this military background was leveraged for enforcement operations and training and recruitment efforts, leading to their reputation as one of Mexico's most violent drug trafficking organizations.

Eventually, as Los Zorros membership grew, the organization became more closely aligned with the drug trade, loosening its ties to the Sinaloa Cartel and transforming into a semi-autonomous drug trafficking organization. There are varying reports about what led to the split, but a disagreement over leadership and direction seems to be the most plausible. By mid-2008 Los Zorros had become completely autonomous from the Sinaloa Cartel.

The report went on to describe hostilities between the two groups that meant not a lick to the current investigation. He kept reading:

This evolution of the drug trafficking organization has led to an essential brand using intimidation tactics, including: narco-banners, torture, and beheadings. Los Zorros often employs such identifiers to instill fear in their victims, furthering their drug trafficking aims through intimidation and fear.

Los Zorros continues to expand their criminal enterprises, going beyond the traditional activities of a trafficking organization. In addition to trafficking multi-ton drug quantities, money shipments and laundering, firearms trafficking, public and private corruption, and use of violence, the DTO's activities, as well as common criminals operating under the brand, now include human smuggling, gasoline and oil theft, and pirating audio and video merchandise.

Elijah smirked. "A real entrepreneurial bunch, aren't they?"

"Look at this," Gina said, reading, "'Los Zorros's influence has breached the US-Mexico border, extending into the United States. While their drug distribution network contains key hubs in Texas, their *interests and influence extend well beyond many non-border states and cities.'"*

"Says here," Elijah added, "that everywhere from Gainesville, Florida, and Miami, to Dubuque, Iowa, and Chicago. Even all the way up to Detroit and Boston and New York City."

"Looks like they've got Saint Louis and Nashville, as well."

"Along with what you'd expect in Texas. Houston, Austin, Fort Worth."

Something else caught his attention. "Whoa. Check this out. *'As former Mexican soldiers, Los Zorros possesses expertise in sophisticated communication. The drug trafficking organization also uses non-verbal communication through identifying symbols, such as the letter Z and certain death cult insignia.'"*

Gina frowned. "That's odd."

"Especially the part about the letter Z."

"The letter Z?" Gina asked. "I don't under—"

Elijah jutted both arms out together as if he were about to dive off a diving board, then bowed his head into a hunch.

Like the letter Z.

"Egads! Our two victims sitting posed in their chairs!"

"Bingo. It wasn't the letter S after all. Just as we wondered."

"Not for sin, but for Los Zorros."

"Dollars to donuts these are our bad hombres."

She kept scrolling, then stopped with a start. "Especially considering this."

Elijah leaned toward the monitor, two words catching his attention: *Dark Spirituality.*

And something else…

"Oh my cheeps!"

Gina hummed with recognition. "Joe Cosgrove is the author, and it connects the *narcotraficantes* to that Santa Muerte death cult."

Now that for sure took the red velvet cake!

He said, "Could be just the link we've been looking for!"

The pair read the report in silence on the spiritual connection between Los Zorros and Santa Muerte, several scrolls through the Word doc filling in the blanks:

---

Santa Muerte ideology has developed in Mexico for approximately a half century and has spread into the United States and Central America. The cult's popularity has increased with its ties to illicit narcotics trafficking in Mexico in the late 1980s and early 1990s. One expert explains, "The Santa Muerte cult could best be described as following a set of ritual practices offered on behalf of a supernatural personification of death…she is comparable in theology to supernatural beings or archangels."

The cult appears to have more European than Aztecan origins, with some individuals describing Santa Muerte as a new age Grim Reaper-type goddess, a bad-girl counterpart to the Virgin of Guadalupe. Her imagery includes that of a robed skeleton carrying a scythe and globe or scales. Many Santa Muerte followers appear benign—typically poor, uneducated, and superstitious individuals who practice a form of unsanctioned saint worship mixed with varying elements of folk Catholicism. However, a sizable minority of worshipers follow the fully criminalized variant of Santa Muerte worship steeped in *narcocultura*.

---

"Egads, check this out…" Gina highlighted a section with the mouse.

"One of the high priests," Elijah said, reading, "was also apparently a muckety-muck in Los Zorros."

"And a decade ago, they called for holy war against the Catholic Church!"

"Egads, is right."

The report went on, documenting the more occult aspects to the death cult: the use of candle magic, herbs, oils, amulets, spiritual energy, and various mystical items. Much of it was familiar to Elijah and his own work with the FBI. Same for Gina, the pair of them specializing in cultic ritual abuse and occult practices, along with their implications for domestic terrorism.

Candles helped focus the Santa Muerte worshiper's concentration and act as a conduit for the death saint to receive their prayers. Smoke was utilized in their rituals, along with alcoholic drinks. Narcotics smeared on statues were thought to help activate them into some sort of golemic use, stone activated by magic into devils and wickedness. The bases of candles and statues were anointed with oils and herbs to enhance their power.

But then...

The final paragraph gave him pause:

---

More extreme forms of worship involve bowls of blood—animal and human—at the altars and smeared on the religious icons and on the devotee as part of a blood pact. Although ritualized killings represent a small minority of murders perpetrated by Mexican cartels and gangs, enough allegedly have taken place to generate alarm.

---

Gina put a hand to her mouth and pointed. Elijah nodded. "I see..."

They read in silence, the HVAC hum and distant conversation down the hallways their only soundtrack:

---

Additional incidents allegedly have occurred involving victims with their skin and hearts removed. Other cases have included individuals castrated and beheaded while alive, lit on fire and burned to death, and butchered and quartered. Sometimes, authorities found only the victim's skin. It remains unclear if these violent killings represent the acts of secular psychopaths or those following some sort of ritualized spiritual purpose.

There are, however, reports of Los Zorros gang members offering over a dozen people as human sacrifices to ensure the magical protection of its members. An old crime scene photo displays a Santa Muerte statuette among the ritualistic tools belonging to the group. An incident once considered anomalous now serves as an early event warning of the growing influence of *narcocultura* in Mexico.

---

Gina sat back. "I think I'm going to be sick…"

Elijah sighed in frustration and ran a hand through his thick hair. Little of this had anything to do with their case, with what was happening in the U.S.. Much less any connection between Los Zorros and three dead ministers.

Frustration was mounting, and their time was running out. They had to get to it.

He grabbed the mouse and took over, scrolling in search of the link.

Scrolling, scrolling, scrolling.

Grin.

"Here we go…"

Gina sat forward. "Whatcha got?"

"Chandler, Arizona," Elijah said. "A kill-team leader for the Los Zorros Cartel engaged in multiple homicides across the border. The man bragged about how he slashed two teenagers with a broken bottle, gathered their blood in a cup, and made a toast to the Santisima Muerte, or death saint. He later disposed of their bodies in a barrel filled with liquid fuel, a method known as a guiso, or stew."

"Certainly sounds like what we found in DC. Sort of." She

took over the mouse, scrolling before announcing, "There's more."

There sure was:

---

Los Zorros considers Santa Muerte their patron saint; for this reason, the more specific the information gathered, the better. It has been reported that tagging prospective victims and their locale with the Santa Muerte insignia, adopted by Los Zorros, has been employed as a means of both intimidation and ultimate repercussions—suggesting a closer link between the two than otherwise thought.

---

The pair finished reading, then fell silent. Not much more after that.

There it was. A gang symbol tagging the turf just outside one of the churches connected with the ministry was also found on a psycho who had tried to take them out. The very same symbol of a major drug cartel from across the border that is also a satanic death cult.

It suddenly all made sense to Elijah.

And it changed everything.

While changing nothing.

Because it confirmed what he had wondered from the start.

What he'd felt from the start.

He exclaimed, "Oh my cheeps! This changes everything!"

"It does?"

The voice was male and from the door.

Elijah's heart sank, a cold flush of fight-or-flight adrenaline racing through his veins.

Cosgrove.

Standing at the door along with Brit.

Elijah stepped around from the man's desk, joined by Gina.

"Wanna tell me what the hell you were doing at my computer?" Cosgrove did not look like a happy camper.

He shrugged. "Oh, you know. Just LOL-ing at some cat videos on my WeShare social media account."

The man turned crimson, clearly not into cat videos.

Gina intercepted any further reply: "It was my fault. I used an old FBI login to expand our understanding of Los Zorros."

"You mean you hacked into my computer to abscond with classified government documents."

"No…" Elijah said, stepping up to the plate in their defense, while literally stepping up to the man in tweed. "We logged into a government computer and merely read classified government documents. Your fault you left it on."

"I stepped out to have a private conversation with the understanding my property would be secured! Nay, the government's property would be secured."

Brit put out a staying hand to ratchet down the temperature. "You both have a lot to answer for. Do you know what kind of trouble you're in? What kind of *federal* trouble?"

Elijah shook his head. "Nope. Diplomatic immunity."

She scoffed. "Whatever. I have a big problem with what you two pulled. I invited you to join—"

"Requested our help, if I understand it right."

Gina sighed. "Eli…"

"*Invited* you to join *my* investigation as a *courtesy* to a *friend*."

He frowned, mumbling, "Any more exclamation points you'd like to throw into that sentence of yours?"

"And *now*—" she went on, narrowing her eyes and folding her arms. A clear power move that also conveyed a bit of piss. "—you go snooping into government documents on secured equipment?"

"It's a good thing, too, otherwise you'd still be spinning your wheels."

"And why is that, Sherlock?"

Elijah grinned with satisfaction. Couldn't help it. Was part of what got him fired by Pendergast, but whatever.

"Because I solved the case."

Cosgrove smirked. "Did you, now…"

"How?" Brit said with too much snoot for Elijah's taste.

So he crossed his arms and leaned against Cosgrove's messy desk, reveling in the spotlight and taking all the time he wanted.

Until Gina nailed him in the ribs. "Get to it, hotshot."

He nodded. "It's elementary, my dear FBI Lady."

# CHAPTER 23

Gina had a hunch she knew what Elijah was going to say. Had wondered if there was some sort of connection from the start, given a priest had been murdered. Because you don't murder a priest unless you're under the influence of some bad juju.

The rulers, the authorities, the cosmic powers of this present darkness that are not of this world.

The spiritual forces of evil in the Unseen Realm.

Satan himself.

But she wanted to hear him say it. And wanted to see the FBI agents' reaction.

"For Pete's sake…" Brit complained. "Tell us what you know."

Elijah went to answer when Gina's phone threw up a shrilly *bring-bring-bring*.

He sighed. "You've gotta stop doing that. You're crimping my style."

Heat raced to her cheeks as she fumbled to answer the phone. It was the mother ship.

"Sorry, but it's HQ."

Brit said, "Say Hi to Silas for me."

Gina put the phone on speaker. "Hello, Silas?"

"Sorry to be disappointing you," a familiar Indian man said, "but it is being your friendly operational support...erm, supporter!"

"Hi, Abraham, whatcha got for us?"

"First of all, none of the names have been checking out thus far from the Arlington Diocese settlement with Father Rafferty. A few of them have passed, several more had convincing alibis, and still most were surprisingly quite heartbroken their former priest had been murdered. Sorry that I am not being more help."

"No worries. Pretty sure that's a rabbit trail anyway, but keep looking."

Elijah asked, "What about the other thing?"

"Righto," Abraham replied. "I am having the lab results for the sample you sent me of that substance from the Saint Thomas crime scene."

Brit startled, spinning to Eli. "Crime scene sample?"

Elijah answered, "Yuppers. Some of the substance on the confessional chair. The one that smelled like reptile pee."

Reddening, the FBI agent narrowed her eyes. "That's my evidence!"

"Technically, our evidence."

"No, it isn't!"

"Yep, it is."

"No."

"Yes."

Brit threw up her hands in a huff and ran one across her pixie cut.

Gina suggested, "How about we let Abraham fill us in on what he discovered."

"Fine. But I could have you arrested for this."

"Nope," said Elijah.

"Abraham," Gina said with intervention before the sticky wicket got even stickier, "what can you tell us?"

"I am being pleased to report," he said proudly, "that it is definitely being reptile urine."

"Egads, what?"

Elijah clenched a fist. "I knew it!"

"Knew what, Sherlock?" Brit asked, folding her arms.

"It's what I was going to suggest. Mammals, like us humans, excrete urea in our urine. Not reptiles. Something to do with their kidney structure. Instead, their pee contains uric acid."

Brit asked, "So, what, there was a lizard running around inside the confessional at the time of the murder?"

"Nope. Something way worse. The evidence proves it."

"I'm confused…" Cosgrove said. "I thought this case was about a death cult drug cartel."

Elijah said, "It is. And it isn't."

"What's that supposed to mean?"

"Yeah, Eli," Gina said. "What are you getting at?"

He turned to her. "What I'm getting, it is. These men, these ministers, were killed by Watcher-spirits."

"Watcher-whos?" Brit said, face twisted up in confusion.

Gina sucked in a measured breath, wondering where her partner was going with this. But also knowing entirely well what he was suggesting.

"Demons, my dear Watson," Elijah went on, "killed the priest, then the other two ministers."

Cosgrove threw back his head and laughed out loud, from the belly.

Brit joined him, closing her eyes and widening her mouth and letting a cackle rip that grated on Gina's every last nerve.

Elijah huffed, folding his arms and running through his familiar finger tick. The one when anxiety arose, and his nerves were fraying.

Thumb to index finger, thumb to middle, thumb to ring finger, thumb to pinkie. Then rinse and repeat.

He kept at it while the peanut gallery kept at their own thing.

Gina intervened before Eli's tick led to a whole other thing that wouldn't be good.

"Maybe we could let him explain," she said with raised voice. "You know, like adults?"

That shut them up, the pair winding down and clearing their throats, but suppressing another round of giggles.

Rolling his eyes, Elijah looked around the room. "Do you have a Bible in all this bureaucratic junk lying around?"

Agent Cosgrove startled. "A what?"

"A Bible. You know, the Word of God. The Good Book. The—"

"I know what you mean," the man snapped, shoving past Eli for his desk. "Was raised Baptist, so of course I do."

"What's this about?" Brit asked.

"You'll see," Gina said.

Cosgrove handed over a black book with crimson-edged pages, *Holy Bible* gold lettering stamped on the cover.

Elijah took it, flipped through it, and frowned. "Not a very good Baptist, it seems…" he muttered. "Hasn't been used once. Crisp pages and no underlines, like the day it was printed."

Cosgrove glanced at the floor and ran a hand through his unkempt hair. "Yeah, well, you could say I've backslidden. So sue me!"

Brit asked, "What's this Watcher-spirit business?"

Elijah flipped through the Bible, looking for his place. "The offspring of the sons of God."

"The sons of God?" Cosgrove said. "Don't you mean the offspring of, just, God?"

"Nope. They concern the other gods in Psalm 82:6 called the sons of the Most High. Elsewhere, they're called the *beney ha-elohim.*"

"Oh, is that all…"

"Sorry. The Hebrew is '*the sons of God.*' Other Jewish literature from the Second Temple period call them Watchers."

Brit furrowed her brow. "Don't you mean angels?"

"Nope. They are what the text says they are. Gods. They outrank angels. The Hebrew word for *angel* is entirely different."

"Are they demons then?"

"Not exactly. Some are indeed fallen spiritual beings, but they outrank demons as well. The details aren't important. Here, why don't I…"

Finding his place in Cosgrove's Bible, Elijah read aloud:

---

When people began to multiply on the face of the ground, and daughters were born to them, the sons of God saw that they were fair; and they took wives for themselves of all that they chose. Then the Lord said, "My spirit shall not abide in mortals forever, for they are flesh; their days shall be one hundred twenty years." The Nephilim were on the earth in those days—and also afterward—when the sons of God went in to the daughters of humans, who bore children to them. These were the heroes that were of old, warriors of renown.

---

"I don't like that translation," he complained, "but that will do."

"What is that?" Brit asked. "It sounded like gods mating with humans."

"That's exactly what it says, from the opening verses in Genesis 6 launching the Great Flood story."

"In the Bible?" Cosgrove asked with surprise.

Elijah nodded. "Yuppers."

"That isn't in any Bible I've ever read!"

Brit smirked. "He read it from *your* Bible, genius."

"Oh, yeah…but that's messed up."

Elijah started bobbing back and forth on his heels with pent up energy. Clearly ready to unleash it on the room. He also started up that tick, his thumb touching each of his fingers before repeating it while he paced.

"What's fascinating about this story in Genesis is that it reflects other kinds of stories. The other major religions and cultures around the world also tell of beings coming down from heaven to mate with women, eventually birthing unusual offspring."

"What kind of unusual offspring?" Brit asked.

Elijah spun on his heels to face her. "Divine-human hybrids birthed with the intention to rule over humanity with divine right. These beings breached the established boundaries, falling from their heavenly positions."

He was raising his voice and gesturing wildly now. Gina smiled to herself, a familiar sight she'd forgotten she'd missed the past few years.

"Those supernatural beings," Elijah said, "the sons of God, or their offspring rather—they can appear in the flesh, manifesting themselves on Earth, and the Bible makes reference to some of these occasions. Ancient religious texts not included in the Bible suggest they can shape-shift."

"Wild…" Cosgrove said.

Elijah flipped to another part of the Bible. Clearing his throat, he read: "'God has taken his place in the divine council; in the midst of the gods he holds judgment…I say, You are gods, children of the Most High, all of you; nevertheless, you shall die like mortals, and fall like any prince.'"

Cosgrove smirked. "Sounds like something straight out of ancient Rome or Greece, with this talk about God ruling over other gods."

Elijah grinned. "Actually, it's a poem from the Holy Scriptures."

"For real? Don't recall that from my Baptist upbringing."

"Where is this poem from?" Brit asked.

"It's a Jewish poem, Psalm 82. My people—"

"Eli is Jewish, by the way," Gina interrupted with explanation. "Well, Messianic."

"Messianic?" Cosgrove asked, face twisted up.

Elijah answered, "It means I've come to realize Yeshua, Jesus, is the Christ. The One who my people have been waiting for since Yahweh's great promises. But that doesn't matter. What does is that my people have maintained a tradition that Yahweh rules over a divine council of lesser gods. You can't deny it. It's in Psalm 82, which is where I first discovered the language."

Elijah started pacing again, bouncing on the balls of his feet with unbounded energy, as if it had been bottled up and now was being unleashed.

Gina grinned. Just like the old days.

"The sons of God and their offspring, the Watcher-spirits, bear tremendous power and capabilities that far exceed our own. Jewish texts reflecting Genesis 6 reveal that rebellious members of Yahweh's divine council, fallen ones, mated with human women to birth a race of superbeings."

"I can attest to this fact," Gina said. "Last year, we saw them in action. Remember the crazy UFOs and alien abductions from last year?"

Took a beat, Brit and Cosgrove staring at them like they were from another planet.

But then it dawned on them.

Brit said, "You mean the government conspiracy that broke open last fall?"

"The one about Uncle Sam using Nazi tech," Cosgrove added, "to raise a race of superbeings?"

"Bingo," Elijah said with a satisfied grin.

"Wild…"

Eli suddenly spun around, then bolted for the sad, well-worn chairs at Cosgrove's desk.

"I need to sit," he announced, then did so.

Gina joined him, as did Cosgrove back in his own chair. Brit stood by his desk, arms folded and drilling Eli with skeptical eyes.

"Go on…" she said.

"Psalm 82 shows," Elijah continued, "God took away the right to rule over Earth from the sons of God. And within them, within the Watchers, there began to well a desire for what had been taken away. They sought to reclaim their dominion, desiring their own ruling successors. Until one day they arrived."

Cosgrove said, "The original extraterrestrials in Genesis 6."

"Bingo. The Watchers descended to Earth in celestial flesh and spent their seed inside the wombs of human women spawning a ruling class of immortal gods, shrouded in the robe of mortal flesh. But Yahweh, the Most High God, their very Maker, would have none of it. He exiled them to the Abyss and sentenced their bastard offspring to death in the great flood of Genesis 6. It is these half-breeds who were the Nephilim, the giant fallen ones. The only other missing piece to the puzzle are the *shedim*."

"What or who are those?" asked Brit.

"Fallen ones…" answered Gina.

Elijah nodded. "Bingo. The Nephilim bastard-born monstrosities had been exterminated, but they were instantly reborn upon death, becoming as their Watcher forebears: immortal, disembodied, uncontrollable. The Bible reveals that after the flood, more members of God's council rebelled and came to Earth, where humanity was again enraptured. Mankind worshiped them as shamanic teachers, divine healers, powerful saviors. They were gods to them."

Taking a breath, he continued, "Still more bastard-born races arose, known from ancient Hebrew texts as the Anakim, Emim, Rephaim, and Zamzummim. Like those before them they were slaughtered, now by Yahweh's very own portion, the children of Israel, who were sent to conquer the lands occupied by these hybrid beings—blooming the *shedim* to frightening numbers, the disembodied spirits of dead Nephilim."

"Which have tormented humanity since," Gina added, all of it making perfect sense now. "And manifested themselves in untold ways across the centuries. Including as extraterrestrial biological entities, like last year."

Elijah smiled. "Bingo. Jewish literature suggests the Watchers and their offspring had creative power. In fact, they possessed advanced knowledge that they pledged to pass along to humanity. A higher level of knowledge from the storehouses of the supernatural Unseen Realm itself. Science, engineering, technology, even magical enchantments. Root plants and potions and medicine."

"Like drugs…" Gina said. "And their effects on the body."

Elijah closed his eyes and tipped back his head. The tell he was about to unload from memory what he'd stuffed away inside his noggin. He quoted:

> *Evil spirits have gone forth from their bodies, because they are born from men, and from the holy Watchers is their original creation. They shall be evil spirits on Earth, and evil spirits they shall be called. And the spirits of the giants afflict, oppress, destroy, attack, do battle, and work destruction upon Earth, causing chaos. These spirits shall rise up against the children of men and against their women, for they have come from them.*

"This was from an ancient Jewish text about Genesis 6," he explained. "Though not of this world, the Watcher-spirits have been wreaking havoc on Earth since the dawn of time. Afflicting, destroying, attacking humanity. Chaos is their aim."

"What does that mean?" Cosgrove asked, voice just above a whisper. Dude was clearly freaked now.

Gina knew the answer. "Spiritual warfare."

Elijah nodded. "Bingo. Which isn't about commanding demons to submit or performing abracadabra magic tricks to put them in their place. Fundamentally, it is about conflict."

"What sort of conflict?" Brit asked.

"A war, really, between two kingdoms. The kingdom of God and the kingdom of Satan."

She scoffed. "Sounds like those Medieval Knights Templar."

"Nope. Because this war isn't about flesh-and-blood actors. Like I've been explaining. The disembodied souls of dead Nephilim are raging against humanity."

"Demons?" Cosgrove asked, swallowing hard and licking his lips.

"Demons. Well, the principalities and powers of this present supernatural darkness. Spiritual warfare is driven by the Great Commission to share God's crazy love, which catalyzes the expansion of the kingdom of God."

"Alright, alright," Brit said, extending her arms and holding them there. "I've heard enough. Let's say you're right. Demons are real and wreaking chaos on our world. What does this have anything to do with this case?"

Elijah answered, "The Gospel of John, chapter 10."

"Huh?"

"'The thief,'" Gina quoted, "'comes only to steal and kill and destroy. I came that they may have life, and have it abundantly.'"

"And don't forget," Elijah added, "the Second Book of Peter, chapter 5: 'Like a roaring lion your adversary the devil prowls around, looking for someone to devour.'"

Cosgrove asked, "This is about these…demons?"

"The Devil and his minions, yes. Their only function is to destroy what is most precious to Yahweh."

"And what is that?" Brit asked.

Eli turned to her. "The very beings who bear his Image."

"You're speaking of humanity."

"Bingo."

Gina nodded. "We heard it straight from Carmen how this

crazy drug concoction, as she put it, is destroying people across the country by devouring their brain. It makes perfect sense that Watcher-spirits would be involved in this stuff. Especially knowing some drug cartel is a conduit for a death cult that channels the demonic wickedness, wanting nothing more than to lay waste to their clientele."

"But what about the dead priest and pastor?"

Elijah answered, "I have a theory about that, too."

Brit frowned. "Go one…"

"In the Gospel of Luke, chapter 22, we read, *'Satan entered into Judas called Iscariot.'* Then again in John's Gospel, chapter 13: *'The devil had already put it into the heart of Judas son of Simon Iscariot to betray him.'*"

Cosgrove said, "Wasn't he one of Jesus' disciples, the one who betrayed him?"

"Bingo Baptist Boy. Judas was so consumed by greed and betrayal. And even though he was a follower of Jesus, he opened a door into his heart for the Devil to gain a foothold. So much so that he entered him and used him as a tool for his evil ends."

"You're talking about, what, possession?" Brit said.

"Technically, maybe. My point is, here we have two followers of Jesus—ministers even, who likewise opened themselves up to the Devil through their sin."

"Sexual abuse and adultery," Gina said.

"We know Father Rafferty abused teenage altar boys for years, and then Pastor Stone had an adulterous affair. No matter how you cut it, the men gave the Devil a foothold in their lives— opening the door for the Evil One to make himself at home and influence them. Even to the point of killing them."

Gina's head was spinning. It all made sense. "Hence, the locked-room mystery. The Watcher-spirits just came and went inside the confessional booth and then the store-front church, then entered through the open door of the men's heart to get them to strip and sit in that silly Z pose, crushing their necks with suffocation."

Elijah nodded, saying nothing more.

Cosgrove shook his head. "Wild..."

Gina added, "And don't forget the Book of Acts, chapter 5, where Luke tells the story about Ananias and Sapphira, and Peter's accusation to Ananias: *'why has Satan filled your heart to lie to the Holy Spirit and to keep back part of the proceeds of the land?'*"

"Oh my cheeps! That's right. Good one, Gina colada!"

She giggled and pushed a stray lock of hair behind her ear, embarrassed at the attention.

"An even starker instance of two rich Christians letting their greed turn into fraud, opening the door for Satan to waltz inside. Just like Judas."

Brit said, "Suppose that does sort of line up with Reverent Atkins. We discovered the man had been embezzling money from the church for years."

"There you go! Three men of the cloth, opening themselves up to the Devil by giving him a foothold in their lives with rampant sin."

"So, what, Satan—I can't believe I'm saying this..." she muttered. "But the Devil possessed them, or something?"

Elijah cocked his head with consideration. "Not sure *possession* is the right term. Certainly gained entrance into their life through their wickedness. Abraham's confirmation that the substance in the confessional booth was reptilian adds further proof."

"How so?"

"There is a Dead Sea Scroll of Jewish literature that describes the Watchers' appearance as *'fearsome—like a serpent.'* So my conjecture is a Watcher-spirit is responsible for their deaths, somehow in partnership with this drug cartel, the doorway opening from their own sinful heart—"

"To give the Cosmic Powers of darkness a foothold to choke them to death," Gina added. "Death by asphyxiation."

Elijah nodded with satisfaction. "Bingo. Something truly not of this world is your perp."

"Wild…" Cosgrove whispered.

"Yes, and I know exactly what we're going to do about it."

Brit frowned. "What's that?"

Elijah took a beat, then a breath, then smiled—a familiar twinkle in his eye letting Gina know things were about to get real.

Then he explained his plan.

# CHAPTER 24

The melodic sounds of a Steinway's black and white ivory floated all around Elijah and his partner. Sweet, round, dark, and rich. The juxtaposition was an odd one, given where they were.

Huddled in a balcony row hovering above the sanctuary of Renovate Community Church, a megachurch in Northern Virginia that sat thousands.

So, to catch a glimpse of the beautiful grand piano down below, faint light glinting off its glossy, polished surface, and to hear those enchanting notes swirling around them—let's just say there was a lot of cognitive dissonance going on alongside the harmonic chords.

Of course, much of that dissonance was from Elijah's own snooty tastes about church buildings. Along with liturgy and prayers, the smells and bells. It's what drew him to Anglicanism after he'd left the Messianic Jewish community on the other side of that fateful Shabbat day. Catholic ecclesial rhythms and trappings (including architecture), combined with Protestant doctrine and teachings.

Not the kind reminiscent of the Bible church they were staking out for the final leg of their Group X case.

Such ecclesial edifices were far more likely to feature twangy electric guitars and a pounding drum set, maybe the rhythmic beat of a djembe or strumming guitar if they wanted to take the mood in a stripped-down indie direction. Definitely not a straight up piano at the center of the stage from Eli's '90s Baptist childhood.

The rest of franchise Evangelical trappings were missing at that late hour. The room was clear of fog. Multi-colored stage lights were dead to the world, with a single spotlight aimed at a grand piano instead, white light slicing through the sanctuary that was more an auditorium, the space shrouded in shadows.

Place would normally be lit up like a Christmas tree, computer-controlled stage lighting normally setting the mood with a lineup of Jesus-is-my-boyfriend songs. Probably even passed out those Stouffer's Communion meal abominations. The little cups of watered-down Welch's grape juice with the stale cracker slapped on top. Don't think that's what Jesus had in mind when he broke the bread and said *'Take, eat; this is my body,'* and when he raised the cup saying, *'Drink from it, all of you; for this is my blood of the new covenant, which is poured out for many for the forgiveness of sins.'*

Nope. Although…

In that moment, something from long ago rose to the surface. The memory of his conversion and the first time he took Communion, as it was called in his neck of the Christian denomination woods.

Popping the top to one of those Stouffer's Communion meals and crunching on that cracker, right before he peeled back the seal to his plastic cup and downed a thimble of barely sweetened Welch's generic stepchild. It was the Baptist way, after all.

And that was right after he'd been baptized into the faith, by Dad. And not one of those hot tubs they drag on stage now, or one of those built in baptismals. A lake, like it should be.

Waiting for the snake to strike, he ran through the great Baptismal Presentation that served his public profession of faith:

*'Do you renounce the devil and all the spiritual forces of wickedness that rebel against God?'*

"I renounce them," he whispered, renewing his vows in the face of the Force that was not of this world.

*'Do you renounce the empty promises and deadly deceits of this world that corrupt and destroy the creatures of God?'*

Again: "I renounce them."

*'Do you renounce the sinful desires of the flesh that draw you from the love of God?'*

"I renounce them," he muttered louder.

*'Do you turn to Jesus Christ and confess him as your Lord and Savior?'*

Elijah nodded. I do.

"You do what?" Gina whispered. "And what do you renounce?"

He startled, catching his breath and tightening his Glock's grip.

"You heard that?"

"Yeah. Sounded like something I recall from Mass."

"You should. I borrowed it from your Catholic playbook. Well, Dad did. During my baptism."

She gasped. "Your dad borrowed Catholic liturgy for an Evangelical baptism?"

He shrugged. "Mom was into that sort of thing. Besides, liturgy is liturgy is liturgy, no matter how you slice it."

The notes suddenly changed to the tune of a familiar hymn, one from way back.

Elijah smiled, the words flooding back from childhood: *'Rock of Ages, cleft for me, let me hide myself in thee.'*

Given what they were up against, an apropos petition to Yeshua Almighty.

Especially for their bait plunking out that tune on the Steinway center stage.

Pastor Ronny Parks. A bald Boomer with bulging muscles and a wicked tan who was the fourth member of Wellspring

Ministry's board of directors. The last man standing, only because he'd been away on business.

It was Elijah's idea to put the man on stage in the middle of the evening. Idea was to use him as bait to attract the Evil One to make a move. Whether it was one of the Devil's minions or some Los Zorros gangbanger, didn't matter. What did was catching the serial minister murderer, stopping the mayhem, and bringing them to justice.

Brit wasn't too keen on using a civilian that way. Totally outside FBI protocol. Which made him press the idea even more and brought Gina on board. FBI Lady left it up to Pastor Parks, so Elijah contacted him straight away.

Gave the man credit where credit was due. Parks immediately agreed. Was enthusiastic even. Counted it his Christian duty to not only avenge the deaths of his ministry colleagues by bringing the perps to justice. But also standing against the darkness by putting up his dukes.

Or, in this case, putting his fingers to ivory.

Of course, Elijah left out the part about the potential for a demonic fight—whether a real manifestation from the Unseen Realm or a possessed psycho like at Cracker Barrel, it wasn't clear. Figured Parks was on a need-to-know basis.

And needing to know about the demonic dimension of the Group X case was something he didn't need to know. In his experience, the Unseen Realm was written off as hocus-pocus nonsense and dismissed as Medieval lunacy, to the detriment of the Church who was called to stand against the darkness. Or otherwise, the Unseen Realm was engaged like Hogwarts or the Jedi, an obsession with binding the Devil and confronting demons and wielding spiritual gifts like Harry Potter or Anakin Skywalker.

Elijah and Gina didn't have time to determine which sort of person Pastor Parks was, or whether he had a more moderating position like him and his partner. All he knew was that a drug cartel might come a calling to take him out, given his ministry

228 J. A. BOUMA

freeing people from their product. The way they figured it, Rafferty and Atkins, Stone and Parks were much like the Apostle Paul when he freed the people of Ephesus from demonic idol worship. When he did, the silversmiths who crafted silver shrines of Artemis, the god worshiped in Ephesus, were none too pleased. After all, their wealth came from people bound by their demonic idol worship, and they tried to kill Paul for the freedom he brought people in Christ.

Looked like the same was unfolding in the DC area, Los Zorros none too pleased with the freedom from demonic addiction those ministers brought people in Christ. Think of the money they'd lose if Jesus was enough for them, satisfying them like the Samaritan woman at the well, instead of P2P—or any other addiction for that matter, whether money or status or drugs.

Freedom in Christ definitely wasn't good for a drug cartel's business.

Or the demonic kind...

So, play Pastor Parks did, transitioning to a rousing chorus of "A Mighty Fortress Is Our God."

The third verse instantly surfaced, another staple hymn from childhood:

> *And though this world, with devils filled,*
> *should threaten to undo us,*
> *we will not fear, for God has willed*
> *his truth to triumph through us.*
> *The prince of darkness grim,*
> *we tremble not for him;*
> *his rage we can endure,*
> *for lo! his doom is sure;*
> *one little word shall fell him.*

"One little word, *Ha-Satan*. One little word..."

A sudden rise in static feedback sent a jolt of surprise racing up his spine.

The radio attached to his hip.

Now it squawked, *"Team Leader to Group X, do you copy?"*

Brit Armstrong.

FBI Lady insisted the operation was an FBI one, with them providing backup. Even though the whole taco was Elijah's idea from the start!

Whatever. Didn't mind in the slightest using his former place of employ to do his bidding and to land their first Group X case in the bag. Even if he was playing second fiddle to a Fed with a pixie cut.

He grabbed the radio and squawked back, "Roger, Roger."

*"We've got company."*

A jolt of excitement skated through his veins, and his mouth tasted like pennies. Pure, unadulterated adrenaline, baby! The kind he remembered from back in his FBI day. When the wide-open possibilities at the start narrowed to a pinprick of resolution.

This was it.

He threw his partner an excited grin. Gina took in a measured breath. "Showtime."

"Bingo." Then he squawked into the squawker: "What kind of company?"

A beat, then: *"Shadows and movement."*

"Just our kind of company," he said to Gina.

Now Gina startled, "Wait, she said *shadows*."

He frowned. "Plural."

"Right."

He returned to the squawker: "How many bogeys?"

*"Bogeys?"* Brit squawked back.

"As in, an unidentified aircraft. Or hostile, in this case."

*"Hard to tell. But they're coming in hot and heavy, so be ready."*

"Oh, we are."

*"So are we. We've got your back."*

Brit and Cosgrove had joined them as backup outside, acting

as a lookout scoping the perimeter as well as four more hands with two more Glocks at the ready to take down the threat. Wasn't enough time to assemble anything more official on such short notice with the waning day. They figured there was a ticking clock on Pastor Parks, just like the rest now that he had returned. Dude was a goner if they didn't intervene.

Brit returned: *"By the way, we got some more info on your Pastor Parks bait."*

"What's that?"

*"Inconsistent reported income on his tax returns compared to standard of living. His Audi and seven-bedroom lake house don't exactly add up to a pastor's salary."*

Gina frowned and took the radio, saying: "Another offering plate pilferer, I presume."

*"Looks that way."*

Elijah shook his head. "Greed and girls are the Devil's playground."

Gina hit him; he yelped. "You're forgetting Rafferty was a horse of a different sinful color."

"Yeah, but Greed, girls, and altar boys doesn't have the same alliterative ring to it."

"Regardless, just goes to show how patterns of sin sure do give the Devil a foothold, a way into someone's life. Like Judas, like Ananias and Sapphira."

"'Do not make room for the Devil,' Paul exhorted in Ephesians. Wise words."

"Sure thing, chicken wing."

"It also just goes to show people are complicated. The four did right by people. They were also scoundrels. Complicated, I tell ya."

Gina nodded. "Don't I know it."

Elijah gestured between them. "Don't *we* know it."

*"Watch your six,"* FBI Lady squawked again. *"You've got company."*

"Roger, Roger."

Elijah shoved the radio at his waist and immediately crossed himself.

As did Gina. "What now?"

"First, a prayer is in order."

"For what?"

He turned to her. "For holy angels."

She took in a measured breath, nodding.

Elijah led them praying while the ethereal piano notes continued rising around them.

"Everlasting God, you have ordained and constituted in a wonderful order the ministries of angels and mortals: Mercifully grant that, as your holy angels always serve and worship you in heaven, so by your appointment they may help and defend us here on earth; through Jesus Christ our Lord, who lives and reigns with you and the Holy Spirit, one God, for ever and ever."

"Amen," Gina said.

"Yee-haw," Elijah said.

And just in time, too. Because something was happening.

Could feel it, deep in his bones—in his very soul.

A pressure, a Force.

A Presence…

The same one that had spread in a sonic wave boom after the hostile from Cracker Barrel kicked the bucket from Gina's well-placed shot.

But that wasn't all.

In between stanzas, Elijah heard the faintest of *clicks* from the sanctuary. Then the padding of feet along the periphery of the auditorium.

Shadows and movement, Brit described it.

Dead on the money.

"There!" Gina whispered, pointing down below.

Elijah craned his head over the balcony, the music continuing, Pastor Parks oblivious to his own demise. For his part, he played it well. Had cojones of steel, that's for sure.

He was gonna need them.

Because padding his way, in the shadows of the dimmed auditorium, were four men in black.

"That's our cue," Gina whispered, Glock already in hand and standing to leave.

Elijah grabbed her arm, but only briefly before letting go. She turned to him with a startled breath.

He said, "Not yet. First, we wait."

"Why?"

"Because I want to give it time to play out."

She went to offer a retort, but relented. "Fine. But only if we get into position. Can't do him much good from up here."

He nodded, and she led the pair across the balcony and down an aisle stage right that would give them a better advantage. He followed, tightening his grip on his Glock before the two settled down a row that gave them the high ground.

Didn't take long before the hostiles gained their own ground, reaching the stage just as they got into position.

"Time's up, *muchacho*," one of the hostiles shouted, voice high and heady and nasally, with a Latin lilt moving toward the center aisle.

The slice of white stage light revealed a short, squat man in a black T-shirt and jeans with a large bald head covered in ink. One at the back in particular caught Elijah's eye.

The cross bisected with a circle ringing the top stem and dotted by four tiny crosses in the center with flaring lines like the sun at the top.

His mouth went dry, and he whispered lowly, "Santa Muerte…"

Pastor Parks faltered at the keys, hitting a sour chord and interrupting his tune.

Too bad, too, because he was just getting to the second verse of "My Hope Is Built on Nothing Less." *'When darkness veils his lovely face, I rest on his unchanging grace,'* was its exhortation. A good one, resting in Christ's grace in the face of the Dark One.

They were going to need that grace that night.

Especially Pastor Parks, by the look of it…

"You've been a bad *hombre*, yes you have," the center hostile said.

Two hostiles reached stage left, while another slid just below Elijah and Gina at stage right. All three aiming squarely at Pastor Parks while the fourth sauntered down the center, unarmed. Dude was picking at his teeth with a toothpick. Totally nonchalant, like he had not a care in the world.

Parks slid the bench back from the piano, kicking up a hideous screech, then stood. Straightening and puffing out his chest, he said, "You…I've seen you on the corner up from the mission. Búho, you call yourself. Owl. One of Salazar's boys peddling that street junk."

Eli smirked. "Owl? What kind of narco name is that?"

Gina shushed him.

The main dude called Búho laughed. "*Buenos ojos, muchacho.* Too bad you didn't see clearly enough to stop messing with our operation when you had the chance. You and your three *amigos.*"

"And what *operation* is that?"

Búho reached the front and leaned a hand against a chair, continuing to pick at his teeth. "Bondage, *muchacho.* Addiction."

Now he pointed at the pastor with that toothpick, the end glistening with saliva.

Totally gross!

"But you offer freedom, which ain't being good for business. And now you must die. I must say, it won't be pretty."

Parks shifted, his puffed chest deflating and that straight back slumping some. "You won't get away with this."

"We have already. Three times now. Thanks to a deal with the Devil."

Gina threw Elijah wide eyes. Not surprised, not even panicked. More like she couldn't believe the confirmation they were right.

He understood her completely.

It was go time.

# CHAPTER 25

n all her years fighting for justice with the FBI and wrestling the darkness to the ground with Elijah back in the day, Gina hadn't seen nothing like she was seeing now.

And that was saying something, given all the crazy the two had witnessed.

Something had suddenly shifted. Like the barometric pressure in the room had ratcheted, and somebody had cranked on the AC without any accompanying HVAC hum, and time had slowed to one of those corny '90s sitcom crawls when doom and gloom were about to show their mugs.

Except…this wasn't a corny '90s sitcom. This was high-def real life. With her and Eli planted on their haunches behind a row of padded church chairs in the dead of night, a storm howling outside with clapping thunder to beat the band.

"Do you feel that?" Elijah asked on a shaky breath.

Gina swallowed hard, her throat raw from dried anticipation. "You mean like we've just stepped through a portal into a Twilight Zone fever dream?"

"Bingo."

"And now—" Búho said, his voice lowering along with his head, eyes slitted and chest heaving heavy, congested breaths, as if he were about to expel something from his lungs. "—take off your clothes."

Did she hear him right? Latin Dude picking his teeth like it was nobody's business just uttered a command to the pastor to strip naked? For reals?

Real as rain, as Brit had said. Confirming what they'd suspected about the others: the doorway into their very soul, opened by their sin, gave a foothold for the Devil to issue them commands. Resulting in their locked-room death.

Pastor Parks shuddered something fierce at the command, as if resisting it while all at once unable to. Like it had some sort of hold on him—from the inside...

Then another thing happened that she wasn't sure was happening.

It was Owl Man, that Búho narco character.

Was he growing in size, getting taller and bulkier?

No, couldn't be. Trick of the lighting, it had to be.

And yet...

Six, seven—even towering eight feet from his five-foot frame, he was. Arms bulging through his black T-shirt and skin glistening with an iridescent glow that reminded her of last year down in that underground hangar in the middle of Nowheresville, Ohio!

The fallen ones, rising from the shadows to enslave humanity...

The memory of that rodeo and the sight of this new one sent her heart galloping forward and head blooming with the truth of the matter.

What they were witnessing—this man, this moment—was not of this world.

"What is happening?" Gina whispered on a shaky breath.

"Not sure," Elijah answered on the same breath. "But whatever it is, I'd say now is as good a time as any to stand against the darkness."

He took his words to heart, rising behind the row of chairs with outstretched Glock.

A real go-getter, that Elijah was. Something she liked about him.

She joined her partner—

And Búho turned their way. As if sensing their presence even before they had made it known.

He drilled them with haunting eyes glowing with an orange wickedness straight from the Abyss.

*"Kill them!"* a Voice erupted from the man. Something roary and snorty, something skittering and screeching.

Something definitely not of this world!

Their own world around them exploded with bullets strafing the walls and chairs. Beside, in back, in front.

Sending them to their knees and praying to the good Lord above the megachurch didn't pinch pennies on those padded chairs!

But not before Elijah pinched of a *one-two-three-four* punch that sent the bad hombre directly down below sinking to his knees, his head snapping back and blooming with an arc of dark crimson.

"Nice shot, hot shot," she said, huddled behind their row of chairs.

He shrugged, catching his breath. "I've kept up my firearms training."

"One down, two to go. Or three, I suppose."

"Two bad hombres with guns and one possessed by the Devil himself."

Gina nodded. "He's the one we've got to worry about."

"Yuppers."

Relentless *rat-a-tat-tats* chewed the chairs around them. Oddly, not the ones they were huddled behind. As if there was some sort of repellent or shield blocking the shots.

Perhaps those angels they'd summoned with their prayer earlier had come to the rescue.

"We need to do something," Elijah said.

Gina nodded. "Suppose they'll run out of bullets sooner or later."

"And when they do—"

A sudden silence filled the space—echoing reverberations of spent rounds tinkling to the floor, joined by howling winds and slapping rain outside, the only soundtrack to their nightmare.

She grinned. Just the window they needed.

"We'll let 'em know who's boss."

Elijah nodded. "Let's roll!"

He was first to his feet, sending a *pop-pop-pop* rejoinder into the void. Then another: *pop-pop-pop.*

And connecting with one of the two armed hostiles who had made it to the center. Two sank into his chest and the other skated across the side of his head, splitting through the skull and spraying his partner with blood and matter.

Which had the effect of triggering his rifle—sending a spray of bullets their way in an arcing last swan song that chewed through the grand piano and sent Pastor Parks stumbling head over heels with a moaning shout of injury.

Gina followed it up with a *one-two-three-four* punch of her own at the final hostile.

Just as he blasted an angry *rat-a-tat-tat* reply.

Catching her in the arm and sending her stumbling backward into the aisle.

So much for those angels.

Elijah turned to her. "Gina colada!"

Pain lanced through her shoulder, and she could feel her heart in her arm, warm and pulsing.

And wet…

Blood seeped out of the wound, a stream of crimson winding its way toward her elbow. She lifted it, the pain intensifying.

Eli just hovered over her on all fours as the world continued reverberating with weapon fire—eyes wide with indecision and one hand running through his tick.

Thumb to index finger, thumb to middle, thumb to ring finger, thumb to pinkie. Rinse and repeat.

His mouth hung open, as if questioning what to do, heaving desperate breaths. She could see him breaking, needing air, even as she lay bleeding out, her hand clenched against her arm doing no good against the wound.

A firm, tight strip of cloth cinched against the gaping hole should do the trick. But she couldn't do it on her own. She needed help.

She needed her partner.

"Don't spiral on me now, Eli…" Gina moaned through gritted teeth.

Just as the *rat-a-tat-tats* wound down to zero.

Shaking him loose from zoning out.

He blinked rapidly, then sprang to his feet.

Launching a well-placed *pop-pop-pop* reply.

From the ground, she could see the final hostile slump to the floor.

Then another: *pop-pop-pop.*

The center boss man flailed before slumping over the front row.

It was over, just like that.

Elijah spun to her. "Gina colada!"

"Got a T-shirt to spare?"

He unbuttoned his shirt and threw it off, then took off his T-shirt and wrapped it around her arm slick with blood.

She started to fade in and out, so she was relieved for the tourniquet measure.

The thumping in her arm increased, as did the pain, but it seemed to hold. Like the little Dutch boy plugging the hole in the damn to save the town, and the day.

Eli was her hero.

He threw his button-down back on and offered her his hand. "Can you stand?"

Gina took it and winced but pushed through. "I think so."

He guided her to her feet. She faltered, the lights dimming in and out, but a deep breath steadied her.

The unholy scene out front did not.

Four bodies and lots of blood littered the sanctuary's front. That wasn't even touching on the mutilated chairs and Communion table and grand piano that had been chewed up and spat out in the melee.

Such sacrilege…

Finishing with his shirt buttons, Elijah helped Gina out of the row, and the pair inched down the stairs to the main floor.

The grand piano obscured their full view from the stage, but Gina caught sight of Pastor Parks's leg in the slicing spotlight sprawled on the floor, unmoving.

Gina gripped her Glock and called out, "Pastor Parks, can you answer—"

A sudden bassy rumble intercepted any reply, slicing through the auditorium, echoing with growing intent. A vibration that began crescendoing into a guttural moan that seemed to be coming from—

From one of the Los Zorros hostiles!

The boss man still slumped against the front row.

Elijah grinned. "Showtime…"

Gina's bowels went watery at the bassy tremble. Her heart jolted forward when the doors burst open.

She spun toward the sudden sounds, arms taut and weapon extended—ready for anything.

Brit Armstrong and Joe Cosgrove were padding toward their position.

Gina backed toward them, weapon trained toward the front now with Elijah doing the same.

"You two alright?" Agent Armstrong asked.

"Peachy, you?" Elijah answered.

Cosgrove eased up on his aim, lowering his arms but holding his Glock steady. "We came as soon as we heard the weapon fire.

Came quicker than we expected. Held back to make sure there weren't any reinforcements."

Another bassy rumble from the front. This time followed by a roary, snorty, skittering screech!

"What the hell is that?" Brit exclaimed.

"Literally," Elijah mumbled.

Brit tightened her grip and glanced back toward the open sanctuary door and around to the ceiling, the howling winds and rapping rain continuing their assault.

Gina knew better. "Sorry to be the bearer of bad news, but I don't think what we just heard came from outside these walls."

She threw her a look. Fear, laced with something else she couldn't place. A knowing look that made her think this wasn't her first rodeo.

An aftershock rattled the room again, carrying with it another deep moan.

Before all at once ceasing into an eerie void.

"Now I'll say it," Cosgrove said, raising his weapon, "what the heck was that?"

Elijah said, "Nothing from this world."

"What do you mean?" Brit said with biting skepticism.

Before he could answer, there was a shuddering from the stage.

And a thunderous *smack!*

The lid to the grand piano slammed shut, throwing up wicked chords that hung with dread.

But that wasn't all of it.

Not by a long shot.

The downed hostile named Búho started shuddering with intensity, vibrating and throwing his arms with rigidity slumped against the pew so that he looked as if he were crucified.

Cosgrove gave a frightened yelp; Brit echoed with her own version.

Elijah was the only one who seemed activated by it all, taking aim with a tightened grip and taking a step toward the supernatural display.

"The Devil is still with this one…" he said on a breathy whisper.

Before Brit could interrogate him, the back set of doors to the sanctuary slammed shut with such force that a large picture of Jesus fell to the floor with a crash.

Cosgrove jumped with a startled scream. He reddened and chuckled. "Whoa, now that was something straight out of *The Exorcist*."

"Probably just an updraft from the HVAC," Brit said.

A rattling from on the stage said otherwise.

A snare drum, along with symbols in all of their percussion glory, startled inside a drum cage.

Cosgrove yelped again. "You think that was caused by an updraft from the HVAC?"

The rattling grew until a mic stand fell over and the piano itself shook again with an aftershock that jolted Búho upright.

With sudden, supernatural levitation, the man's body began moving with a wicked arch, its arms stiffly outstretched and belly reaching dramatically toward the ceiling, head firmly planted on a front row chair with feet on the floor while the rest of it bent like a wishbone.

"I thought he was dead…" said Gina.

Eli turned to her—

A scream cutting off any reply.

It was Búho. Howling, frantic, hysterical. Eyes bulging from their sockets and mouth wide with horrifying abandon.

Almost like an owl, his namesake.

A hideous roary, snorty, skittering screech that sounded not of this world.

"Sweet mother of Melchizedek!" Elijah said with a jump.

Gina grabbed his arm, which he yanked back.

Then Eli did something she did not expect.

He stepped forward on cool, cautious steps. "Stand back. All of you."

"Eli…" Gina said, "what are you doing?"

He took a breath, then a beat, then said: "Standing against the darkness."

# CHAPTER 26

Elijah took a deep breath. This was it. The moment he'd been waiting for from the start.

Hero at the mercy of the villain.

Sort of a trope of bargain-bin Kindle yarns, but it usually proved true in his former line of work. Well, at least for the agents in the field. He'd always been a desk junkie, like his former partner.

Not now.

Now the shiznit was about to hit the fan.

Had already hit the fan when that bullet hit his partner. Reminded him of that moment when the bullet struck Dad between the eyes, blood blooming from the wound and his body slumping to the floor, even while his soul flew into the arms of Jesus Christ.

Brain screamed when he saw Gina lying on the floor like that, crimson slicking her arm and face lancing with pain. Took everything within him not to spiral into a meltdown. Had to have been Yeshua Almighty himself steeling his nerves and keeping his head on straight. Because without Jesus gifting the Holy Spirit's steadying power, who knew what would've happened.

Actually, he did. And it scared the crap out of him...

Couldn't think about that now. Needed to keep his head in the game. Because a spawn of Satan himself was rising from the dead.

Readying to do Lord only knew what.

Spreading a commanding arm, Elijah pushed Cosgrove out of the way while inching closer to Búho. The man towered above them from the front. Hulking and heaving heavy breaths, reeking even from there of the same reptilian musk and piss he'd sniffed inside that confessional booth, then again in the storefront church.

Could hardly believe his eyes. It was just like the fallen one they had seen last year in that cray-cray Air Force bunker. The Watcher-spirit who had been wreaking havoc with humanity thanks to Nazi occult shenanigans.

Only this one was different. Just as ugly but occupying the body of that owl man he had shot.

Sweet mother of Melchizedek, this could get ugly...

With his other hand, he slipped a gold crucifix out from the inside of his shirt. Something he had picked up from a shop in Rome years ago on a trip with his parents before Dad was murdered. Golden and glinting in the white spotlight.

Figured it would come in handy for what came next.

And it did.

Búho jolted backward at the sight. The hulking figure bowed his head toward the Christian icon and fixed it with a penetrating gaze, eyes narrowed and dark with glaring ill intent.

Then a sound emanated from his being. Which sounded eerily familiar.

A cross between a strangled sheep and irate mama grizzly bear. A roary, snorty, skittering screech.

A thing from nightmares...

Búho growled and glared at Elijah, then gnashed his teeth at him.

He stood, resolute and unmoving, arm outstretched with the crucifix.

"The Lord Jesus Christ rebuke you, O Satan!"

Búho shuttered backward, throwing his bulky arms glistening with an iridescent glow and sludgy slim against his face —as if shielding itself from the name of Jesus.

The Being held them a beat before opening them up wide and lashing out with a wicked gnashing of his teeth—roaring and snorting and screeching. A cross between a bear and a boar and hawk.

"What is going on?" Brit asked with strain, lips quivering with a mixture of shock and horror and fear.

Gina replied with a choking whisper, "It looks like Eli was right. The Devil is with this one. And the pastor gave him a reason to be pissed. They all did."

"But why?" Cosgrove squeaked.

Keeping his gazed fixed on the possessed narco, Elijah answered, "They were undoing his work, Wellspring Ministry. Setting captives free from the binding power of drugs, giving them back their dignity, and restoring them to the way God intended them to be. Whole humans, flexing their flourishing identities as his Image Bearers."

"The Devil, the Adversary," Gina added, "roams the earth like a roaring lion seeking people to devour. To use up, spit out, shatter, and leave for dead, enveloping them in chaos. Same for Los Zorros."

All at once, Búho suddenly fell silent. No more muttering, no more screaming. No more writhing and flailing about, all movement and motion seeming to hang in one dramatic suspension of time.

But not for long.

Búho began talking again. When he did, a new persona emerged. Something rose up within him, guttural and gravelly, like that of a deep-throated man whose voice was being masked from identity on those undercover news shows.

*"He is mine, this one,"* the Voice hissed. *"Mine! Same for the pastor. All four of them."*

Elijah's mind swam with confusion at the truth of what it all meant. But it also crystalized with a singular thought.

This man was possessed.

And he had to stop him.

"Who are you?" Elijah said.

A wicked laugh bubbled up within the man. Low and growly and mocking.

"I command you, in the name of Jesus Christ, reveal yourself!"

Búho snarled and bared his teeth at Elijah, who thrust the crucifix in his direction again, repeating his command: "The Lord rebuke you, O Satan!"

Then he added a prayer, pleading with the Holy Trinity for assistance: "Oh God, come to my assistance! Oh Lord, make haste to help me! Oh Everlasting God, who have ordained and created the ministries of angels and men in wonderful order: Mercifully grant that, as your holy angels serve you in heaven, they may help and defend us on earth at your command. Through our Lord Jesus Christ, your son, who lives and reigns with you in the unity of the Holy Spirit, one God, forever and ever. Amen."

Another guttural moan followed by a high-pitched screech echoed throughout the sanctuary. The grizzly bear strangling the sheep—the roary, snorty, skittering screech that had come from the psycho at Cracker Barrel!

Lord Jesus Christ, Son of God...do something!

All at once, Búho's head started flailing from side to side, cocking back at odd, inhuman angles.

Gina rushed forward on instinct, but Elijah held her back.

"Stand back, Gina colada!" he commanded.

"We can't just stand here," she pleaded. "We've got to do something!"

"I am."

"But—"

She was cut off by another screech slicing through the confusion, followed by a weak cry.

"Help me!" came a squeaky voice from the stage, meek and mousy and full of trapped dismay, trailed by pleading cries that heaved the man's body up and down with a mournful shudder.

Pastor Parks!

It was as if the man was trying to break free, harassed by whatever had possessed Búho.

A Power not of this world…

Then the Voice returned, the one of demonic intent: *"You humans have your own sense of time,"* it hissed with the same guttural growl. *"I have plenty of time. I have all the time in the world. I've been biding it, saving it, stashing it away with this one. With them all…"*

Elijah shook his head with wide-eyed confusion.

Gina asked, "What is it talking—"

She was interrupted by the Voice shifting into a staccato whisper: *"It's the pastor I want."* The Being stared straight into Elijah with those haunting, slitted eyes brimming with a menacing wickedness.

The Voice boomed now: *"Not only his body but his SOUL, for all that he has wreaked. Saving people from my chaos—from stealing, from DESTROYING their lives through my revelation-insight into mind-altering potions!"*

As the Voice spoke, Búho jerked his head from side to side, as if carried along on strings by a halting puppeteer until Elijah thought his head would pop off.

He was right! The Voice seemed to confirm his suspicion. The Cosmic Powers of this present supernatural darkness had been in on this *inexplicitus* case from hot Hades.

Elijah swallowed, confronting the demonic Power. "So this was your doing, all of it—the show of things, their deaths?"

A low, guttural laugh filled the sanctuary—bassy, haunting, the stuff of nightmares—and a wide, wicked grin spread across his face.

But no answer. Not yet. So Elijah pressed on.

"But how, with the locked rooms and no signs of entry? And the clothes, the Z pose—all of it…how?"

Búho shrugged, but the Voice did all the talking: *"Was easy peasy, really. The power of suggestion—aaaannnd my voissssse. Sweet nothings whispered into their hearts primed through years disobeying the Nameless One, coaxing them to obey my every word."*

Had to admit, the Voice was enchanting, inviting, ensnaring. A forked tongue dripping with poison but sounding like honey —a deathtrap for the unsuspecting.

*"You can't begin to imagine what's possible when we gain a foothold in someone's life! Look what we did to the Nameless One, thanks to the breach opened through one of his followers."*

Judas, the possessed disciple who'd betrayed Jesus to death. Which was all Elijah needed to confirm his suspicions. The foothold those men gave the Devil literally cost them their lives.

The man's motions suddenly slowed. His head began swaying from front to back like a viper hypnotized by the fabled wind instrument of a snake charmer.

*"God can't save him,"* the Voice within screeched. *"Do you understand that? He's mine, Elijah Fox!"*

The mention of his name by that hideous voice sent a frigid shudder through Elijah's bowels. Thought he'd lose them then and there.

"Who are you?" he asked on a shaky breath.

A bassy cackle erupted from the Being before him.

Holding the crucifix outstretched, he pressed, "In the name of Jesus Christ, what is your name?"

The Being staggered back, as if sucker-punched or hit by a sledgehammer, doubling over and bracing a hand against the front row.

Then again: "I command you in Jesus' name—reveal yourself!"

Búho finally relented.

*"Chaos!"* the Voice erupted in a roary, snorty, skittering screech.

Sounded about right.

The face sneered at him, adding: *"And I have seen you before, Elijah Fox. Small and mousy and cowering in a country church deep in the backwoods of Kentucky."*

Now it was his turn to be sucker-punched.

All the air in his lungs was knocked out of him at those words.

Because it could only mean one thing.

*"Oh yes,"* the Voice cackled. *"That pathetic weakling of a father of yours, putting him down like a dog, the same way these others went — that was my doing, just like the others! Wringing the life from those pathetic ministers' necks, literally!"*

Búho spread a hand toward his fallen soldiers.

*"Those in bondage to me and my ways had started to find release through his ministry. So, dear ol' dad got a bullet between the eyes by one of my own. "*

Búho took a step toward him, the hulking figure shimmering like an angel of light making for Elijah.

He was petrified, speechless.

The Voice went on, *"Couldn't very well let him carry on, now could I? None of them. And fortunate for me, I had an all too willing partner to carry out my dirty work."*

"Los Zorros," Brit said, voice betraying her stun.

"Santa Muerte," Cosgrove echoed from behind.

"Chaos…" Gina whispered.

Elijah staggered at the revelation and chest constricted with pain, his heart throbbing and lungs searching for air. His head bloomed with memory, the images of that fateful day swirling in a kaleidoscope of pain and agony, with injury and death.

Bloody, crimson, black.

This was the Being responsible for his father's death!

Chaos had killed Dad…

He narrowed his eyes and thrust the crucifix on an outstretched arm.

"I order you in the name of Jesus Christ to leave this man!"

That roary, snorty, skittering screech erupted from the Being. It staggered but remained upright.

Elijah approached it, commanding louder: "I order you in the name of Jesus Christ to come out of this man!"

Without warning, there was another bassy rumble that shook the room. Klieg lights from above crashed down to the floor, glass shattering and splintering. More on-stage instruments clattered to the floor as the rumble continued.

In the middle of the melee, Búho suddenly arched his back. His face transformed into a series of menacing expressions—cheekbones and lips and eyebrows contorting in ways not thought possible.

The house lights faded up and down, the single spotlight slicing on-stage dimmed and flickered before brightening back again, sending jolting bolts of fear ricocheting up Elijah's spine.

But he held fast, feet planted on the floor and arm stiff with the cross of Christ.

Brit gave a startled scream, followed closely by Cosgrove.

The writhing continued. It was almost as if Búho was fighting within himself. As if something inside was fighting for his very soul.

"Eli…" Gina yelled. "End this!"

Elijah began praying aloud, beseeching Jesus Christ and his blood to combat the very forces of hell.

"Almighty and eternal God," he shouted with all of the authority given him by Jesus Christ himself, "who appointed your only-begotten Son the Redeemer of the world, and willed to be appeased by his blood: Grant, we beseech you, that we may so honor this, the price of our redemption, and by its virtue be so defended from the evils of our present life, so as to enjoy its fruit in heaven forevermore, through the name of Christ Our Lord. Amen."

A cackle broke out from Búho's lips, spinning into hysterical giggling, almost like a spoiled child. Soon, his body started heaving with guffawing belly laughs from deep inside.

Elijah, crucifix still held outright, switched to quoting a portion of Scripture, Psalm 27:

> *The Lord is my light and my salvation;*
> *whom shall I fear?*
> *The Lord is the stronghold of my life;*
> *of whom shall I be afraid?*
> *When evildoers assail me*
> *to devour my flesh—*
> *my adversaries and foes—*
> *they shall stumble and fall.*

The cackling continued, but seemed to be more pained, as if the Voice within Búho was recoiling from the Word of God being proclaimed against it.

Then there was a turn.

*"We shall meet again…"* the Voice suddenly screamed.

Right before Búho wilted to the floor as if he had fainted, his body crumbling in a heaping pile of spent limbs.

The man went still. The puppet strings had been cut.

Deader than a doornail, he was.

"Is it over?" Cosgrove squeaked.

Elijah took in a measured breath, sighing and slipping the cross around his head.

He turned to his partner. She looked white and frail, one hand clutching his T-shirt wrapped around her arm stained crimson. But she was standing, on her own and tall.

Against the darkness, alongside him.

She said, "That was nutso to the maxo."

"That's one way of putting it…"

He went to her and took her other arm, slinging it around his shoulder.

His body tingled from the touch, not being one who welcomed such a thing. Didn't matter in the slightest.

Even Gina seemed OK with it. She did take a faltering breath, looking like she might protest. But then she threw him a grin. "Thanks for the helping hand."

He returned the smile. "You bet."

She glanced behind, Brit and Cosgrove already on the stage and tending to the pastor, who was moaning but conscious. "Welp, looks like we did one thing right."

"Nope. Two things," Elijah said.

"What's that?"

"We saved someone's life and solved the case."

"Not bad for our first investigation. But, that revelation—" She winced, adjusting her hold on Elijah's shoulder. "Your dad…"

Dad…

The word caught in his chest. Emotion wanted to spring to his eyes. But he wouldn't let it. Wouldn't lose it.

Not now. Not ever.

He shook it away, another word re-centering him.

Chaos.

*That* was the deeper revelation. That there had been a Force behind Dad's death.

From the Unseen Realm…

All the revelation he needed to saddle up and get back to it.

To stand against the darkness.

But that could wait. One more thing to do before the night was out.

"Come on," Elijah said, "let's get you to a hospital."

Gina smiled and nodded, then they hobbled out of the sanctuary and into the rainy night. Together. Just like old times.

Now he smiled.

He could get used to this.

# CHAPTER 27

A steady hum permeated the dimly lit, modest chapel of Indiana limestone, filling the sacred space with a sense of sacred significance.

Exactly what Elijah needed after all the crazy.

Little flames danced on four long candles near the solid white limestone altar in front of an intricate limestone facade of miniature statues of the four Gospel writers, behind oak altar rails with kneeling cushions patterned in red and gold. Beautiful stained-glass windows depicting biblical scenes in crimson red and leafy green, golden yellow and indigo blue hung void of their awe-inspiring light, the sun still slumbering along with the rest of the world.

Elijah continued meditating—eyes closed, legs outstretched, arms folded—sitting on a polished oak pew in the third row of the Bethlehem Chapel a floor beneath the National Cathedral, America's church and headquarters of the Order of Thaddeus, the mother ship to his and Gina's upstart investigative outfit.

After checking Gina into an emergency room, and his partner shooed him away, he'd beelined it for the sacred space. Needed to after what they'd been through.

After what *he*'d been through with that Watcher-spirit…

254 J. A. BOUMA

So there he sat, flickering candles his only light in the late night that had crested into the next day's early morning, the low HVAC hum the only soundtrack to his worship.

After another minute of silent contemplation, Elijah opened his eyes and grabbed the well-worn, red prayer book that would guide his prayer and contemplation. He carefully turned its browned pages until he reached the lectionary for the evening. He breathed in deeply through his mouth, then slowly exhaled through his nose to center himself.

"Worship the Lord in the splendor of his holiness," he said quietly, "tremble before him, all the earth. Let us confess our sins against God and our neighbor."

He closed his eyes and ran through his list of sins, both of omission and commission.

He continued by reciting the prayer of confession, then recited the next several phrases from memory: "O God, make speed to save us; Lord, make haste to help us. Glory to the Father, and to the Son, and to the Holy Spirit." He crossed himself, then added: "As it was in the beginning, is now, and will be forever."

"Amen," he mumbled, crossing himself again.

He opened his eyes, wondering if the help he had been searching for from the Holy Trinity would ever reach him.

Turning to the back of the prayer book, Elijah searched for the evening Psalter—then smiled knowingly.

Psalm 27. The passage he had quoted against Chaos.

Elijah scooted to the edge of his seat and read aloud: "The Lord is my light and my salvation; whom shall I fear?"

What a fitting way to end the day after his stand against the darkness.

He continued:

---

The Lord is the stronghold of my life;
of whom shall I be afraid?

When evildoers assail me
to devour my flesh—
my adversaries and foes—
they shall stumble and fall.
Though an army encamp against me,
my heart shall not fear;
though war rise up against me,
yet I will be confident.

---

"Glory to the Father, and to the Son, and to the Holy Spirit," he said again, crossing himself as he had done before. "As it was in the beginning, is now, and will be forever. Amen."

A sound caught his attention. A footfall coming from the back. He glanced over his shoulder to see the source.

"Mind if I join you?" It was Silas Grey, Order Master, walking down the aisle.

"Sure," Elijah said, moving down the row to give him room.

Silas took a seat, a slight smile hanging on his face as he stared forward. Elijah joined him, wondering what he was thinking.

He said, "After hearing your report from Abraham, I figured I'd find you here."

Elijah shifted and turned to him. "Why is that?"

"Because this is the very spot I came to pray and contemplate in silence after my first operation with SEPIO."

"It's a good spot for that sort of thing."

"Sure is." He returned his gaze forward, centering on the Gospel writers' miniature statues.

The two sat in silence for a few beats.

Elijah finally broke it: "The darkness is advancing, I fear."

Silas nodded, saying nothing more.

"I felt it last year, down in that classified military hangar."

Silas turned to him. "We *witnessed it* down in that classified military hangar, remember?"

Elijah chuckled. "Touché. And then again in a megachurch across the Potomac. Live and in person. In full-on, high-definition color. The manifestation of pure, unadulterated evil. And I don't know what to do about it. What we *can* do about it."

Silas didn't miss a beat: "Stand firm, is what. That's what we'll do. That's what *you're* going to do, you and Gina and all of Group X."

"I suppose..."

"Do you know how many times the New Testament references standing firm or standing against the Evil One?"

"Twenty times," Elijah answered without missing a beat. "To be exact..."

He chuckled with a smile. "There you go. Seems like as good as any mission starting place for the Church's investigative agency."

Elijah considered that. Their mission standing firm in the face of rising evil, standing against a rising darkness from the Unseen Realm. He wondered if he was ready, if he was able.

He flat wasn't sure...

"Given the stakes—" Silas gestured toward the red book. "It's also all the more reason to spend time in quiet contemplation. After all, it's only in the daily moments with the Lord that we truly prepare to stand against the darkness."

Stand against the darkness...

The very language Elijah had used for his and Gina's Group X work.

Elijah nodded and handed him the crimson prayer book. "Why don't you close out our time."

Silas smiled. "It'd be my pleasure."

Taking the prayer book, the Order Master's voice filled the sacred, limestone space: "And now, O God and Father of all, whom the whole heavens adore: Let the whole earth also worship you, all nations obey you, all tongues confess and bless you, and men and women everywhere love you and serve you in peace; through Jesus Christ our Lord."

"Amen," Silas whispered, crossing himself.

Elijah echoed in agreement, both with his lips and fingers. "Amen."

He desired nothing more than to be the answer to this prayer.

What he couldn't tell Silas was that he secretly wondered how best to realize it. And whether he had anything to offer him, the Order, Group X.

Or the Lord.

Was he ready, was he able?

He flat wasn't sure.

Only time would tell.

# EPILOGUE

I move in the shadows with posthaste.

Because that's what is called for.

Not the shadow-moving part; the posthaste part. For that is what Wormwood commanded.

Not sure if I should worry. Guessing I should have packed my bags and run. Not that it would have mattered; the Principal has eyes everywhere, roaming too and fro.

So posthaste I move, bobbing and weaving through the streets, avoiding the Subjects like the plague (boy, do I hate the Human!) before climbing the side of some glass and steel monstrosity. Scampering really, until I tire to the point I give into unfurling my wings and soar to the pinnacle.

Not supposed to do that, and I recall why as I reach top—just barely. Something about the atmospheric differentiation between the Unseen Realm and this one. Don't get the physics behind it, only that I nearly tumble to my demise, hooking a claw at the edge in time to pull myself up top.

Where Wormwood is waiting.

My breath is stolen from me at the sight. At his height and build, his majesty and beauty. Something to behold, he is.

Clearly the Shining One has rubbed off on his top lieutenant, the Principal and shimmering specimen of the fallen ones from yore.

He turns to me—eyes as piercing as diamonds cutting through me.

Nearly stumbled to my demise

"You're late," is all he says.

I swallow, hard. Then stiffen. If there is anything I know of Wormwood, it's that weakness is worse than failure.

Wormwood will not get the best of me.

I simply say, "I know."

No, 'Forgive me, Your Imminence.' Or, 'Apologies, My Principal.'

Our kind do not ask for forgiveness.

He spins back to his view, and I join him.

The city is sprawled below us, the capital of the most powerful nation on the planet. At last for now. We know how long empires last. We've been around to see plenty rise and fall over the years—raising the hopes and dreams for countless Watchers before dashing them to the ground.

It hustles and bustles beneath us, those sheeple scurrying about their worthless, meaningless, vain tasks.

I want to retch. Not only at the sight of all those worthless beasts, but also because I know I failed to live up to my name-sake amongst them.

To create the Chaos Wormwood expects of me.

"What should we do?" I say, swallowing and shifting on uncertain legs, but lifting my head high.

No weakness, no forgiveness.

I add: "What should I do?"

Wormwood looks out into the city. Beyond the horizon.

"Did I ever tell you," he says, "how I came into this business?"

"No…no, you didn't."

"You could say it was a family affair. It was my uncle's doing, you know. Training me, guiding me in the ways of the Cosmic Powers."

He fell silent, just standing and staring.

Then he continues, "One of the many dilemmas facing the High Command for so long was whether or not we should conceal ourselves. We hadn't always, you see, but for a stretch we did. Now…"

Wormwood sweeps a hand across the air, a power and majesty behind it that sends a shiver through me. Laugher escapes him. Growly, almost giddy. Delighted.

"I recall what a former Principal from ages past wrote—my very benefactor, actually, in a series of cherished correspondence. He offered this insight: *'On the one hand, when the human creature does not believe we exist, all of the terrorism of our designs and magic is lost. On the other, when the human is a believer then we fail at making them trust only in the material world and skeptical of what is Unseen.'"*

He gives his head a shake, a wide grin spreading across his face. "Now…Now we have emotionalized and mythologized their Science to such an extent that they are indeed the Materialist Magician that High Command had been longing for so long! They worship what they vaguely call *Forces*, what lives and moves and has its being in this world, ones they can control through Science—all the while denying the existence of *Spirits*, the Cosmic Powers racing from the Unseen Realm into this pitiful one."

He turns to me, face wide with delight. "In other words, us!"

I'm not sure what he is getting at, but I nod anyway. Seems safer that way.

His face falls, and he returns to his view.

"When the sheeple scurrying about below think of devils and demons,

I shrug. "Men in tights, with horns and a forked tail welding a pitchfork."

"Exactly! The sheeple are completely in the dark, disbelieving in our existence while putting their faith in forces they can control. Or so they think. They have rationalized the Cosmic Powers in neat and tidy, yet entirely mushy and malleable categories—psychology, sociology, inequity, and whatnot. Which deny the true power, the true existence of the Unseen Realm."

"Meaning…he cannot believe in us. He's rationalized our existence away. We are free to do our thing."

"Exactly. Which brings me to your question."

"What shall we do?"

He nods. "Keep going, that's what."

"Keep going?"

He turns to me and grins, those diamond eyes I found so enchanting narrowing now into haunting slits of fearsome power.

"*Yeeeethhh*. Keep going. In all the obvious ways the Cosmic Powers have gifted us. Fomenting discord, provoking despair, binding to desire, and…creating chaos."

I stiffen at his mention of my name. He drills me with a stare I cannot escape from, his eyes making his point. Then he turns away, and there is nothing more said.

A sigh of relief slips; I cannot help it. Thought my backside was fried for sure!

I say, "Onward, it is then."

He grins. "Indeed. Onward…"

# ACKNOWLEDGMENTS

I want to give a sincere, heart-felt "Thank you!" shout out to two people who helped make this story happen thanks to their generous support through the Kickstarter campaign that helped launch this book and series: Dana Day and Seth Alexander.

Backing this project not only helped me finalize the story in order to put it out into the world, it also gave me a shot in the arm with a goodly dose of encouragement. So, thanks for both! Fans and supporters like you are why I'm able to do what I do.

# AUTHOR'S NOTE

This first case for Group X was inspired by an article from the November 2021 issue of *The Atlantic*. In "I Don't Know That I Would Even Call It Meth Anymore" Sam Quinones chronicles the dehumanizing rise of a virulent form of methamphetamine that has ravaged entire neighborhoods throughout America, the Phenyl-2-propanone (aka P2P) that I reference in chapter 22. Much more than even the opioid epidemic, though the two are linked. Its insights into how social workers have navigated the explosion of drug addiction informed chapters 15 and 16.

Reading the 8,000 word article, I couldn't help but think about the manner in which Satan and his minions devour humanity—through a number of means. There seems to be at least some sort of spiritually wicked element to the way in which Image Bearers are ravaged by addiction—trusting that what Jesus says about the Thief is true: *'[He] comes only to steal and kill and destroy'* (John 10:10). That the Devil *'prowls around, looking for someone to devour'* (1 Peter 5:8) is a sober reminder of our true enemy, which I find fits the ravenous ills of addiction in all of its forms.

Now, let me be clear: I do not want to suggest drug addiction is entirely spiritual, and if one were to give their life to Jesus

Christ—believing him to be their Savior and submitting to him as Lord—that addiction (in all of its forms) would magically disappear. Not at all. There are biological and genetic, social, medical, and psychological dynamics at work in such struggles.

However, I do want to suggest there is indeed a supernatural dimension to the manner in which drug use—and, again, addictions in all their forms—dehumanize a person, ravage the soul, and play havoc with communities as small as couples and families and as large as neighborhoods, states, and entire countries. This dimension has been forgotten, even disbelieved in favor of purely natural rationalizing. I hoped to bring at least some light to bear on how our real Enemy might use addiction to steal, kill, and destroy people.

Los Zorros is a fictional cartel loosely modeled after Los Zetas, including their Z calling card and connection with Santa Muerte, a real cultic influence on *narcocultura*. Much of that insight came from an official FBI Law Enforcement Bulletin compiled by Robert J. Bunker in 2013. In it, he outlines the frightening rise of a dark spirituality alongside narco trafficking. I used those insights, quoting from the paper in chapter 22.

Another thing to mention: it is always a risk for any writer to represent characters from certain walks of life. Naomi Torres (from my *Order of Thaddeus* series) is one such character, a Latino woman. Elijah and Gina were two more, autistic people whose characters came to me in the writing process of a different story, *Fallen Ones*. I spent time reading autistic people's stories and getting to know their experiences in the world to get them right. I particularly wanted to listen to their pain points when it comes to representation in the media, not wanting to fall into the same traps.

Hopefully, I represented them justly, writing unique, individual characters that shed some light on how they image their Creator in the world and their unique challenges expressing their personhood. However, if I fell down on the mark, and you yourself are autistic who can offer me insight into better representation, do contact me and help me understand how I can better write the stories of autistic Image Bearers.

I will also say that writing these two characters and exploring their stories gave me a chance to explore my own story. During the course of research, I myself tested for autistic tendencies. I also placed along the autism spectrum in a way that gave me further clarity about myself and also gave me interest in delving deeper into this aspect of my own story. While I would not claim to be an autistic person, nor have I been clinically diagnosed, this process writing these stories was an interesting journey for me personally.

Finally, if you caught the C. S. Lewis reference to our illustrious demon Principal, Wormwood, good for you! I alluded to the demon nephew at the receiving end of fatherly wisdom from his uncle Screwtape, featured in *The Screwtape Letters*, with a nod to his insights in the epilogue from chapter 7. Wormwood is also mentioned in Revelation 8, a star that falls to earth, possibly (and probably) a spiritual being making an appearance during the Apocalypse—inspiring this Principal character in my own story.

As with all of my stories, I like to take elements of the real world and spin it in a way to tell a compelling, propulsive page-turner. I hope you enjoyed this first foray into supernatural suspense.

# GET YOUR FREE THRILLER

**Building a relationship with my readers is a joy of writing!**
Join my insider group for updates, giveaways, and your free
novel—a full-length, action-adventure conspiracy mystery in my
*Order of Thaddeus* thriller series.

Just tell me where to send it. Follow this link to subscribe:
www.jabouma.com/free

## CONTINUE THE NEXT CASE!

In a case ripped from the headlines that speaks prophetically to
our age, Group X must solve another unfathomable mystery
menacing one small town and confront a haunting, fearsome
darkness from consuming more innocent lives.

**Read *The Darkest Valley* today: bouma.us/gx2**

# ENJOY NOT OF THIS WORLD?

A big thanks for joining Elijah Fox and Gina Anderson on their investigation saving the world! **Here's what's next:**

**Want to join Elijah Fox and Gina Anderson solving more supernatural mysteries?** Dive into solving more Group X cases: www.groupxcases.com.

A prequel case from their FBI days, *Luck Be the Ladies*, is ready to solve at:
http://bouma.us/luck

If you loved the book and have a moment to spare, **a short review is much appreciated.** Nothing fancy, just your honest take. Spreading the word is probably the #1 way you can help independent authors like me and help others enjoy the story.

# ALSO BY J. A. BOUMA

Nobody should have to read bad religious fiction—whether it's cheesy plots with pat answers or misrepresentations of the Christian faith and the Bible. So J. A. Bouma tells compelling, propulsive stories that thrill as much as inspire, offering a dose of insight along the way.

### *Order of Thaddeus* Action-Adventure Thriller Series

Holy Shroud • Book 1

The Thirteenth Apostle • Book 2

Hidden Covenant • Book 3

American God • Book 4

Grail of Power • Book 5

Templars Rising • Book 6

Rite of Darkness • Book 7

Gospel Zero • Book 8

The Emperor's Code • Book 9

Deadly Hope • Book 10

Fallen Ones • Book 11

The Eden Legacy • Book 12

Silas Grey Collection 1 (Books 1-3)

Silas Grey Collection 2 (Books 4-6)

Silas Grey Collection 3 (Books 7-9)

Backstories: Short Story Collection 1

Martyrs Bones: Short Story Collection 2

### *Group X Cases* Supernatural Suspense Series

Not of This World • Book 1

The Darkest Valley • Book 2

Luck Be the Ladies • Novelette

***Ichthus Chronicles* Sci-Fi Apocalyptic Series**

Apostasy Rising / Season 1, Episode 1

Apostasy Rising / Season 1, Episode 2

Apostasy Rising / Season 1, Episode 3

Apostasy Rising / Season 1, Episode 4

Apostasy Rising / Full Season 1 (Episodes 1 to 4)

Apocalypse Rising / Season 2, Episode 1

Apocalypse Rising / Season 2, Episode 2

Apocalypse Rising / Season 2, Episode 3

Apocalypse Rising / Season 2, Episode 4

Apocalypse Rising / Full Season 2 (Episodes 1 to 4)

***Faith Reimagined* Spiritual Coming-of-Age Series**

A Reimagined Faith • Book 1

A Rediscovered Faith • Book 2

***Mill Creek Junction* Short Story Series**

The New Normal • Collection 1

My Name's Johnny Pope • Collection 2

Joy to the Junction! • Collection 3

The Ties that Bind Us • Collection 4

A Matter of Justice • Collection 5

Get all the latest short stories at: www.millcreekjunction.com

Find all of my latest book releases at: www.jabouma.com

## ABOUT THE AUTHOR

J. A. Bouma believes nobody should have to read bad religious fiction—whether it's cheesy plots with pat answers or misrepresentations of the Christian faith and the Bible. So he tells compelling, propulsive stories that thrill as much as inspire, while offering a dose of insight along the way.

As a former congressional staffer and pastor, and award-nominated bestselling author of over forty religious fiction and nonfiction books, he blends a love for ideas and adventure, exploration and discovery, thrill and thought. With graduate degrees in Christian thought and the Bible, and armed with a voracious appetite for most mainstream genres, he tells stories you'll read with abandon and recommend with pride—exploring the tension of faith and doubt, spirituality and culture, belief and practice, and the gritty drama that is our collective pilgrim story.

When not putting fingers to keyboard, he loves vintage jazz vinyl, a glass of Malbec, and an epic read—preferably together. He lives in Grand Rapids with his wife, two kiddos, and rambunctious boxer-pug-terrier.

www.jabouma.com • jeremy@jabouma.com

facebook.com/jaboumabooks
twitter.com/bouma
amazon.com/author/jabouma